CHOSEN

Book One

LAWRENCE SIMPSON

ISBN-13: 978-1-7330446-0-8

This is a work of fiction.
No aspect of this story depicts real persons living or dead. Any similarity is coincidental. The use of place names is entirely fictional.

For my Uncle Robert, who told me he was proud of me on a dark night
long ago.

CHAPTER ONE

The accident took him by surprise. John was a careful driver at sixteen years of age. His father had taught him to drive while moving hay and supplies around the farm, and this Friday evening his parents had him chauffeur them into town for dinner and a movie.

The Presbyterian Church held a nice potluck dinner and played old movies once a month. John looked forward to the evening. The movie tonight was *Father Goose* starring Cary Grant and Leslie Caron, and his parents were fans.

The weather forecast suggested thunderstorms later that night, but their plans were indoors. They planned to be home long before the weather rolled in.

John drove and listened to his parents talk happily together about their week. He smelled his Mom's broccoli casserole, wrapped in a foil covered baking dish, sitting on the passenger front seat of their extended cab farm truck.

The evening air was cool in the middle of October, and John worked the heater control to keep the interior warm. The dark trees to either side of the road, barely outlined in the truck headlights, danced in the quickening wind. He did not take his eyes off the road. He took his duty of driving his parents into town seriously. He could feel their amused pride in him, as he carefully negotiated the curving two-lane road. He felt happy in that moment, like he was doing exactly what he was meant to be doing.

He averted his eyes at a bright flash.

He woke up on the ground, confused. A light mist fell from the sky producing a small cloud of steam from the overturned truck and a tick, tick, tick from the still warm engine in the evening silence.

John thought of his parents. Oh God, his bloody and unconscious parents were in the truck. He could see both of them as lightning flared overhead. His heart echoed the pounding thunder. The rain mixed with his tears and smeared across his face in wind driven gusts.

John tried to wake them, but their shallow breathing was the only response to his efforts. He knew from first aid training that he wasn't supposed to move them. His parents would be better sheltered in the truck from the approaching thunderstorm than out on the side of the road. He grasped the rolled up blankets kept under the rear seat of the truck and covered his parents to help them stay warm.

He had no way to call for help. There was nobody around except for the Kincaid house up the road. The fields across the fence actually belonged to Senator Kincaid, the biggest landowner in the area. Everyone knew him, and, unfortunately, his son, Paul.

John did his best to stay away from Paul Kincaid. But tonight, he needed help, and there was nowhere else to turn. He started toward the Kincaid house several hundred yards up the road. His light denim jacket soaked up the rain, and he began shivering. His right knee felt sore under a tear in his jeans which sported some dried blood at the frayed edges. He thought of his parents and walked faster.

Approaching the house, there was light everywhere. Multiple cars and trucks were parked along the long driveway. Oh yeah, he remembered. Paul was having a party tonight, a senior's only event. Well, sophomore or not, he was going to get help. Hurrying up the driveway, he ignored his throbbing right knee. Hearing music and voices inside the house, he pounded on the door willing someone to open.

Finally, a girl he recognized from high school opened the front door. She smirked at him.

"You're too young for this party," she said.

He pushed in past her. At sixteen he was tall for his age. He looked around, frantic.

"Where's the phone," he asked. "I have to call for help."

He remembered the girl's name was Darlene. Her face flushed and her words slightly slurred.

"There's a phone ina kitchen," she said. "but you shouldn't go back there."

She pointed to the back of the house.

He pushed through the crowded rooms jammed with swaying jubilant teens, finally seeing the kitchen ahead.

Two senior boys with bared teeth blocked his path. They challenged him almost in unison.

"What are you doing in here?" asked one of them. "Paul didn't invite you, no way."

"My parents are hurt," said John. "There was an accident out on the road, and I have to call for help."

He had to get to that phone.

The football players parted, shrugging their broad shoulders, and John squeezed between the burly linemen. Spying the phone on the wall, he slid forward and picked up the handset. He started to dial for help, but there was no dial tone.

He slammed the phone down in frustration. Either the phone was out because of the storm or a handset was off somewhere else in the house. He decided to shout for help to see if the other students would help him, but it was useless, they were all too inebriated to care.

Maybe I can find Paul he thought, and ask him to give me a ride? Heck, I could get a couple of these guys to help me get my parents. We could use doors from the house for backboards, rig up cervical collars, and drive straight to the hospital. The police could come later.

However, he didn't see anyone sober that he would trust to drive a car. He had a learners permit only. Never mind that. He would drive illegally if he could get keys and some help saving his parents.

John turned to the football players.

"Where's Paul?" he asked. "I need to talk with him."

"He don't need you bothering him now," said one of them. "He's got serious business going on upstairs with the Ice Queen."

"Yeah, she's getting melted tonight," said the other ox of a senior as they slapped hands and howled in unison. They started chanting, "Ice Queen" over and over. The chanting grew louder as several of the nearby students echoed the call with added snide remarks followed by more laughter.

John felt nauseous. He understood then. Paul Kincaid was the only son of a state senator and a senior at the local high school. He thought of himself as God's gift to women and was always bragging about this conquest or that. He didn't care who overheard. He thought himself above any consequences because of his father.

John had heard Paul talking with some of his buddies about his ability to score, and how he had a source for a special something that made any girl want it, even beg for it, and he was only too happy to oblige.

John knew Paul had his sights set on Jessica Holloman. She was a senior and a neighbor. Her family lived in a small trailer down the road from his family's farm. She was quiet, beautiful, and very intelligent. John had spoken to her probably a half-dozen times, but he remembered every moment in detail.

What he couldn't understand was why she would be here. He knew she had ignored every advance Paul had made. He had seen her cold shoulder Kincaid at school more than once. If she was here, she was in danger. Now, he had two reasons to find Paul.

John shouldered his way quickly through the throng of stumbling schoolmates. Thunder boomed overhead outside the expansive house, and rain danced against the windows. Escaping from the intended embrace of a sozzled girl, he climbed the winding stairwell leading from the entry hallway to the second floor.

He had never been in the Kincaid house before and didn't know the individual rooms. He started opening doors along the hallway. How many bedrooms does this house have, thought John, amid the muttered "hey" and "get your own room" from couples in various positions of entanglement?

Finally, he was at the last door. He heard muffled voices. He turned the knob, but the door wouldn't open. With time running out and thinking of his parents and Jessica, John kicked in the door. He was tall and whipcord thin at sixteen, but strong from daily work on the farm.

He barged into a version of hell. Paul Kincaid stood motionless holding his pants unbuckled about his waist, startled at John's entrance. There were two other senior classmates in the room all in various stages of undress. Jessica was on the bed, disrobed from the waist down. She mumbled incomplete sentences around glassy eyes and rubbed her abdomen and hips.

"What are you doing here?" asked Paul. "How dare you come into my home uninvited!"

Paul shouted out of fear or anger. John couldn't decide and didn't care. The senator's son had been found out and was cornered. John knew he wouldn't be getting any help from Paul Kincaid now or ever. He advanced on Paul. The two other boys dashed out of the room just as the lights went out.

Shrieks sounded from panicked teens downstairs, but John had no ear for that. He needed car keys and had already decided he was taking Jessica to the hospital with his parents. Any punishment for Paul Kincaid and the others could wait. He only hoped his parents were still alive.

A flash of lightning shown briefly through the bedroom window warning him of Paul's swing. He took the blow glancing off his shoulder as he turned to the right.

John struck back then, righteous anger fueling hammer like blows matching the lightning outside in quickness. Paul went down to the floor wheezing.

John reached into the pocket of Paul's trousers and found car keys. He left him groaning on the floor. Wrapping the blankets around Jessica, he lifted her off the bed. She didn't seem to understand what he was doing, but there was no way he was leaving her in this house of horror. He would call her parents once she was at the hospital.

Carrying Jessica, wrapped in blankets, down the stairs in the darkened house lit only briefly by lightning stabbing through the windows, proved difficult. John thought he was going to fall several times, but somehow he managed to reach the entry hall. The front door slammed open. He could see cars and trucks weaving away from the property as the teens abandoned the now dark house. Gusts of cold wind whipped into the entry hall carrying rain onto the high thread count Persian rug.

He managed to get Jessica into the back seat of Paul Kincaid's Cadillac Escalade. Adjusting the seat, he drove down the drive way and turned left, following the road until he arrived at his family's over-turned truck. He prayed he was dreaming, and he wouldn't find them, but they hadn't moved from where he left them.

Jessica sprawled in the Escalade's rear seat with bubbles of saliva at the corner of her mouth, but she was breathing as near as he could tell. He covered her with the bedding and belted her in as best he could.

He folded down the third row seats of the Escalade and opened the rear hatch to get his parents into the truck. He turned to get his parents and stumbled, feeling very lightheaded. Everything went bright around him, and then, blackness.

As his senses returned, he realized he had placed his parents in the back of the SUV. He really didn't have much time to think about his weird blackout spell. Maybe he was going into shock? He did feel numb and lightheaded. John shut the doors, adjusted the driver's seat, and headed for the county hospital.

"Hang on Mom and Dad," he said, not knowing if they could hear him. "Jessica, it will be all right."

John felt powerless to help them. He concentrated on his driving, willing the prowling panic back into the corner of his brain, not to be let out until unlocked. He could feel it pressing against the bars of his caged mind, bowing the door inward, but no, he would not give in to despair. He said a quiet prayer for strength and healing for his passengers.

He reached the county hospital intact and pulled in front of the Emergency entrance. He jumped out of the truck and ran around and in through the glass doors, which slid open at his approach.

"Help!" he shouted. "My parents are hurt!"

After a moment of hesitation, nurses and assistants rushed out to the Escalade. As soon as they saw his passengers, the rush of hands from the staff multiplied. His parents and Jessica were placed on stretchers and rushed inside.

His mother and father were taken into the resuscitation room. The drawn faces of the emergency department staff spoke volumes, confirming John's worst fears. Still, he hoped.

While the doctor and nurses labored for his parents, he sat beside Jessica. She mumbled incoherently at times, but mostly, she remained still on the hospital stretcher breathing slowly. Her monitor echoed the second hand of the clock on the wall, each second, each heartbeat here and gone forever, he thought.

Jessica paused her breathing just as the lights flickered briefly. The clock on the wall paused. John heard increased activity from the trauma room, and he knew his parents were leaving this world as they lived in it, side by side.

Later, much later, even years later, he would remember sitting there holding her hand.

CHAPTER TWO

Seventeen years later ...

John Stone slumped in his desk attempting to avoid another provocative question from Professor Paul Kincaid. He knew it was not possible to hide in a college classroom, but he could hope for the best. When he discovered Kincaid was a professor at Great Western University, he almost changed his enrollment plans, but he decided he would most likely not ever come in contact with Kincaid. Seventeen years, he thought, was not enough time to forget.

He needed this history class to complete his teaching degree. He'd asked several history majors and gotten a recommendation for Professor Avery. The first five weeks of class had been reasonable. However, when he showed up for today's class, there was Paul Kincaid filling in for Avery, who had taken leave for illness.

John tried telling himself the past was the past. He had worked hard to purge any bitterness from his system. Instead of punishment for their activities against Jessica Holloman that terrible night, Paul Kincaid and his followers convinced many, including Judge Birchen, of their innocence.

There was no crime if Jessica was a willing participant, and half the senior class recounted how Jessica was the life of the party, laughing gaily as she walked upstairs with Paul and his friends, giggling that she was going to change some things about her life that night.

Somehow, it had been John who wound up in trouble. Accused of assaulting Paul Kincaid and stealing his SUV, he was also prosecuted by the county attorney for negligent homicide as the driver in the accident that took the lives of his parents. John ended up being sentenced to juvenile detention at McCracken, and eventually, he was sent to Green River pending his eighteenth birthday.

The farm that his mother and father worked as a legacy for him was put up for auction. He heard later that Senator Kincaid purchased his family property to add to his already sizable estate.

John worked through his anger in that first year at corrections surviving the attacks of the other boys and self-made gangs. Fortunately his father had taught him how to fight, and he was naturally strong. He didn't win all the fights, but he won enough to gain some respect and serve out his time until he was eighteen.

When a judge offered him the chance to expunge his record if he joined the military at age eighteen, John jumped at the chance. The judge also offered him a chance to change his name. He suggested it would make it easier for him to have a fresh start going forward.

John felt a bit guilty giving up his family name. He had lost everything else, but his instincts told him the judge was trying to be kind when he asked what his new name would be.

"John Stone," he had replied.

Stone like his heart, he thought.

Now here he was face to face with Paul Kincaid again and all he could think of was a dark rainy night, and the betrayal of a young girl.

Amazingly, Kincaid didn't seem to know him. John knew he looked different after seventeen years. He had grown up in a rough school, and his face reflected many lessons. And of course, his name was different. The judge had been correct.

He suspected he would be dropping this class. Still, he thought, maybe he could make it through the class if he kept his head down. How bad could it be?

The answer became clear to him over the next two hours. Now honorably discharged from the army, John already stood out from most of the other students, because of his age, having spent much of the last seventeen years in the military, most of it deployed overseas.

He knew his worldview differed from many of his classmates at Great Western University. He wasn't out to change anybody's ideas of right and wrong, but he couldn't deny his core convictions tempered in the fire of multiple trials. John found question after question thrown his way ranging from the American Civil War to the Vietnam era and ending with the war in Afghanistan. He did his best to answer.

Professor Kincaid stood up at the front of the class with a smile on his face that reminded John of Sylvester, the feral stray cat years ago at Green River, toying with a mouse.

He could see Professor Kincaid's glee in his answers. He heard gasps from the students around him and a muttered "that's hate speech, man" coming from somewhere to the left of him. Probably from the pale slacker sporting the dreadlocks. It was the first time John could remember hearing him contribute in class.

Kincaid placed his hands clasped together under his chin, hesitated for a moment as if in thought, and then held his hands outstretched in a settle down class motion to ward off further interruption from the other students.

"So you think America's involvement in Afghanistan was justified?" asked Kincaid.

His phrasing and tone indicated his disbelief that any person could give any answer other than complete and total disagreement.

John shifted a bit in his seat, remembering explosions splintering a stone and clay wall, threatening to push away his current surroundings. He centered in his seat and forced himself not to grip the sides of the desk too tightly.

"Violence is always the last and worst option in dissent," he said.

Professor Kincaid seemed about to continue, when the chime sounded for end of period.

"Well that is an interesting position from someone with your history." Professor Kincaid continued, addressing the entire class, "Read from your text and give me a one page paper on causes and justifications for American involvement in the Vietnam War for Wednesday."

John gathered his book and belongings into his backpack and started out the door to follow the rest of the students when Professor Kincaid called his name.

"A moment please, Mr. Stone."

John paused and turned from his planned room exit. He had an introductory physics class in twenty minutes and didn't want to arrive late. He feared despite all his self-control, he couldn't quite address Paul Kincaid politely in a private setting.

"I hope you don't mind being part of our discussion," said Kincaid. "I know we haven't met previously, but I always find class discussions to be most illuminating when every viewpoint is brought forward. I will be especially interested in reading your interpretation of the points in the current chapter."

John nodded, which was all he felt he could do and contain his emotions even now, seventeen years later. He turned and exited class through the door into the hallway.

"Until Wednesday, Mr. Stone."

Professor Kincaid still had a smile, more like a smirk on his face.

John walked into the hallway and found several students from class standing in his way. They were bunched up, and a well muscled guy on the right bounced up and down on the balls of his feet. John thought the brawny guy was on the football team, as he had heard him talking about practice before class.

"You need to learn your history, army man," said the beefy boy with the short neck.

"That's right!" said Mr. Dreadlocks.

"You tell him, Ronnie," said a girl hanging on to the back of football boy's jacket.

John looked at each of them, and without saying a word, moved to his left and around the group just as bouncing boy stepped toward him.

He moved down the hall and down the stairs. He thought they might follow him, but apparently, they were content to loudly mutter about stupid soldier boy rednecks.

He needed this class. Why was it always the self-proclaimed victims who advocated violence first?

Looking behind him, he didn't see anyone coming down the stairs, but he could hear some more exclamations. Let them have their victory, he thought as he took the stairs two at a time. I don't care, but I guess I will have to consider dropping the class. Now, I'll have to find a way to catch up next semester, he thought.

John checked his watch again as he paced down the hill to the science building. The sun peeked through the overhead tree canopy, birdsong filled the air, and the scent of flowers cascaded in the morning air. Showers of color along the foundation bordering the walk pushed away memories of young children begging in the streets overseas. Warmed away by the morning sunshine, his emotions over his interaction with Professor Kincaid faded.

John reminded himself again how fortunate he was to be here and have a chance to continue his life. The time in rehabilitation after his end in the army was long and difficult, but lying in the hospital bed and learning to walk again had given him plenty of time to think and plan. He wanted a quiet life now, and he hoped that his love of history would sustain him in a teaching career.

First, he needed to finish his degree. That meant making it to class on time.

He picked up his pace.

CHAPTER THREE

Fortunately, the science building was just a few hundred meters down the hill. John looked up at the faded red brick and cream concrete accents as he neared the glass entrance doors. Built in 1928, the aged red brick and concrete exterior sported ivy climbing up the exterior of the building, lending a stately and academic aura.

The solid cornerstones in the building foundation reflected the opinion of the students and instructors within that science was built on a sturdy foundation of Galileo, Newton, and Einstein. The inside looked a bit dated reflecting its last interior renovation in the late seventies.

John took his seat in the far corner of a first floor classroom where he could see the door leaving no one behind him out of habit. Something he had learned out of necessity in his previous life. This was his fifth week in this class, and he knew there was an attached laboratory due this afternoon. He noticed the vivacious coed sitting in the left front had moved back to the seat in front of him.

She was pretty enough to gather attention in any setting. He refused to believe she had moved for any reason related to him. Probably trying to escape the attentions of the three preppy looking students sitting in the middle front forming their own island, he thought.

They were conversing loudly prior to class and laughing as they glanced her way. John could guess what they were saying more or less, but decided not to share. No reason to upset her further. He saw her cringe at one of their comments. Perhaps that group prompted her move back to his corner of the room after all.

An instructor other than Mr. Woerner walked into class, and John saw an older man with a full head of gray hair and average height, lean like a runner except for a bit of softness about his middle. He smiled and placed a copy of their physics text, new and seemingly unopened, on the clean table in front of him.

"Good Morning. I am Dr. Horace Maxwell, and this class comprises introductory physics. I know you've had your first few sessions taught by Mr. Woerner. He was kind enough to get the semester started for me, as I was feeling a bit under the weather. He tells me he has covered the basics of static and motion systems and natural forces such as gravity. Today we will discuss the qualities of light."

Professor Maxwell's eyes glowed with enthusiasm as he vigorously explained that light was both wave and particle, depending on the measurement, and its velocity remained constant no matter how it was observed. He started on the board behind him and continued around the room moving from concept to concept in an amazing summary of the classical double slit experiment, which left John struggling to keep up and hoping he could teach like that someday.

As Professor Maxwell finished up his discussion, a teenager entered the classroom and stood off to the side. The professor introduced the young man to the class as his research assistant, Jacob, who would assist during the lab in the afternoon.

John, thought the young man looked about the same age he was when he took his bus ride to Fort Benning. After getting off that bus and trying to line up, he ran to get his bags, and didn't stop running for five months until he finished infantry training. The lessons there, and the crucible that was basic training, forged him at the time and almost prepared him for what was to come later. Shaking his head slightly he thought, how could someone so young be assisting a college professor in teaching other students. John felt old and dumb.

He noticed the trio of students look their way again. He couldn't blame anyone for wanting to look at the coed as she was California blond wrapped in midwestern sweet, but the dark eyes of the taller middle one, whom John had mentally tagged as the leader, seemed to linger. John couldn't help but stare back. The staring contest continued until the student huffed and turned back to look at Professor Maxwell, who was discussing the location and mechanics of the physics lab and the experiment for today, which would involve coherent light and illustrate some of the principles discussed in class. Each of them was to partner up with one or two other students for the experiment stations.

"You are John, right?"

The young coed had turned and was talking to him.

"Yes," he replied.

"I'm Samantha," she said. "I was wondering if you would like to be my partner?" She blushed. "I mean in the physics lab. Do you have a partner yet?"

John knew he needed to work with someone for the lab this afternoon. He wasn't particular, as long as he could get the work done in a satisfactory fashion.

"Sure Miss Samantha, we can partner up for the lab," he said. "I don't have much experience in physics, so I hope you can carry us."

She beamed and said, "Oh, I love science, and I know we'll do okay. Just call me Sam. Everyone does."

Her smile was open, and John tried to remember when he felt so enthused about anything. Been a long time, he thought. Her joy for life was contagious, and he found his spirits lift even more from his earlier history class experience. He began to look forward to the afternoon.

The student who had been staring walked toward Samantha and stood in front of her. John thought he looked a bit awkward standing there.

"I'm Conrad Thurston," he said. "My friends and I would like you to work with us."

Samantha seemed surprised and hesitant to respond.

Conrad repeated himself.

"C'mon," he said. "It'll be fun."

John eyed Conrad and his two friends who had come back to join him.

"She already has me as a lab partner," said John. "Thanks for asking."

Conrad stared at John. His eyes smoldered, and the corners of his mouth pursed tightly. Abruptly, he shouldered his way through his friends and stomped out of the classroom. They turned to follow.

Samantha exhaled her relief at the end of the brief confrontation.

"Wow," she said. "Thanks for that. I'm so glad I asked you to be my lab partner. That guy won't leave me alone, since I met him during rush week. One dance, and he thinks he owns me. I've actually been dreading coming to class even though I was excited to get Dr. Maxwell for an instructor."

She took a breath and continued.

"Why don't I meet you at the front entrance hallway at a quarter of three. We can walk up to the lab together?"

"Sure," said John. "I'll see you at 1445 hrs.

He replied in military time reflexively. But Samantha seemed to understand. She smiled as she gathered her belongings and left the classroom.

John checked his watch. He should be able to catch Isaac at the snack shack for a quick bite, and then, maybe have enough time to swing by the administration building to look at his options regarding the history class. He hated to let himself be run off by Kincaid again, but honestly, he wanted to avoid any contact with him going forward. He just didn't know if he had enough self-control. After his exit from the army, he didn't need anyone else worrying over his mental health.

The Snack Shack was sandwiched in between the campus post office and the fine arts building conveniently across from a small copse of trees and picnic tables shaded during the afternoon sunshine. It was a favorite hangout for students and campus squirrels. Grabbing a turkey club wrap and a bottle of water, John found an empty spot at one of the tables and waited for Isaac.

A group of students were finishing up at another table. He recognized one of the students from his history class sitting with them, the young lady so enamored with Ronnie earlier. She noticed him and bent her head to talk with her fellow students in close conversation.

One by one they got up and walked by John on their way to deposit refuse in the lone trash can. Each of them managed to drop something on or near the table where he was sitting. One of them brushed close enough to jostle him and muttered "racist" under his breath just loud enough for John to hear. They gathered by the trashcan as a group, and when John ignored them, one of them walked away, then another, and finally all were gone save his history classmate. John couldn't remember her name? She continued to stare at him as he opened his wrap.

"Hey, John, you couldn't find a cleaner place to sit, brother?"

Isaac sat down across from John. Looking at the staring young coed, Isaac addressed John.

"Hey, what's with her?" he asked.

John smiled.

"I think she's trying to decide if we're twins," John replied.

Isaac reared his head back and laughed. Isaac scaled out at two hundred and forty pounds of muscle. John was taller but knew he never wanted to get in a hand-to-hand match with the densely muscled black man.

Isaac was the first male in his family to attend a university, and, like John, he was using his GI benefits for tuition. He had been an aircraft and diesel mechanic in the Air Force, was studying engineering, and was John's dormitory roommate.

John glanced over, and saw his history classmate stomp off, muttering in confusion over the supposedly racist anglo sitting and laughing with the giant black man.

Isaac recovered enough to speak.

"You remember about tomorrow, right?" he asked. "I could use a hand getting my truck out to the airport."

Isaac earned good money working at the airport on weekends and sometimes weeknights when he could squeeze in the hours. His aviation maintenance certification from the military continued to pay off for him. Tomorrow morning was Friday, but Isaac had some time. John knew there was a job his roommate was trying to finish, and his truck was giving him some electrical issues. Isaac wanted to use the equipment at the airport to track down the gremlin in his truck's ignition system. He might look like a big muscle bound guy, but John had already figured out that Isaac was a very smart operator who managed to give the appearance he was just drifting along.

"Yeah. I'll be ready in the morning," said John.

He picked up his leavings and some of the trash left around him by the other students. He hated to leave a mess on general principles.

"I'm heading over to admin, and then I've got lab later this evening," he said. "See ya later, Isaac."

Walking over to the Admin building, John kept his head on a swivel out of long habit, which is how he noticed Conrad trailing about fifty meters back. Interesting, thought John. Probably a coincidence, except he didn't believe in coincidences.

When he turned to look again, there was no sign of the student. Okay, maybe just a bit paranoid, he told himself, but being paranoid had kept him alive for years and was part of his nature now.

Shaking his head, he pushed into the double glass doors at ground level for administration and hoped he wasn't too late to drop what was now Kincaid's history class.

CHAPTER FOUR

S'ear'r was elated. In his mission, he had been awakened from dimming six times, and only one of the habitable worlds found showed sentient life, an aquatic species without a written language. They did live on a beautiful world perfect for expansion for the Chos'n. Searcher had no doubt that they had been swept away in the aftermath of his reported discovery.

Interesting happened when life was found. Life meant a fertile world and new ideas and technology to offer to his kind. Life also meant food, which was always in short supply and necessary to fuel the growing Chos'n empire.

Across known space, species which survived infancy to send objects into the n'btw'een were few. Such finds became a priority to evaluate as risk versus prize. Rarely, a species was observed carefully and allowed to continue to develop for a time in pursuit of a technological advancement that complimented the plans of L'ment'l. However, no species would be allowed to make their way to interstellar travel to challenge the destiny of the Chos'n.

Ship had wakened S'ear'r after detecting weak electromagnetic signals. The signals were really just wisps without obvious direction, but the small and primitive probe craft Ship had caught held further information.

The probe's construction suggested a pre-composites culture with no suggestion of nanotechnology. An attached metallic disc displayed information about the origin solar system, which was likely the present system not a light turning away. Audible broadcasts in unknown languages were present. Visuals were strange, but binary coding and math with base ten and basic electronic flight control systems were all different but similar and workable.

S'ear'r weighed options.

Ship was quick to point out that protocol called for communication upon discovery of possible life forms, but that would take a sizable power burst and might be noticed. However, current indications suggested it unlikely that this contact had advanced sufficiently to be able to detect any subspace communication this far out from its primary.

Ship insisted they were obligated to report life detection. S'ear'r agreed. Yes, send a detection signal, and then maybe slowly drift in limiting their ambient light and heat signature until closer to source of signals. They would advance and gather more information for a more comprehensive report.

The last pass through this part of space was more than a thousand passings ago. No sentient life had been detected then, but now, they had found a satellite space probe. That suggested very rapid development, unprecedented in S'ear'r and Ship's understanding of known Chos'n history. Interesting. Ship agreed, abuzz with anticipation.

Recorded life was known in the n'btw'een, but no known contacts in this area made this very interesting indeed. First chance to accomplish mission, yes, this was very exciting.

S'ear'r called up calculations from Ship, and a plan for approach was made and agreed upon. A slight reorientation and change in direction was accomplished, and a descent initiated following the gravity well of the nearby star, called Sol by this race, moving at fractional velocity and utilizing minimal resources. More calculations were reviewed for fuel, power consumption, and reserves. Yes, they both agreed it was reasonable to proceed.

CHAPTER FIVE

The man no longer begged for his life as he swung, hanging by his wrists, from the overhead beams in his great room. Shadows rebounded from the cream painted walls and danced in the light from the candles about the room.

Vincent had found the candles in the dining room in the third drawer of the exquisite cherrywood buffet chest. The decorative candles were just right to cast enough flickering illumination as he worked at performing his assigned task. Vincent felt the silver carving knives were a bonus and decided they would add encouragement for the man to share information. Silver had long represented purity, and this man was to be made pure in his absolution.

Vincent had been briefed. The target worked in government and was in a position to know many secrets reflecting the trust placed in him. Unfortunately, the man had decided to share some of those confidences in a misguided atonement for perceived wrongdoing by the administration.

Vincent understood that a man had to believe in his work, that what he did was in the right. Apparently, this man felt he couldn't live with his involvement in certain actions at the government level and wanted to bare his soul. Very well, thought Vincent, he would help him in that goal.

The man looked ragged in the flickering light. The deep lacerations Vincent allowed the carving knives to produce made a beautiful pattern, and the target was near the end now, repeating his words softly. Vincent strained to hear, hoping that in the man's moment of suffering he might be sharing enlightenment.

"Our Father Who art in Heaven, Hallowed be thy name ...."

The man's voice trailed off, alternating between whisper and moan.

Vincent felt sad. He had hoped that the man might see in his last knowing moments how his actions defined him. Each of us chose, door-by-door, the direction of our lives every day. Vincent knew this, knew there was no God, no devil, no supernatural, only the choices each person made and the natural consequences. He knew this because he had once suffered as this man did now. Vincent had tried to pray then as well.

Surely, this man could reach the same conclusion, could see as Vincent had seen. There was no right or wrong. All morality was relative, but loyalty, well, loyalty was an absolute. Break that code, and no punishment was too terrible.

Vincent was loyal. He had been rescued from the deepest pit of despair as he swung in the air, feet off the ground, wrists and shoulders burning, leading the way to death's door and begging for him to follow. In the clarity of that moment, when he was to be freed from his torment as his captors led him down to his knees, one of them unsheathing a sword and another videotaping him, he had felt a moment of enlightenment, an emptiness so profound that he felt husk like, a shell without any redeeming memory in support of a coming afterlife, left only with the anticipation of relief from his torment.

Vincent remembered the pain of his knees on the stone floor and the whisper of the unsheathed blade as one of his captors narrated his end. Then, Vincent heard his executioner pause and speak angrily as another fighter interrupted him. A blindfold was placed, and he was pulled to his feet and partly dragged out of the building into the blinding warmth of sunshine.

Later, after the unofficial prisoner exchange, after medical attention and debriefing, and while lying in his quarters at night pretending to sleep, Vincent finally understood. He no longer believed in the God of Isaac, Abraham, and Joseph, if he ever did. His receptacle for that childhood instruction had been hollowed out along with his sense of self in the fires of torment?

No, the only thing that made sense to him was loyalty. He was alive because of the efforts of his employers, and he remained grateful. Given the opportunity to repay their kindness to him, Vincent performed his assigned tasks with efficiency. He believed in equality for his targets. All were given the chance for absolution, to find clarity in their last fleeting instants as he had done.

"Jeffrey, please pay attention. This is important," said Vincent. "Is there anything else you have to tell me now that our evening is coming to an end? You can trust me with all your secrets. I hope you know that by now."

He didn't really expect the man to divulge anything else useful, but this honored his personal code, each target given full opportunity to find their own truth to salve their soul, for if they believed there was some all powerful deity to face on the eternal journey, then best to do so with a clean conscience.

Vincent hoped the target's wife was at peace. Her end had been necessary to ensure full cooperation from the man. While inflicting needed pain on the man's wife had not affected Vincent in the least, the man had quickly confessed to all in very specific fashion. Vincent was true to his word to end her suffering, allowing her to precede her husband.

Vincent had seen the hope leave the man's eyes as he gazed at his wife sprawled on the great room floor so still in her testament to his failure.

"Please, please let it end, please let it end," the man said.

Vincent did admire politeness. He allowed a moment's grace as he maneuvered behind the man using the candlelight to allow his target to see his reflection in the polished silver of the carving knife, just before Vincent sliced through the man's throat, feeling the knife slide across the anterior cervical vertebrae.

The night's work was almost finished, but Vincent still had to take a moment to reexamine the scene, going over all movements in his minds eye, his mask intact, no cameras hidden or otherwise, for he had asked about that. He had worn gloves of course and a gray plastic rain jacket, uncomfortable, but helpful in keeping any incriminating splatter of DNA off him. His employers in the shadows of government had seen to it that his fingerprints and military records were expunged, facilitating his nonexistence.

This target's computer records and hidden thumb drive were in Vincent's possession now, and he would upload the records to his own server as a backup. He was loyal, but not stupid. He knew his masters could turn on him, and would, if they thought it would benefit them. He kept meticulous records as leverage in case he began to feel his virtual nonexistence about to become a reality.

He also had an eye toward his retirement knowing he wouldn't be able to do this forever, after all, he was only a man, and a worker not only earns his pay, but, also, his rest. His records might help with his retirement plans. Always good to have options, he thought.

His assignment had been specific, track the man, find him, isolate him, obtain all information and eliminate him, making it seem a random crime. The man's wife had been at home. That was a surprise to Vincent. His information suggested she was receiving inpatient chemotherapy overnight. Still, he prided himself on his ability to adapt, something he had learned long ago in another part of the world.

Vincent finished the scene by splashing some obscure references on the walls of the great room. He thought it very courteous to allow the police something to work with as they performed their investigation, but no real evidence could remain. His goal was to give the appearance of drug crazed perpetrators and a home invasion gone bad. He left a scented candle burning as he let himself out through the back door. The candle's pleasant aroma almost masked the coppery scent of blood on the woven carpet at the center of the great room.

Shame about the carpet, he thought.

CHAPTER SIX

"I don't know if I can do this." said Samantha. She was holding a lancet in her right hand like a pencil. "I tend to faint at the sight of blood, especially my own."

John smiled and reached for the lancet and an alcohol swab. The experiment called for a pinprick of blood from each of them to be placed on individual microscopic slides. Using a known grid and a laser beam, the diameter of each lab partner's red blood cells could be calculated.

John and Samantha were in their own small room, one of several enclosures in the laboratory. A faint smell of disinfectant lingered from the night cleaning, reminding him one more time of the hospital as he lay in bed hoping for the feeling in his legs to return.

"Allow me," he said, taking her hand in his, and nodding at the experiment setup, said, "So, this is what you do for fun, eh?"

He chuckled when she winced at the finger stick. Placing the drop of blood on the slide, he took his gloves off.

Samantha lined up the diffraction grid, checked her alignment on the laser apparatus, and nodded for him to fire it up.

"No, this is just interesting," she said. "I really like computers.

That's my passion. I want to develop the next great computer revolution."

John thought that was a fine ambition, and with her enthusiasm, who knew? Certainly, anyone would agree that Samantha would look good on stage at an annual technology exposition.

"Samantha, I think you just might," he said, earning a brilliant smile from her.

John double-checked that they were both wearing safety glasses and flipped the power switch for the two milliwatt laser, which emitted a fine red beam of coherent light striking the diffraction grid with the slide of blood in the center and throwing concentric circles on the screen behind.

He was even more impressed when Samantha pulled out her laptop computer and began to input their numbers for the experiment. When calculated, their lab sheet was sent on for grading. By this point, he was feeling smug about letting Sam talk him into being her lab partner.

Checking outside their cubicle, he noticed the lab assistant, Jacob, walk between the different groups working on the experiment and approach the same trio of noisy students working together. Conrad immediately waved Jacob away when he approached them. He spoke a few words, and his partners burst out in laughter.

"Those three are trouble," said Samantha. "They act like the world owes them, and they can do no wrong. The one on the right scares me the most. They're worse when they're together. A couple of girls at the dorm warned me."

She was rubbing her arms, her eyes slightly magnified in the ballistic eyewear.

"Is that why you asked me to be your lab partner?"

"Well, yes, partly. You seemed older, more self assured, and you don't creep on me with your eyes."

Jacob walked over to their station.

"Is there anything you need?" he asked. "Have any questions?"

He addressed them both, but spent most of his time trying not to look at Samantha.

"No, this seems straightforward," she said. "The professor's explanation in class was helpful. He's a good teacher. Are you in school here? How do you know him? You look so young to be instructing at the university level?"

"I've known the professor most of my life," said Jacob. "He's family to me. I guess I'm lucky, cause he tutors me at home sometimes."

Samantha looked puzzled, so Jacob went on.

"He's my grandfather," he said.

"But, where are you in the university curriculum?" asked Sam. "I mean what level? You're not a grad student are you? I mean, how could you be? No one finishes four years of college in twelve months?"

Jacob shrugged his shoulders.

"Well, I tested out of some classes, and my grandfather lets me help in this lab because I really enjoy working with lasers. And computers." said Jacob, looking at her laptop. "Tell me what software you are using to interface with the school system, because that can't be a standard operating system?"

Samantha began to show him the custom interface software she had designed for her computer, and they were quickly light years beyond John's computer knowledge base. Samantha got very excited when Jacob told her of a computer project he was working on and made him promise to show her his work. They were ready to leave an hour early, and John noticed jealous looks from some of the other students, especially the terrible trio as he had come to think of them.

"Thanks again, John," said Samantha. "I'll see you Tuesday."

Samantha walked down the hall. John noticed the three loud guys from class eyeing her and laughing together. He started to say he would walk with her, but was surprised when Jacob spoke up.

"Hey Samantha, you left your lab journal," said Jacob.

The young lab assistant ran to catch up with her.

"Thank you, Jacob," she said. "You are so sweet."

John could see Jacob's blush as he walked with Samantha through the laboratory door into the hallway. They were chatting back and forth.

As the two of them continued down the hall, the three laughing students left the lab, swiftly caught up with Samantha and Jacob, and moved in front of them. Conrad, the taller one, began to talk in earnest to Samantha, while the other two flanked Jacob. Conrad's voice carried down the hall.

"You know," he said. "We're throwing a party tonight." He continued, "You should come over to the house with us."

John was surprised when Jacob addressed the three young men.

"Hey guys," said Jacob. "I don't think she's interested?"

"That's all right, Jacob." said Samantha, looking at the three guys blocking her in the hallway. "No thanks. Get out of our way, and leave us alone!"

John registered all this in a moment for he had seen it too many times. He glided toward the group. He could feel the pulse at his temples keeping time with the wall clock in the hall, and the second hand seemed to slow. He noted Samantha's flushed face and her emphatic "No!" to Conrad's continued words.

John knew what was about to happen, and for a fleeting moment, he had the thought that he shouldn't get involved. After all, he had formed a plan to live his life quietly, but he dismissed the thought as unworthy seeing Samantha, her hands on her hips, square up to the three students.

The trio seemed surprised at first, but then Conrad grasped Samantha's wrist in his hand to pull her along with him.

When Conrad completed the grab to Samantha's arm, Samantha moved her hand in a circle to the outside of his arm, and, turning her body to the left, she placed her right hand on Conrad's left upper arm. He tumbled into the empty space she created as she turned. He went down hard, John noticed.

One of the other two, punched Jacob in the face while the last one attempted to jump on Jacob as well. John arrived at that moment. Pulling on the jumper's hair, he yanked the attacker backwards in a long fall down to the gray and white linoleum floor. Stocky attacker number two pulled a spring knife from behind his back, as John used his left arm to push Jacob and Samantha away from the range of the knife while Conrad was struggling to get up from the floor.

Troublemaker two, as John now thought of him, lunged at him with the knife. He stepped to the outside, his right hand knife edge parrying the weapon arm, then grasping the young man's wrist as the knife moved past his midsection, John slid his left arm up and across the young man's neck effectively creating a fulcrum at his shoulder. He felt a pop as the attacker's shoulder joint cleaved and felt the fight go out of the man, but John didn't let go of the assailant until the knife dropped to the floor.

Turning to the leader attempting to get off the floor and continue his attack, John kicked him in the face feeling the crunch of his nose under his boot. Conrad went down again and stayed down this time. All three attackers were on the floor. Samantha was looking at Jacob's face where he had been punched.

John felt his heart rate increase and external sounds came back to him as the adrenaline began to fade. He recognized the familiar washed out feeling in his limbs and the mild nausea that always accompanied violence for him.

He noted the horrified facial expressions of some students who were hanging back about ten meters down the hall. Some were holding cell phones in extended hands. John thought he would need to be sure to get some names and phone numbers for statements for when the police arrived. So much for a peaceful day, he thought.

He surveyed the scene. He had suffered no injury. Samantha looked a bit tremulous. John knew it was the adrenalin rush waning after her response, and where did that joint throw come from? The girl had some training previously, he thought. He observed Jacob, who was holding his face, looking at Samantha with his mouth partly open.

Someone must have called security, he thought, when a campus police officer came out of the stairwell and walked rapidly down the hall toward the scene.

"What's going on here?" asked the officer?

John could see the officer's name tag read P. Murray.

"We were attacked by those three guys!" said Samantha.

Officer Murray looked at the terrible trio. One sat against the wall cradling his right arm, one held his bleeding head and looked woozy, and one sitting against the wall, holding his back and nose.

Conrad, who was pinching his swollen nose, said, "We were walking down hall from lab, and this crazy girl jumped in our faces. The next thing, we are being attacked. That one—" he pointed at John "—came up from behind and threw Dale to the ground and broke Franklin's arm."

Officer Murray looked at the bystanders and said, "Okay, no one is to leave this area. I'll need statements from each of you."

He then keyed his radio, requesting backup for an altercation scene in the science building second floor hallway and to roll an ambulance as well while eyeing the three sitting on the floor. It was then that he saw the knife on the hallway floor.

"Okay, who pulled the knife?" asked Murray.

"He did," said Samantha. "That one pulled the knife and tried to stab John, and John broke his arm when he disarmed him."

John winced as Samantha spoke, he would rather have verbalized the story, but he understood she was trying to help.

"Is that right?" asked Officer Murray, looking at John.

"Yes, Officer, pretty much correct," he said.

The campus police officer looked at John carefully.

"You a student here?" he asked.

"Yes," replied John. "I just started this semester."

Samantha was looking at Jacob's face. He was going to have a black eye for sure.

"What's your story, then?" asked Officer Murray.

Two more campus police officers entered the hallway from the stairwell, and a siren could be heard outside the building. Murray turned briefly to the two officers from campus security, gave them an update, and they started talking with the assembled bystanders one by one.

"Sorry about that," said Officer Murray. "Please tell me about yourself and what happened."

"Just out of service and trying to get my life restarted," said John. "Here to work on a degree and a career. I came out of the lab and saw these three—" John pointed to the terrible trio "—step in front of those two." John nodded at Samantha and Jacob. John repeated what he had heard Conrad say to Samantha and Jacob.

"You heard what they were saying?" asked Murray.

"Yeah, most of it," said John. "Anyway, the taller one grabbed the girl, and she threw him on the floor."

Murray cocked his head to the side.

"Really," said John. "You had to see it to believe it."

John went on to tell the officer that Jacob tried to protect the girl, but the one called Dale sucker punched him in the face. John went on minimizing his role, but stating he involved himself when the trio started laying hands on Samantha and Jacob.

"Is that when that one tried to stab you?" asked Officer Murray, and he pointed to Franklin,

"Yes, I was fortunate to avoid the knife and grab his arm, but in the tussle for control of the knife, his arm broke, kind of," said John.

Officer Murray grinned ever so slightly and said, "Stay right here for now, will you? I've got to talk to these other two."

John nodded and walked over to lean against the hallway wall. He saw the paramedics emerge from an elevator pushing a stretcher bearing equipment bags. After an initial assessment, they wrapped up Franklin's right arm in a sling and placed a woozy Dale on a stretcher. They left for the hospital accompanied by one of the campus police officers. Conrad followed them, muttering about a lawsuit against John and the university while holding his back and nose.

John noticed some of the students looking at him and whispering. He half closed his eyes and took a cleansing breath willing the adrenaline dump to dissipate. His counselor during his rehabilitation meant well, and really, she was good at her job even if he wasn't the best patient. As she had taught him, he took another breath and allowed his mind to drift focusing on a dark point in the distance letting himself, and only himself, exist as all his focus and concerns drifted into that dark spot. He felt at peace for a moment aware of everything around him but disconnected in a healing way. His mind wandered.

Once again he saw her, dark hair and eyes, running, looking back in terror, not at him but at what was behind him. He tried to call to her, urging her to run faster, but ....

"John did you hear me?" asked Samantha, interrupting his thoughts.

She and Jacob leaned against the wall beside him. Samantha reached over and hugged him.

"Thank you," she said.

Jacob nodded in agreement while rubbing his face.

"I don't know if you needed my help the way you took care of that first guy," said John. "Where did you learn how to move like that?"

"My brother insisted I learn jujitsu when I was younger," said Samantha. "He wanted me to be able to take care of myself. I guess some of it stayed with me."

She smiled weakly.

John turned to Jacob and said, "I heard you try and talk those guys down? That was the right thing to do."

"I picked it up from watching too much television," replied Jacob, looking uncomfortable.

John noticed several of the milling students in the hallway still had cell phones out recording the aftermath. Don't they have classes to attend or other things in their lives, he thought?

"Jacob, are you hurt?"

John saw Professor Maxwell standing in front of them, looking concerned. He guessed the professor heard the commotion in the hall and walked from the lab.

"I'm all right, Granddad," said Jacob. "Just took a shiner is all. Nothing bad. We're both okay, Samantha and I, thanks to him."

Jacob waved his hand toward John, with an introduction.

John stood up to shake Professor Maxwell's offered hand.

"Mr. Stone, it appears I owe you my gratitude," said Professor Maxwell. "I'm in your debt."

Officer Murray came back up to them and said, "The other statements are matching up. I've got your contact information, so you are free to leave for now."

"Thank you, Officer," said Professor Maxwell.

The professor addressed John and Samantha.

"Perhaps we could walk up to my private lab to get away from this for a moment?" he said.

John was good with that. Anywhere other than here, he thought, as he turned away from more cell phone camera flashes.

CHAPTER SEVEN

Richard Reynolds loved working at the Jet Propulsion Laboratory. It was his dream job. Growing up in Iowa on his parent's farm, and not being a great athlete or terribly popular in high school, his one solace had been watching the stars at night.

He was hooked after his parents gifted him a small refractor telescope at age ten for Christmas. He checked every book out at the local library on astronomy and and built his own larger telescope, an eight inch Dobsonian reflector. He ground and polished the glass blank for the primary mirror.

He still had that telescope, although he didn't get as much time to use it now that he was working, and it took up a fair amount of room in his too expensive single bedroom Southern California apartment.

Richard worked as an IT consultant and software engineer at NASA's Jet Propulsion Laboratory (JPL). He was captivated by the work going on here and dreamed of making a great contribution to space exploration. If asked to go to Mars in a colonizing effort, he would say yes in a heartbeat. Meanwhile, he would make sure everyone's computers remained safe from viruses and inadvertent self destruction by the people working at JPL, in that way no different than any other company in America.

Richard always took a moment to check on Voyager I, which checked in every thirty-six to forty-eight hours depending on the earth's rotation and timing. He knew this wasn't really his job, but he felt he was playing a small part in his dream by checking on the data streams, even though Voyager I wasn't expected to send any significant data from its position in interstellar space. Most of Voyager's instruments had been shut down to save on the probe's waning battery life after more than four decades of service.

Whoa, he thought, what's this? There was way more data coming in from Voyager I than expected. He saw that the infrared sensor, magnetometer, and even partial television camera data were present? That didn't make sense, unless Voyager I detected something with the magnetometer and caused the flight management system to autonomously turn on the other instruments. The system had recorded thirty-seven seconds of data, then it shut off abruptly. Usually there was a coded END transmit in the data to show completion, but this transmission while unusual for content and amount, was also unusual in its sudden cessation. It was almost as if Voyager I ran into something, something large enough to trigger the magnetometer and cause it to come to life. But what? In its present location, there really shouldn't be anything there.

Pushing his glasses up on the bridge of his nose out of habit, he muttered to himself, another habit at work that some found annoying, he knew. He would need to get the team involved. Of course that wasn't really his job either. He was allowed to monitor, but not analyze, incoming data.

Still, they never told him he couldn't look at the data for his own education. He copied the raw feed onto an approved thumb drive and carried it over to the supervisor's office and knocked on the door. Surely, it would be okay to ask a question for education. Yeah that's the way to play this, he thought, as he pushed the door open in his excitement.

"Hey Dr. Lowell, I picked this up from Voyager I this afternoon," said Richard. "It's really odd. I thought you might want to know."

Dr. Lowell was in an animated conversation with his personal secretary, Janet, and frowned when he saw Richard enter his office.

"Yes, Richard, what is it?" said the director.

Richard brought him up to date on the interrupted data dump from Voyager I and, taking a breath, said, "I think we should consider the possibility that Voyager I has come in contact with something, maybe run into something out there?"

Director Lowell sighed.

"Richard, have we fully interpreted the data stream yet?" the director asked.

Richard nodded no, and Lowell continued.

"Well then, shouldn't we do that before we jump to any conclusions? Thank you for bringing this to my attention. I will have the team look at it first thing in the morning. Your job is to keep the computers running, correct?"

"Yes sir," replied Richard.

Janet was looking at him like he had a mouse in his pocket instead of his pocket protector.

"Well, why are you bringing me this information?" asked the director. "Why do you even have it? Shouldn't one of the analysts be bringing this to me? We've talked about this once before. We have a certain way of doing things here, Richard, certain channels we go through. Do we understand each other?"

Obviously dismissed from the office, Richard nodded yes and headed back to his work, but he couldn't get past his certainty that Voyager I had come in contact with something, and it would be prudent to go ahead and start searching for an explanation.

Richard decided to implement a program he had been working on in his spare time, which would monitor various radio telescope data feeds as well as visual telescope reports. He wanted to mine the data himself for anything unusual. Maybe nothing would come of it, but if whatever Voyager I came in contact with was large enough, there might be some evidence of it at some point.

He sat at his desk and brought up his private files and booted up the program. He had debugged the program repeatedly, and everything seemed to be running smoothly. Strictly speaking, he wasn't supposed to load up personal programs on the company computers. However, he convinced himself that this was for a good reason. After all, this wasn't some computer game, and he used the most up to date anti-viral and anti-malware software on his machines at home to prevent any contamination.

He pressed the ENTER key after some further thought and watched the program load onto the mainframe in shadow mode, which made it work in the background only when the server CPU wasn't occupied elsewhere. If an anomaly presented in the data, he should be one of the first to know.

He thought about involving his sister, Samantha. She was away at school, and he was so proud of her. She was head and shoulders above him and everyone he knew in computer programming and database architecture. He felt sure she had great things in her future.

He would give her a call this evening.

CHAPTER EIGHT

Professor Maxwell led them to the end stairwell where they followed him slowly up the stairs at his pace. Emerging into the third floor hallway and turning left, they came to a locked double door. The elderly professor took out a key and opened the door.

"Officer Murray says he has what he needs for now, but be sure he can get in touch with you," said the professor. "I'm so sorry this happened to you. Jacob, maybe an icepack for that eye, and I know your mother is going to be upset with me as well. If either of you need to make a call, you can do so from my office."

"I probably should call my parents," said Samantha. "They'll be worried if I don't let them know about this."

Entering the lab, John saw an eight by fifteen meter room with the same gray and white tile floor and white painted block walls interrupted by five tinted windows spaced around the exterior walls allowing one to see, but not touch, the outside. The interior walls held finished pine two by four and plywood shelving holding various pieces of equipment with dials and gauges and screens. It all looked expensive.

The ceiling was the typical drop ceiling present in academic buildings all over the world and looked to be clean without any water stains.

In the center of the room, facing the far wall, was a setup similar to their red blood cell laser experiment, but the equipment looked far more robust.

"Are you measuring a giant's red blood cells?" John pointed to the center table setup.

Jacob glanced at Professor Maxwell, before answering.

"Not quite," he said, without further explanation.

The professor's office was off to the left, and Dr. Maxwell ushered Samantha into the office so she could phone her parents. They could see her talking on the phone. She had tears in her eyes as she got off the phone with a muffled "I love you too."

Jacob walked into the office and guided Samantha to the couch against the wall. He pointed to a folded stack of sheets, blanket, and pillow beside the couch if she needed them. He opened a small refrigerator against the far wall sitting under a poster of Albert Einstein quoting something about "God not playing dice with the Universe." He pulled a bottle of water out to give to Samantha.

"What about you, Jacob?" she asked as she took the water.

"No, I'm good, but maybe Granddad or John?"

He offered both of them water. John accepted one and took a sip.

He was about to comment on the relationship between Jacob and Professor Maxwell, when the lab door opened and in walked Jessica.

He had dreamed of her for so long, he couldn't believe she was real. She was older, but so was he. If anything, she looked more beautiful to him. She was about medium height with dark auburn hair, and her eyes flashed green. She ignored him completely, as she invaded the office like she was striding onto Omaha Beach in June 1944.

"Max, is Jacob with you?" she asked. "Is he all right? I heard there was a fight or something? I came as soon as I heard."

Before Professor Maxwell could reply, Jessica saw Jacob in the office and gasped.

"Oh, what happened, Son?" she asked. "Are you okay? Your face! Are you hurt otherwise?"

Jessica examined her son's arms and ribs as she spoke to reassure herself.

Jacob suffered her to hug him and blushed again.

"I'm all right, Mom, just a little excitement," he said. "This is how us physicists roll, don't you know?"

Jacob looked over her shoulder at Samantha and John and introduced his mother, Jessica Maxwell.

Jessica turned and glanced at them briefly, and then insisted on hearing everything that happened after she decided Jacob seemed okay other than a black eye.

"I don't understand," she said. "Why did those students attack you, Jacob?"

"I think they were more interested in Samantha. I was just in the way."

"Oh?" she asked.

Jessica folded her arms and pivoted with her left foot forward and focused her attention on Samantha clearly waiting for some sort of explanation.

"I don't know," said Samantha. "Those jerks acted like I was going with them whether I wanted or not, but Jacob helped me, Mrs. Maxwell. He stood up to those guys. He was very brave. I'm glad he was there, or all three of them would have ganged up on me, I guess."

Samantha shrugged her shoulders and smiled at Jacob.

John couldn't believe his eyes. It was Jessica, and Jacob was her son? Of course, he realized, she had married after all this time. He had thought of her so many times. There were moments in the past, when he thought he might not survive another day, and the thought of her sustained him. And she didn't recognize him. She looked a bit unsure at Samantha's response.

How could she know me?

It's been seventeen years and my name is different. Maybe I should just leave well enough alone, and just as John was thinking of excusing himself, Jessica turned her full focus on him. Her cheeks flushed, and her hands were on her hips. Very nice hips, John thought, but quickly made sure he was looking at her face. I remember those eyes, he thought.

"Mr. Stone is it?" she asked. "If I'm hearing correctly, you were involved in this incident also? Could you not have prevented my son from being beaten?"

"Mom, that's not fair. John—" said Jacob starting to speak, but he was interrupted by Jessica.

"I should think he is perfectly capable of speaking for himself," said Jessica, looking daggers at him. "Well?"

John stretched up to his full six foot two inch height and looked down at Jessica. He knew it would irritate her, but she looked so cute angry as she bluffed out like a mama grizzly bear.

No, she didn't recognize him, which was probably good, he thought.

"Miss Jessica, your son acted like a man," said John. "You should be proud of him. Samantha is a wildcat in a fight. I wouldn't want to tangle with her. Maybe like you, I bet. I tried to help, but I guess I just wasn't fast enough."

Jessica hummphed and turned to face Professor Maxwell.

"Dad, are you all right?" she asked. "You don't need this kind of excitement after the last few months."

She ignored John completely and began to talk quietly with Professor Maxwell while John turned to Jacob, who shrugged his shoulders as if to say what can you do? She's my Mom.

John moved over to Jacob and asked, "I heard you call Professor Maxwell granddad, and your mom called him Dad?"

Jacob went on to explain briefly that Professor Maxwell and his wife Sarah took Jessica and Jacob into their home when he was still a baby. John noticed Samantha taking in every word.

"Your mom never married?" asked John.

He tried not to let any emotion creep into his question. Still he saw Samantha giving him a "what's up with that question" look. Magically, she turned her attention back to Jacob.

"So, Jacob, you're seventeen, and you are helping to teach Professor Maxwell's classes?" she asked.

Jacob looked down for a moment, looked at the two of them and said, "Well, I went through school kinda fast, and I was able to start at university here a bit early is all. It helps having granddad as a teacher at home. He's really good to us."

John realized that was the most he had heard Jacob speak. He was about to ask more, when Jessica stepped in to face John again. She stretched up on her toes to look him in the eye. Professor Maxwell tried to speak, but Jessica was beside herself.

"They pulled a knife?" she said. "Jacob could have been killed!"

Her eyes looked more green with her face pale.

John held both hands down and out in a placating gesture.

"Well, yes, Miss Jessica, but the young man with the knife seemed more intent on harming me than your son, but yes, there was danger, and your son acted very responsibly."

"I'll keep my own counsel on what is responsible behavior for my son. I'm not sure it would have escalated if you hadn't involved yourself," said Jessica. "I don't think I want my son around you any longer."

John put his hands behind his back with his head down, but otherwise stood at attention.

"Yes ma'am, as you wish."

He raised his head to look at the others present.

"Thanks Sam, Jacob, Professor, I'll be leaving now. Samantha, you okay? Need me to get you home?"

Samantha saw Jacob hesitate to speak in his mother's presence, so she replied, "Yes, I guess that would be helpful. I feel a little wiped out. I don't live far from here."

Samantha gathered her belongings and began to walk out of the office. She paused, faced Jacob, and stood up on the balls of her feet and kissed his cheek.

"Thank you for standing up for me," she said. "I'll see you in class."

John saw Jessica's lips tighten at the gentle and very sweet kiss Samantha gave Jacob, who left off rubbing his left orbit and touched his face where she kissed him. Professor Maxwell tried to hide his smile when Jessica turned to face him again.

John kept his thoughts to himself as he walked Samantha home to her dormitory in what was known as the "valley of the dolls" on campus. Several girl's dorms ringed a grassy area dotted with trees, crossing sidewalks, and scattered flowerbeds. The beautiful morning earlier had delivered a mild evening, cool with long shadows and a faint smell of wood smoke in the air from something burning. He noticed the encroaching shadows brought about by the trees and buildings while noting every possible concealment spot for ambush as they walked to her residence.

Samantha nervously chatted a bit on the way to her dorm. She sounded tired now. She hugged John.

"Thank you again," she said. "I know you saved both of us from something very unpleasant. Jacob's mother was wrong to blame you."

"She's a mother in fear for her child," he said. "She needed a target for venting, and I was handy. Been a long time coming for her. It's all right. Good-night lab partner."

John waved to Samantha.

Samantha waved back to him while using her campus identification to key into her dormitory entrance.

John walked back to his dorm, deep in thought. Maybe it was a blessing Jessica didn't remember him. Really, it was just as well. He still felt grateful. She didn't know it, but she had saved his life so many times already. He was happy just seeing her again.

The knife attack was an escalation for sure. Jessica was correct about that, and maybe he shouldn't have intervened, but John was too familiar with violence. He knew he had read the situation correctly. Those three were out of control. He guessed the result of coming from permissive families with too much money and power. It was an old story not limited to one culture. He knew that for a fact thinking of the Kincaid family, Jessica, and their shared past.

Well, maybe he would find out more in the morning. John kept to his thoughts, still searching his surroundings out of habit as he walked back to his dormitory.

CHAPTER NINE

"We have to act, Dean. We'll need to release a statement regarding this tonight," said Professor Paul Kincaid.

Kincaid sat in a leather chair in the dean's office in the Campus Administration Building. Paul had called the dean, the university advisory attorney and two of the most senior trustees, shortly after finding out about the altercation in the science building from Campus Police Chief Roberts.

The Dean of the University, Kenneth Paulson, sat behind his desk, his hands folding and unfolding a brochure proclaiming the wonders of a European river cruise. The dean hesitated, turned his head and said, "Chief, do you have anything to add?"

Chief Roberts sat in a comfortable office armchair with his legs crossed, his left hand resting on his knee.

"We've questioned just about all the student witnesses in the hallway and gotten just as many accounts," he said. "Eyewitness testimony is often inconsistent."

"So, we don't know who threw the first punch?" asked Professor Kincaid.

Chief Roberts shifted position in his chair, uncrossed his legs, and leaned forward slightly.

"No, we have no clear agreement between the witness accounts," he said. "There is one cell phone video which begins when another student, a John Stone, became involved." Roberts flipped a page or two in the notebook that he was holding. "The video does show one of the involved students lunging at Stone with a knife."

"Was this Stone hurt?" asked Phillip McPhearson, one of the trustees at the meeting.

"No, surprisingly, he managed to avoid being hurt," said Chief Roberts. "However, student Dale Winston suffered a concussion and scalp laceration. Student Conrad Thurston suffered a mild concussion, a broken nose, and a strained back. Student Franklin Bryce, the one with the knife, suffered a dislocated and fractured right shoulder and will need surgery. Turns out that the Bryce boy had some trouble in the past as a juvenile."

"Oh dear," said the dean. "All three of those boys are from prominent families who are members of the Founders Club."

Kincaid knew what that meant. The university facilitated scholarships in all sorts of ways. What went unsaid was sometimes those scholarships were accompanied by generous charitable donations to the university. The Founders Club comprised some of the largest beneficent donors to the university. Paul inferred the dean was trying to think how to spin this public relations crisis, and Paul knew just how to take advantage.

"Dean, you know there may be a backlash from several of our student groups given the prominence of the three students," said Kincaid.

"Yes, yes, I know," said the dean, nodding his head in agreement. "Chief, what is the position of the investigation so far?"

"There is no general consensus among the witnesses for the beginning of the altercation, but they say that the students did confront Samantha Reynolds and Jacob Maxwell. When you add in the knife, which clearly belonged to student Franklin Bryce, and the video of that event, there is support for self defense. However, there are enough conflicting accounts that an inquiry could go either way."

McPhearson leaned forward and said, "Wait, is that Professor Maxwell's grandson, Jacob?"

"Yes. I'm afraid so. It's fortunate that nothing points to him instigating any of this, so I think we can take away the worry over how Horace will react as I understand his grandson will be okay," said the other trustee. "Perhaps we can just wait to let this sort itself out?"

Professor Kincaid said, "That won't do at all. I've already received calls from two news organizations regarding this incident, and they won't be the last. We need to wrap this up quickly."

The dean leaned forward picking up the crumpled cruise brochure again in his hands and said, "How so?"

"The most expedient answer for the university is that this Stone fellow escalated the situation by involving himself unnecessarily. I have him as a student in my Focused American History class, and Mr. Stone proved his ability to be a hothead just this morning," said Professor Kincaid. "Besides, he is a military veteran, and we know how unstable they can be."

Robert Sandifer, a local bank chief executive officer and long time trustee to the college, shifted around in his chair, almost as if he couldn't find a comfortable place to be, and asked, "What are you suggesting?"

Professor Kincaid said, "I'm saying that we quietly share a few thoughts with some of our more active and involved students, and they will help us be sure this resolves in the favor of those three students whose families will likely demonstrate how grateful they are to the university for standing up for their sons."

Always use a crisis to good advantage thought Paul. That's what his father taught him, on the few occasions he paid attention to him.

The dean sat back in thought for a moment.

"Okay, I think that is reasonable," said Dean Paulson. "With the video from student cell phones posted on the internet, we won't be able to handle this discreetly. Since we can't be completely sure how this occurred, we will take the official position that Mr. Stone should not have involved himself, but when he did, the situation escalated, and three students were injured. The rest will sort itself out. Now, let's discuss any anticipated issues."

An hour later a satisfied Professor Paul Kincaid pushed open the glass door exit from the University Administration Building. The dean had deferred any final decisions until hearing again from all present at the meeting.

Clearly, he wasn't comfortable with the situation and felt trapped with any decision going forward, but in the end, the overwhelming fear of negative publicity worked its magic, and the decision was to follow Kincaid's plan, discreetly of course. For just a moment, Paul considered that his senator father would be proud of him. Like his father, he would make an immortal legacy for himself.

Certainly, this situation was made to work to his advantage. He could point blame to that insufferable tackling dummy Stone and leverage Jacob against Professor Maxwell, who stood in his path to succeed as Dean of the University.

Maxwell had the ear of several on the regents board, mostly because of the sizable research grants he had brought to the university, but now, Paul could manipulate the aging professor with leverage on the boy. Kincaid almost cackled as he rubbed his hands together. He could play the boy's involvement off on his mother as well.

Yes, that would be very good. Jessica had been an insufferable busy body into his activities at the university since that duplicitous young coed betrayed him by speaking about their agreement. Katie had been delicious, but hardly worth the risk. If only Jessica could see, could understand. Well, now at least, he had a way to fight back, and he determined to use this fortunate incident for all it was worth.

Now, he was off to home, and maybe, a late movie. Life was good with a quiet house, he thought. I'm better off since the wife left me. The prenup held, so good riddance. No more marriage for me, especially with all the pretty and naive coeds coming through every year.

Tomorrow will be a good day. I can start taking care of business. I may speak with Jessica at the library. She wouldn't like a public scene so better to talk with her there. Maybe I can persuade her to meet for dinner. She's always said no to me, but not this time.

No. Not this time.

CHAPTER TEN

Jessica was still angry when they got back home. She had stopped being afraid for herself long ago, but a threat to her family, Jacob or Max, that made her fearful, and being afraid made her angry. She knew she was being unreasonable toward John Stone, but Jacob could have been hurt severely.

Jessica set about making something simple in the kitchen for them to eat. She was emotionally exhausted from the day's events, so something quick. She mixed batter and threw in some apple spice and bits of dried apple for pancakes. She put some bacon slices in the broiler. Breakfast for supper was something they all liked occasionally.

Jessica knew letting Jacob attend the university was necessary for him, but she had tried to shield him for so long. She and Max had long discussed this. Sarah too, while she was with them. Jessica had a daily fear that Jacob would reveal too much of himself, and now, he had been attacked.

She set the plates out on the table calling to Jacob and Max who were out in the barn behind the house. They both spent so much time in their "workshop" as they called it, but at least they were bonding.

She wasn't blind. She had seen the way her son looked at Samantha. Okay, the young coed was cute, and obviously bright, but what was she like inside. Jacob was very inexperienced and utterly without guile. Jessica didn't want him hurt if she could avoid it.

She called over the intercom to the workshop again for the boys to come in. Sometimes they got so wrapped up in their work, they simply didn't hear her. She had a rule of not calling more than three times for them, figuring eventually, their stomachs would lead them back in.

Max and Jacob both came through the driveway side door. Max rubbed his hands together and smiled.

"Smells good, daughter," said Max. "Thank you."

Jacob added his thanks while washing his hands after Max, and they both sat down.

Holding hands, they said a quick blessing in practiced unison.

"Bless us O Lord for this food and all thy bounty, through Christ our Lord, Amen."

Max looked over at the photograph of Sarah on the wall and said a few silent thoughts, as was his routine. He applied himself to a plate of pancakes and bacon and a cup of tea.

They ate quietly, unusually so. Jessica realized the two of them were picking up on her mood.

"Okay, I get it Jacob," she said. "You couldn't help what happened. Are you unhurt, really?"

"Mom, I'm alright," said Jacob. "I slipped the guy's punch when I saw it coming, but really didn't have to do anything else, as John was there."

Jessica could see Jacob's facial bruising was already fading. He had always healed quickly.

"John is it?" she asked.

"Well, yeah, I was talking to him in the lab, and he asked me to call him John. He was in the military for a long time, I think."

"How do you know that?" she asked.

"He mentioned being out of country for a while, and I heard Samantha asking him what he did before coming to university. You know he's just about your age, Mom."

Max listened, working on another pancake, but paused to add, "I'm glad he intervened, Jessica. We were fortunate he was there."

Jessica thought to herself. Am I really so off base here? She was beginning to regret her words to the somehow familiar and well-built man. Now, why did she think that?

"Anyway, Samantha says he's really nice," said Jacob. She says he seems a bit sad though. She says he doesn't like to talk about himself very much."

Jacob nibbled a piece of bacon.

"Oh, and what else does Samantha say?" asked Jessica, teasing her son.

"She said she was really excited to be in granddad's class, and she couldn't believe I was helping."

Max interjected, "Jacob, I think everyone is a bit surprised to see someone as young as you at university. This won't be the last time for that reaction."

Exactly, she thought. This is what she had talked to Max about, how they needed to keep Jacob's abilities away from the rest of the world. Putting him out in a public situation would put him at risk.

When Jessica realized she was pregnant, the full enormity of what had happened that terrible night came due. She found herself momentarily reliving the days and weeks after. Her parents had brought her home from the hospital, and her exam had been inconclusive. She had endured the snide remarks at school along with the isolation, and at home, her father had essentially told her to get out of his house.

"I'm not going to have no tramp living with us," he said.

So, she had left home pregnant, with some money she had managed to hide from her teen baby sitting jobs and the small amount of cash her mother had pressed into her hand on the morning that she left. Somehow her mother had known Jessica was leaving. Her mother quietly told her she loved her, and said she was sorry. Her mother didn't want to wake her father. He was sleeping off another drinking episode.

Jessica gave birth to Jacob in a neighboring town and was sheltered in her poverty at a local church until she and Jacob moved on to the city on advice of the pastor. She made her way to a shelter with child care for young families, hoping she might be able to find some work.

Sarah had found both of them there. Jessica remembered Sarah holding Jacob. He was not yet six months old. He reached up his chubby hand to touch her, and Sarah's face had taken on a look of wonder. Jessica looked over at the photograph on the wall behind the empty chair and silently gave her thanks to Sarah again.

"Granddad," said Jacob. "Samantha is a great computer programmer. I told you, right?"

Jacob waited for Max to respond.

"I see. You think she can be of help?" Max asked, and Jacob simply nodded yes.

"Mom, Mr. Stone asked me if you ever married?"

Jacob stirred a bite of pancake in some syrup on his plate and tried not to smile.

Jessica put her hands on the table.

"I don't see what difference that could possibly make to him," she said.

"Well, Mom, I was just wondering, I mean, did you notice that he and I look a little alike. Samantha noticed it, and after she said something, well, I could see it too."

Max kept his silence.

Jessica knew where this was going. From time to time, Jacob would wonder over his father's identity. He would never ask outright, but sometimes, like this, he would hint. He was convinced for a while that James Stuart was his father after seeing *It's a Wonderful Life* for the first time. It remained one of their favorite Christmas movies.

"Jacob, are you finished eating?" asked Jessica, redirecting the course of the conversation.

She had never told Jacob or Max the details of that night at the party. She couldn't remember everything, and what she did remember was a hazy horror.

Truth is, she didn't know who Jacob's father was, and she desperately wanted to spare him that shame, so she just refused to talk about it. Better he think his father was a movie actor or a famous sports figure. Better for him and less painful for her. At least, that's what she kept telling herself.

CHAPTER ELEVEN

Back at the dormitory, which was the tallest building on campus, John walked into the hallway downstairs only to have several people clap for him.

"Way to go, dude!" along with shouts of "Way to kick ass, man!" came from several of the loitering students in the lobby.

John started to walk toward the elevator bank, when a young man and woman approached him and stepped into his path.

"Are you John Stone? Could we talk with you for a moment? I'm Brittany Burkholter, and this is Steve Johnston. We're from the *Campus Vine* and would like to interview you."

The *Vine* was the campus newspaper, and the last organization John wanted to contact him. The young woman held a small solid state recorder in her left hand which suggested to John that she was right hand dominant. He could see nothing in her other hand which she moved to emphasize some of her words. She was wearing a simple shirt, skirt, and flats. Steve held a go pro HD video camera. He was wearing a short sleeve t-shirt, sandals, and tan cargo shorts. Obviously, he remained the man behind the camera.

John considered his options. He could walk past them without comment, which they would undoubtedly film and include in the electronic campus newspaper, or he could answer a few questions, which might turn into a fiasco. It all depended on their attitudes.

"I can talk for a moment," said John. "What can I help you with?"

John motioned to the lounges they had been sitting on. He and Brittany sat down while Steve kept his camera on the two of them.

"We've all seen cell phone video from the altercation in the science building, but no one has talked with you," she said. "I was hoping to get your take on what happened and on the protest building on campus."

John looked at Brittany. She sat calmly, and he detected no agenda. Her question was straightforward.

"Ok, I'll answer," said John. "But first, may I ask what you think?"

"I don't know what to think exactly," she said. "There are several versions of cell phone video out which show you throwing those guys around, and I know they went to the hospital. Were you hurt?"

Brittany seemed genuinely concerned.

"No, I was fortunate. Others less so," said John.

He proceeded to share the altercation in the hall from memory glossing over his own involvement except for the facts and omitting the names of Samantha and Jacob. He wanted to keep them out of the limelight.

"One of them tried to stab you?" she asked. "I didn't see that on any of the versions I saw."

"That's because the cell phone versions you saw on the internet are edited for an agenda, Miss Brittany. People want others to believe what they want them to believe."

"So you defended yourself and others is what you are saying?" she said. "You didn't instigate an attack against those three students?"

"That is correct," said John.

"Thank you, Mr. John Stone," she said. Turning to her cameraman, she added, "This is Brittany Burkholter reporting for the *Campus Vine*.

John stood, and Steve, the cameraman said, "You really expect us to believe those three students attacked you in the hallway for no reason at all? Do you know how angry people are over this? How can you even walk around here? Why aren't you in jail?"

John subconsciously evaluated the cameraman for threat noting his pressured speech and pupillary dilation, but John saw no fist clenching, bouncing, or pacing and judged the young man was venting. He was about to reply, when Brittany jumped in.

"Steve, you know we talked about this before we came here," she said. "That's not professional."

"Professional, hell!" exclaimed Steve. "This guy is a berserker on our campus. None of us are safe with him here. I don't care if you're trying to brown nose your way to a job after college, the truth needs to come out here."

Steve stepped closer to Brittany, and looked down at her. He was about to say more, but Tom Mosier, the assistant dorm director who had been observing from the front desk, interrupted him. Tom walked up as soon as Steve started blustering.

"Everything okay over here?" asked Tom.

John said, "I believe Mr. Johnston was getting a bit excited expressing an opinion is all."

Steve's lips grimaced like he was choking on poison.

John looked at the young female reporter and said, "Miss Brittany, are you all right?"

Brittany had a chance to distance herself from her cameraman as she stepped back. Her eyes spit flames at Steve.

"Thank you, Mr. Stone," she said. "Yes, I think we are finished here."

She continued to glare at Steve, and John couldn't help but smile. He had seen that look just recently on Jessica's face and knew it was universal language for dark clouds ahead. He was glad it wasn't directed at him.

Brittany exited the dormitory lobby with Steve stomping behind her.

John faced Tom and said, "Thanks for that. I probably shouldn't have stopped to talk to them, but there didn't seem to be a good alternative."

Tom motioned for him to come into his office. He shrugged and followed him, although John was thinking a short nap sounded good.

His mind started to wander. The drop process at administration hadn't gone smoothly. He had been asked to come back Monday as the computer was giving them some trouble, and no one would be available tomorrow, Friday. Monday was the last day for drop/add requests. He probably should at least make some effort on that paper due for history, just in case he ended up not being able to drop the class.

Tom Mosier was a clean-shaven, affable man, a couple years younger than John, and had the lean build and medium height of a distance runner. John had met him two weeks into the semester during a trash chute fire in the dorm. Waking up to the alarm John had grabbed his go bag and took a hand in getting some of the students from the upper floors out of the building while ducking his head to stay out of the smoke gathering towards the ceiling.

Standing outside in the cool night air with eight hundred sleepy and grousing students surrounded by strobe red lights from the fire trucks allowed some time for conversation. Tom had come over to thank him, and had asked John about himself. They exchanged brief back-stories.

The next day, Tom left a message for John to come by the office. During their conversation, he learned Tom was working his way through his graduate MBA with administrative work at the dormitory for the university.

Tom was a runner and training for the Olympic trials in the coming year in the marathon event. He offered John a resident assistant position after watching him work with some of the students that night, but John had politely declined saying he didn't want any responsibility beyond getting himself through school.

John liked to run in the morning for fitness and had gone out for a couple of runs with Tom, but he found himself dropping behind after about two miles. The assistant dorm director was on another level when it came to running.

John shut the door to the office.

Tom sat in his desk chair.

"I received a call earlier from campus police chief Roberts concerning what happened in the science building today," said Tom. "He wanted to know if I knew anything about you and if you are a troublemaker?"

John said, "And?"

"I told him I haven't had any trouble from you," said Tom, looking at John. "Are you a troublemaker?"

The assistant dorm director smiled.

"Really, are you okay?" asked Tom.

"I'm a little tired," said John, shrugging his shoulders.

Tom said, "I'm not supposed to tell you, but there will likely be a hearing over what happened. The academic council is pushing for it on the grounds you acted without proper cause."

John's look said it all.

"I know, I know, but I was told this in confidence by Officer Murray when he came by earlier to interview me. He also said you might be an okay guy. Of course I already knew that, but it says a lot coming from him." Tom continued. "Did you know there is video of at least part of it?"

John knew there were no cameras in the hallway as he had checked early in the semester out of habit.

"That young reporter mentioned someone with a cell phone," said John.

"Yes", said Tom, looking at him with more interest. "I think administration tried to suppress it, but it's already gone to the web, so good luck with that."

Tom turned his laptop around showing John a cell phone video showing part of the altercation. The knife was clearly visible being held by Franklin. The action between John and the knife wielding student blurred on the camera making it difficult to see clearly until Franklin was on the floor holding his arm.

"You know, you move pretty fast for an old man," said Tom. "Anyway, watch your back. I can guess the administration here would love for this to be a non-event, but with the cell phone videos already going viral, you can bet they will do whatever makes them look best. I suspect the administration will not hesitate to pin any and all fault on you if they can. With that video out, there will be some fuss, and the families of those boys have some powerful friends. I'd like to avoid any trouble here in the dorm."

"Honestly, trouble is the last thing I want," said John.

Tom nodded his thanks at hearing that statement.

"For the moment, you are at the center of the storm," he said. "Let me know if you need anything."

"That could cause problems for you, couldn't it?" asked John.

"Some cost I can live with, some not. Get some rest," said Tom.

John was feeling the full after effects of the adrenaline rush earlier now. He wasn't nineteen anymore. He leaned against the elevator on the way up to his floor. He needed to work on that paper for Kincaid's class, but first a nap if possible.

He let himself in his room, happy for the quiet. Isaac was either working or at the library, and once again he felt grateful at having found such a decent guy as a room mate and for gaining a room on the graduate student's third floor. He lived high enough to be away from the noise on campus but far below the generally younger and rowdier students.

He stretched out on his bed and wondered if he could have prevented the confrontation in the science building earlier today. He knew those boys were trouble, but couldn't have foreseen they would act out so. Now, he was in the middle of controversy again. Something he had told himself to avoid after leaving the military.

The last mission had gone wrong so quickly. How could the enemy have known they were going to that village that day. They were obviously warned and set up for ambush. John had worked hard to develop relationships with the local people while helping them to overcome their fear of the radicals. But someone had given them up.

As John drifted off to sleep, he saw their convoy pulling up to the small village, with his squad split into four up armored Humvees. The mission was recovery of an asset and his family. John knew the family well, having visited them several times. They were good people living in a bad situation. When command passed down word to extract them, John volunteered to go out and bring them in to the safety of the forward base, knowing that Ali and his family had to be in danger.

Should have known, thought John as he struggled to sleep. Should have known. He hated sleeping because of the dreams. During rehab, he had lied to the counselors telling them the dreams were gone. He had sensed the U. S. Army would not cut him loose from rehab and therapy otherwise. He shifted regretfully in his sleep.

John was urging a teen aged girl with dark eyes and hair streaming behind her to run even faster as he followed holding his rifle in his right hand. Her mother, an older image of her daughter, turned to look behind them, eyes wide in terror as she held her son and tried to run faster.

The woman transformed into an auburn haired woman with blue green eyes beckoning him closer, ever closer, until she whispered into his ear.

"Stay away from my son."

CHAPTER TWELVE

John woke the next morning to the sounds of soft rock radio and humming from the far side of the room. He had slept through the night. New students at university were required to live in the dorms for at least a year. He didn't mind that much as he didn't have many belongings having spent years living in dorm like conditions in the military. His roommate, Isaac Abraham Washington, puttered around the far side of the room.

"Sorry if I woke you," said Isaac. "Probably time you got out of the sack anyway you slacker. Want a strawberry pop tart?"

"You, sir, are entirely too cheerful in the morning," said John, stretching his shoulders and back. He put his sweats on for a morning run. "No thanks, I'll just be out for a few minutes, and then we can get going."

He knew the best way to get his run in the morning, was to stretch and go without delay. John made his way downstairs and used the barricade pylons in front of the dormitory to stretch his hamstrings, then he started running slowly to warm up. He planned his day out while he ran. No class for him this morning, but he had an economics class this afternoon, and then the library to work on that history paper, he thought.

John knew he was lucky to know Isaac. He had requested a roommate with former military experience, thinking they would be closer in age and have something in common. That proved to be a smart move. Isaac was a burly and cheerful man from a loud and loving family. He was also a handy guy to have around, as his military occupational specialty had given him experience working on helicopters and fixed wing aircraft for six years. Before that he worked as a mechanic in his father's garage as a teenager. Isaac had plans for a mechanical engineering degree, and John had no doubt he would succeed given any reasonable chance.

Twenty-four minutes and three miles around campus later, John was back at the dorm and heading up to his room and a shower. He needed to hurry as Isaac had asked him to follow him out to the airport in case his car tried to quit on him.

Of course, John gave his roommate grief for a mechanic having trouble with his own vehicle, but anyone could have car trouble, and Isaac's 1982 Bronco was having some electrical issues. Isaac seemed confident that he could trace out the problem given the equipment in the mechanic's hanger at the airport. He thought he would have time to work on his truck after he finished his work on one of the air school's trainer aircraft.

John thought Isaac a very steady man who liked to give the appearance of a happy go lucky guy. Planning ahead to use his certification in the military to supplement his GI Bill and help defray his college expenses just supported his idea that his roommate had it together.

Finishing his shower quickly, John said, "Ready to go if you are."

Isaac was ready, and they headed out. As they were leaving the dorm, John noticed a group of students paying attention to him while he and Isaac ran cables from John's Toyota pickup and jump-started the Bronco.

Isaac crossed his fingers as he started the engine, which turned over. He listened to it for a moment and when it continued to run, he said, "Well, let's try it.

Isaac was concerned his truck might die on him driving over to the airport, and John was driving escort in case his friend became stranded. The Bronco sounded okay to him, but he wasn't great with engines. John noted the students onlookers had moved on. He tapped the dash of his pickup, thankful he wasn't having any problems with his truck.

Isaac pulled up to the hanger for the flight school, and John parked his truck in one of the spaces in front of the hanger on the other side of the airport fencing. Isaac helped him get in using his keycard and showed him around the hanger. There were several models of aircraft all carefully parked with little room between wingtips to make the most of the available space. The Beechcraft King Air twin was the largest aircraft in the hanger and commanded its own corner on the far side. Faint old oil spots on the concrete floor were visible, but overall, the hanger was much cleaner than John expected. Isaac was working on a Cessna trainer which needed a new alternator and didn't promise to be a long job.

"I admire your planning in getting a useful skill from the army that you can earn money with after getting out," said John. "I only learned how to blow things up."

Isaac reached into the toolbox on the table against the wall for a seven sixteenths inch wrench and began taking the bolts off the airframe holding the alternator in place. He had already disconnected the battery cables.

"I saw you take out the guy with the knife on that video," said Isaac. "I think that's a pretty useful skill set."

"Well, not generally much call for breaking heads in the civilian world," said John, standing behind Isaac and looking over his shoulder. "I'd be just as happy to not ever be in any kind of fight again. Nobody wins in a fight."

"But sometimes you have to defend yourself and others. Sometimes you don't get a choice. Right? And who says you get to win, mi hermano. You only get to choose," said Isaac, grunting as he pulled on the mounting bracket to clear the alternator.

John could see why Isaac had such stout shoulders working like this. He considered his roommate's words.

"I could have walked away or not gotten involved," John said out loud.

Isaac turned back from carrying the old alternator to the workbench against the hanger wall. He stopped and looked at him.

"You are not wired that way, amigo," said Isaac. "That's why you joined the army, chose infantry, and worked your way into the rangers right? You wanted to make a difference. Well you made a difference yesterday." Isaac held out his hand for a fist bump from John. "Now, come make a difference, and help me with the belt tensioner after I get this part back on the frame."

Isaac carefully placed the new alternator onto its position in the Cessna Skyhawk.

The were both sweating in the mildly humid morning air when Isaac finished retightening the alternator retaining bolts and checked the new belt for proper tension. Grabbing the new battery, he tightened the leads on the posts and checked voltage with a multimeter.

"Well, I see someone's working this morning? How's it looking, Isaac?"

The question came from a smiling woman walking toward them wearing a white shirt with pilot wings on her left chest. John guessed her age at twenty-six, and she looked as fresh as a sunrise in Brazil. He had heard Isaac mention Isabella a couple of times, and now he understood his roommate's interest.

"We are almost done, Miss Isabella," said Isaac. "This is my friend, John. We go to school together, and he came out to help me this morning."

John thought his roommate seemed very focused on the young pilot, and he understood. With her bright smile, expressive dark eyes, mocha complexion, and dark hair, she would garner attention anywhere.

"We are just about to pull the plane out of the hanger and do final checks. Hopefully, twenty minutes and finished," said Isaac.

Isabella checked her watch, smiled, and said, "Sounds good. I have a student pilot due in forty-five minutes. Thank you Isaac, and John, is it?"

She turned to go back into the front office. John saw Isaac looking after her until she was at the door. She looked back over her shoulder and smiled before walking into the office.

"So you're working here for the money, eh?" said John.

Isaac's dark skin hid his blush partly as he shrugged his shoulders.

"You ask her out yet?" asked John.

"She is beautiful and smart, and I'm a mecanico," muttered Isaac. Isaac's father was African American and his mother was from Columbia. Isaac spoke and thought in both English and Spanish much of the time.

"You two are a perfect match. You fix 'em and she flies them," said John. "Maybe she is looking for a fixer upper in her life?"

John teased, and Isaac hit him lightly in his shoulder.

They un-chocked the wheels and carefully pulled the plane out of the hanger being sure the wings cleared. Pulling and pushing the Cessna Skyhawk over to a tarmac T-spot to clear the hanger of any potential prop wash, they both climbed into the narrow cabin. Isaac set the parking brake, turned on the master switch, checked the amperage readout, flipped on the fuel pump switch to get the necessary five pounds fuel pressure, turned off the fuel pump, and turned on the tail beacon light.

Opening the door on the left side, he yelled the traditional "clear prop" and looked all around the plane from the inside as well before turning the ignition key with both feet on the brake rudder pedals. The engine started right up, and after letting it warm up at one thousand revolutions per minute, he advanced throttle with full brakes to eighteen hundred rpm and looked at the amperage and all the instruments. Satisfied, Isaac backed off the throttle gradually to one thousand rpm again and leaned out the mixture causing the engine to starve of fuel. He turned off the ignition and the master switch.

"Looks like we have it finished," said Isaac. "Thank you."

"This is interesting work," said John. "Besides, I owe you for helping me with my truck. I have to get back to campus. You going to be okay out here alone with Miss Isabella?"

Isaac was tying down the Skyhawk.

"Ahh, get out of here slacker," said Isaac. "And keep your eyes peeled. I heard some talk I don't like. Some of the students are stirring things up for you, I think."

John nodded to him.

"Thanks," said John. "See you back at the dorm later."

There were several vocal groups on campus. Not surprising they are out for my scalp given yesterday, he thought. He started his truck up and headed back to campus.

CHAPTER THIRTEEN

When John returned to campus, he had time to grab a sandwich and make it to a blessedly uneventful economics class. He refilled his water bottle from a fountain, and checked his pack for a nutrition bar. He made his way over to the library to find some peace and quiet and knock out the history paper on American involvement in the Vietnam War.

He had the text with him, and he read the chapter again, but didn't understand the limited discussion. He knew the subject was complex. He had a feeling that no matter what he wrote, Paul Kincaid would find a way to discredit it.

John didn't like to say the word quit, but sometimes a strategic retreat could salvage a floundering campaign. It might take him an extra semester, but if he tried to take the course next fall or in the spring with a different instructor things might be smoother. Of course, since he hadn't actually been able to drop the class yet, he wanted to be ready with the assignment in case he ran into difficulty.

John found his way to the history section of the library and set up temporary base camp at an unused desk. He had a life giving coffee with him, and he made sure to figure out the location of the nearest restroom. Now, to get some work done. Perusing the shelves he pulled several tomes that looked as if they might help. Sadly, he thought, this might not be the last time he had to juggle classes to escape the pervasive politically correct environment inherent in secondary education. But regardless, if Kincaid was going to be instructing the class, John did not trust himself for the rest of the semester.

John had been working for about two hours and making good progress in the quiet when he became aware of voices coming from the stacks off to his right. He tried to ignore them, but when he heard "Get your hand off me!" in a female voice, he decided he would have to investigate.

Approaching the book shelving from his side he could hear the conversation grow louder. Walking around the stacks, John saw Professor Kincaid had backed Jessica against the shelving. John imagined he could see blood seeping out of the creases of Kincaid's engorged face shadowed red with the overhead fluorescent lighting. His right hand gripped Jessica's left arm at her biceps.

"I don't care what you think you can do, Paul," she said. "I will never have dinner or anything else with you. I don't trust you, and no, I'm not going to let Katie's statement slide. From what I hear, there are others. That's what this is about, isn't it. You're afraid they'll come together and speak out, and then you and your little game will be through here."

"Jessica, you need to believe me," said Kincaid. "I have the dean's ear, and now, I have the leverage to get your precious boy thrown out of this school, and maybe you and your adopted father as well. You need to show a little more cooperation."

John stalked around the corner of the shelving like a panther. Seeing Professor Kincaid with a hold on Jessica's left arm, John coiled inside judging distance, his face flat, almost expressionless.

"Professor Kincaid, I believe Miss Jessica asked you to unhand her," he said and glided forward closing the three meter distance between them quickly. "That might be a good idea, now!"

Professor Kincaid paled and let go of Jessica's arm.

"Think about what we've talked about," said Kincaid. "Don't make a mistake again."

He huffed and backed up while keeping his eyes on John, then turned and quickly walked away.

"Are you hurt?" asked John.

Jessica looked at John standing beside her. He looked as calm and detached as if he were ordering a coffee, but there was something frightening behind his eyes, something best left untold. Jessica's hand trembled as she rubbed her left arm. She felt terribly embarrassed at being in a position to need help from this strangely familiar man again, and she couldn't seem to help herself.

"Yes I'm all right," she said. "I didn't need your help. You seem to have a habit of inserting yourself in other people's business, Mr. Stone."

"You're right. I really should change that about myself," he said. "If you're all right, I'll excuse myself for now."

John turned to walk away.

Jessica hesitated, struggling within herself. She reached out with her right hand and gently touched his upper arm.

"Please wait," she said. "John is it? I don't mean to seem ungrateful. I'm glad that man is gone. I try to avoid him when I can. It's unfortunate that we teach at the same university. Thank you for intervening just now. I'm sorry about the way I acted yesterday with you. I saw the video and realize you probably helped save Jacob from worse than a black eye."

"You were scared for your son. No need to apologize," said John, bending down to pick up the texts Jessica had dropped in the unexpected confrontation with Professor Kincaid. "I don't mean to pry, but what did he mean when he told you not to make a mistake again?"

She looked uncertain.

John immediately said, "You're right, maybe that's too personal." He shrugged his shoulders. "If you don't want to talk about it ...?"

"I've known Paul Kincaid since High School," she said. "His father was and still is a state Senator, and Paul thought he ruled the roost. He didn't take it well when I wouldn't date him. I guess he's never gotten over it."

She bit her lip, looking like she wanted to say more.

"Well I could see where a guy might have a hard time getting over you."

Oh man, did I just say that?

Feeling his face flush, he looked away and decided it might be a good time for an exit.

"Well, if you're okay," he said. "I guess I better get back to it and start trying to figure out another plan for my history credit."

"Would you like to come to dinner with us tonight?" asked Jessica, surprising herself. "Jacob can't hardly stop talking about you and that girl, what's her name, Samantha? I guess it's the least we could do. Here, let me write down our address. We're having spaghetti tonight."

"Ahh, okay, I like spaghetti," said John. "What time? Oh, I forgot, I'm supposed to have dinner with my roommate tonight."

He felt like he was a reed in the wind, swaying.

If she bites her lip again, I might just have to sit down.

"Jessica hesitated a moment and said, "Well, bring him or her along. There should be enough."

He smiled and said, "It's a him, and you haven't seen Isaac eat. But I'll ask him. Thank you for the invitation. Is there anything we can bring?"

"Just yourselves," she said. "We'll see you at seven then."

John walked around the bookshelves and gathered up his notes and belongings, thinking he didn't have to worry about the decision to drop history or not. He would need a substitute class to keep the minimum hours for his G.I. Bill benefits.

Thinking he would settle that Monday morning, John headed back to his dormitory, taking the opportunity to call Isaac and inform him of the change in dinner plans. Isaac was delighted and began to tease John over the phone. His roommate was still at the airport working, but planned to meet John at the given address.

John took a quick shower, and decided to get his economics reading done. He just finished the reading assignment when he heard a knock at the door.

He found Brittany standing there with a half smile.

"I'm sorry about yesterday's interview," she said. "Is it all right if we talk off the record?"

John motioned her to come into the dorm room. Isaac and John both kept their room neat, a holdover from their military training.

Brittany took a seat on the offered chair, and John tried not to look at her bottom as she maneuvered for the seat. He was sure he wasn't the only guy to ever have to do that. Probably every guy around her since she was eighteen he would guess.

"So this is where the infamous John Stone lives."

"Not much different than barracks life in the past," he replied.

"I want to say I'm sorry for Steve again," she said. "He is so self-righteous and a horse's ass sometimes."

"Does he have as much passion for you?" asked John.

Brittany's eyes widened, and he knew he had interpreted the back history between her cameraman and her correctly.

"How did you know?"

"It's not hard to see there is some history between you two. He was overly familiar with you and seemed a bit too possessive during the interview. Just a guess."

"Yes, we dated some, but not in the last two months."

"And, he's not happy about that, I would guess?" asked John.

"He's just so possessive, and he's always around. I could never breathe."

Brittany rubbed her folded hands together as she spoke. She looked down and her shoulders slumped slightly.

"I'm surprised that you used him as your cameraman yesterday?"

"There wasn't any choice," she said. "The other two suddenly had other assignments. If I didn't know better, I would think that Steve arranged for that. You know, I think sometimes he still follows me around. I could swear I've seen him around the women's dorm sometimes in the evenings, and I've gotten some funny texts on my phone. I don't know. He's not who I thought he was."

"Is that why you're here now," John asked?

"I don't know," she said. "I guess maybe, partly, I mean, you just seem so much more experienced than others around here. There's something about you. Even downstairs, I knew you were about a hair from yanking Steve back away from me, right?"

She seemed very assured in her opinion. She looked squarely at John.

He shrugged.

"Well, who knows," he said. "I'm glad it didn't come to that. Probably just as well. They'd be protesting in front of my dorm room, and then, you know, hard to take a shower and all."

John was talking about the central bath and shower unit on each floor requiring everyone to leave their room to access the bathroom in his dormitory.

She laughed, and said, "See, that's what I mean. You treat serious matters lightly, and I don't know. It's nice to feel safe for a moment, you know."

"Miss Brittany, I want you to talk about this with campus security," said John. "There's an officer I know. His last name is Murray. I can give you his number. He seems to be a straight shooter from what I've seen. I think you need to get some of your concern out there for the record. Tell him I asked you to call him. I don't think you should associate with Steve any longer. Pass over assignments if he is going to be involved. Talk with your editor, if needed, so he understands. Don't give Steve any encouragement whatsoever. Okay?"

She nodded up and down. She took down Officer Murray's cell phone number and said she would call him. John wrote down his cell phone number and Isaac's number. He would tell Isaac later. He gave them to her.

"I kinda hoped you were giving me your number so I would call you again?" she said and waited for his answer.

"Miss Brittany, you are so beautiful and sweet you make my heart hurt just to be near you. I suspect you affect men all the time, and are used to that. You get to choose which man you want to be with, now and in the future. Don't ever settle for anyone who doesn't treat you with the love and respect you deserve."

She leaned over and kissed him on the cheek.

"I don't know," she said. "I may have found him already."

He smiled, and held his arms out and hugged her tight, and said, "You can call me, Isaac, or Officer Murray anytime you need us, okay?"

John paused and in a more serious tone, he said, "And Miss Brittany, you need to be aware of your surroundings all the time. Never let yourself be caught out alone, especially in the dark or shadows, or off in some building, right?"

Brittany saluted him and said, "Yes sir."

She got up from the chair and hugged John again.

"Don't worry," she said. "I won't let them slant my article or change the facts just to fit what some of them want."

"Now, you're a journalist," said John.

CHAPTER FOURTEEN

Vincent sighed as he thought over his pending meeting with his employer. He had pulled into the private underground parking structure beneath a nondescript office building which housed the agency just outside of the Washington, D.C. beltway. He hardly ever came into the office anymore. He liked not having a visible presence and felt safer in the shadows.

He had come to terms with his anonymity as a necessary cost of performing his work for the agency. He had learned to kill efficiently in the military and never endured much in the way of remorse or concern. Taking a life didn't faze him. He figured it was his job, and he prided himself on being good at his work.

He was not foolish enough to think that he was secure just because he was good at his job. He was safe only as long as he was more asset than liability. The more he knew personally, the more threat he was to others in higher positions of power, who could be vulnerable. But, that worked for him as well.

Knowledge is power. Vincent had secreted several capsules of incriminating information with mechanisms to have them come to light in the event he failed to make scheduled contacts ensuring his current well being. He considered that operational prudence.

He was happy he was able to finish the recent job without fuss. He had seen the morning news account regarding the tragic death of the husband and wife at home, and how the police were searching for clues related to the break in and robbery. What was important was the story he had staged was working so far. The key was to leave some evidence, but nothing specific and nothing suggesting some other reason for their deaths.

He wondered why he had been called in? His employers didn't want him to be seen. Officially, he was dead and didn't exist anymore. In fact, he had endured some painful plastic surgery to alter his appearance. His facial scar and left eye ptosis remained. He thought of them as badges of honor, remnants of his ordeal on behalf of his country. His fingerprints had been altered by a weak acid solution, and he was sworn to secrecy on pain of death.

He was officially dead complete with a military funeral visited by a priest and military color guard and no one else. No great loss he reckoned, but what else was he to do? He was a trained killer. The army had helped with that, and he didn't really have any other skills. Besides, he enjoyed his work. He knew he had a gift. He had known it ever since that trouble as a teenager. That bully wouldn't be bothering anyone on this plane again.

The stone and smoke glass interior of the office building belied the aging exterior appearance. Vincent approached the elevator bank, presented his ID to the suited man on duty at the security desk, and walked through the metal detectors. The polished dark marble facade surrounding the elevator reflected his appearance, square jaw line, dark eyebrows, slightly drooping left upper eyelid, darker hair cut close in a military style, and his once crooked nose appearing slight narrower and aquiline. The thin facial scar on his left face from orbital ridge to chin remained. Amazing what a small change in bone structure could do to alter appearance. He doubted his family, if he had any, would recognize him.

Entering the surprisingly small waiting room, he was waved into the office by the secretary. Vincent found the director on the phone, and he gestured for Vincent to take a seat. He waited patiently. The director might be anything other than direct, but he was generally straightforward with Vincent. No mention was made of the recent job, which was typical. Vincent would either see money in his account on completion, or if the work were unsatisfactory, he likely wouldn't wake up one morning.

"Have you seen this?" asked the director.

He tapped his keyboard, and the screen on the sidewall showed the news coverage of the incident at the university and subsequent coverage of the campus university unrest with a close up of John Stone. The news went on to discuss some sensitive details of Stone's military service, especially his last mission and discharge from the military on medical issues. The coverage implied that Stone might be suffering from post traumatic stress disorder and wasn't the most stable individual.

Vincent had known John was trying to go to school. He had kept tabs, always toying with the idea of paying his former friend a visit. He had heard of the campus incident on the news this morning while driving in to the meeting.

"You know we can't have this kind of exposure. I just got off the phone with some very nervous people who don't tolerate this kind of leak. It makes us look weak. I don't have to tell you how risky this can be for both of us," the director said. "It was a mistake letting Stone live."

Vincent considered for a moment. John surviving the ambush had been unexpected, but his injuries and lack of memory for the event had suggested leaving him alone was the best course of action at the time. No, the real problem wasn't John, but the intrusion into his sealed military records.

Vincent said, "Source?"

He knew there must be a line on how the military information leaked.

"We tracked it to a request from Senator Kincaid's office, one of his staff who was a student under a particular professor at the same university," said the director. "The professor apparently wants Stone gone from the university and is fomenting discontent, which is causing pain for us."

"So, we want this professor to disappear?" asked Vincent.

"No, the professors name is Paul Kincaid," said the director. "He is Senator Kincaid's only son."

Vincent knew Senator Kincaid was rumored to be a confidant of the president. The senior senator pro tempore also headed up the Senate Finance Committee and seemed to know where most of the bodies in Washington were buried based on his influence and success.

"Has Senator Kincaid talked with his son?" asked Vincent.

The director clasped his hands with fingers touching and overlying his upper chest and leaned back in his chair.

"Senator Kincaid and his son aren't terribly close," said the director. "The senator hopes to talk to his son indirectly through us."

"And Stone?" asked Vincent.

"I thought he was a friend of yours," said the director.

"So did I. He saved my life more than once," said Vincent. "We fought together in Afghanistan. He thinks I'm dead. Like to keep it that way, I guess."

"So no personal vendettas against Stone?" asked the director as he pushed a memory stick across the desk.

Vincent picked up the data stick. He would study the file in more detail later.

"I'm a company man," said Vincent. "You know that."

The director nodded his head and pointed at the file.

"That is what we have on Professor Kincaid," he said. "I've included some current information on Stone as well as any known associates and family. I would leave Stone out of this for now. I think it is better that he doesn't know you exist. No reason to give him thoughts that last mission was anything more than he remembers. See if you can get Professor Kincaid to bow out of this, and let it all blow over. That would be best for everyone, including you, me, and him."

"Got it," said Vincent. "Intimidation with discretion, but no permanent marks."

"Oh, by the way, the FBI is involved in the investigation already, so stay clear of them," said the director.

Vincent drove back home after the meeting and gathered his necessaries for his assignment. He left within the hour, and while driving towards his target, he sifted through the meeting in his mind again. Why bring him in to the office? They could have sent instructions in the usual way? He was here now. He would scout his opportunities and plan as he always did. He couldn't help wondering if, this time, someone was planning for him?

CHAPTER FIFTEEN

S'ear'r found great joy in transiting this new solar system. Ship had suggested a path above the elliptic plane. Doctrine amassed through contact experience over the last thousand passings suggested most warning devices and nets were placed within the ecliptic plane, especially in early space faring species.

S'ear'r had conceded Ship that point, however, he pointed out the nature of the exploration probe Ship had recovered. It seemed unlikely that the beings that constructed such a probe had advanced to the level of subspace warning nets or gravitic sensors. S'ear'r also pointed out the opportunity for harvesting fuel. Diving into the ecliptic plane and back out might bring more notice than quietly approaching amidst the outer planets and asteroids.

In the end S'ear'r succeeded in convincing Ship of the benefits of an ecliptic approach, and, now Ship approached a an outer gas giant. A beautiful blue ball of a planet, called Neptune by the sentient species in this system according to the probe. Sensors suggested the atmosphere to be eighty percent hydrogen along with helium and methane, all useful replenishment storage for the fusion furnace and converters. Normally Ship handled this sort of harvesting while S'ear'r was dimmed, unaware and in stasis.

Of course, S'ear'r still had Ship handle the process rather than trying to perform it manually. Ship was much more capable of the minute attitude control necessary to perform a safe harvesting. The process was soon completed. S'ear'r made sure to complement Ship on the competent handling of the refueling process.

Dimmed as he was much of the time during their mission, S'ear'r had still spent tens of passings living with Ship and wished to continue a good working relationship with the vessel's Artificial Intelligence. The organics used in construction of Ship had once been part of a sentient being, but a more limited interface and matrix were used with Ship to produce a competent automated intelligence. Ship Artificial Intelligence also served as a fail safe making deviation from their mission difficult, if not impossible.

S'ear'r had ultimate decision capacity on their mission, but if his decisions jeopardized their mission or deviated from protocol without a clear and overriding reason, Ship would contest and ultimately override any serious dereliction of duty. S'ear'r so far had enjoyed a good relationship with Ship and did not anticipate any such issues. S'ear'r wanted only success and had high hopes for their current investigation.

Ship had suggested, and S'ear'r agreed, to avoid high velocity or sudden course changes. As much as possible, they would follow a gravity well course into the inner system.

S'ear'r delighted in the beautiful ringed gas giant and the even larger gas giant farther into the system. He imagined Chos'n harvesting factories for all of these planets. So far this system looked useful, but there were many systems with gas giants for harvest. The real prize was a habitable world. The information on the probe disc hinted at conditions similar to the Chos'n home world, and if so, S'ear'r felt sure his success would be assured.

S'ear'r wondered quietly if he might be allowed a life contract if this mission proved successful. He could dare to hope. Most of his kind did not make it to purpose other than as fodder for others. He had risen above that fate and was still alive, closer in nature to the great L'ment'l, although he would never give voice to such. Quiet rumors suggested the leader did not suffer comparison to her well, and S'ear'r had no wish to be deconstructed.

No, if he was allowed to dream, it always came back to obtaining a life contract and being allowed to live out his days with someone compatible and kind, perhaps to be given the rare privilege of cultivating their own children. Traditional reproduction was a great privilege reserved for those L'ment'l deemed worthy through genetic trait or success in glorious purpose.

Perhaps this find would be of such value and gain him that reward. S'ear'r thought of M'lit'a again. During his twenty-two passings of preparation, his only remembered highlight was her friendship. S'ear'r did not understand why she wanted to spend any effort with him, as he thought himself unworthy of her. He had actually trembled whenever she came close. They talked of many things, both in their studies and beyond. In his dreams, it was always M'lit'a as his life partner.

S'ear'r had known she would succeed in purpose and was not surprised when she had been selected and tasked. She was truly brilliant and was chosen for the sciences, a noble pursuit.

He remembered seeing her that last time. She had held his hands talon to talon, remarkable to S'ear'r as physical contact between male and female was forbidden outside of a life contract. Still, she reached out and held his fingers in hers and simply looked at him. He still remembered her eyes, luminous, understanding and kind. Her eyes had sustained him through many passings.

Then the guardians came to escort her for purpose, and her face changed. Her eyelids drooped, her features flattened, and then she was gone.

S'ear'r remembered feeling sadness at her leaving, but also happiness knowing she would survive in purpose. If not chosen for purpose, one was deconstructed at the age of twenty-two passings. This was the fate S'ear'r expected for himself. But, still he could be happy if M'lit'a survived.

S'ear'r was confused when he was selected for purpose on the eve of his twenty-second birth date. He had been preparing himself for deconstruction, willing himself to allow his body the purpose of nurturing others.

He still did not understand why he was selected. He did not excel at anything beyond being able to stay on task. He couldn't explain it, but he would force himself to stay focused when all of his classmates had given up. S'ear'r couldn't imagine how that quality would be useful in purpose until the selection guardians explained to him his assigned tasking. Since the unstated alternative to purpose was deconstruction the next day, S'ear'r had been delighted to accept.

S'ear'r wondered if M'lit'a was happy. She had probably earned a life contract with another already, but he allowed himself some hope in the promise remembered in her eyes and the feel of her long fingers touching his. Those thoughts he kept private and did not share with Ship or L'ment'l. Those thoughts were only for him.

CHAPTER SIXTEEN

Jessica was distracted at work the rest of the afternoon. She had to re-file some documents three times before she actually did it right.

Paul Kincaid's threats upset her. She knew, even when they were teenagers, he was to be avoided. This was not the first time he had approached her trying to pressure her into .... She knew what he wanted, had always wanted.

Oh, how she regretted going to that senior party. Instead of pressure, Paul had some of the other girls convince her into showing up by telling her she would regret not being at one of the last parties of her high school senior year.

She foolishly thought she would be safe with all the other people present at the party. She had underestimated him that night. She didn't remember much after arriving at the party. She wasn't a big drinker of alcohol, really not at all. The drink she was offered by one of the girls tasted like iced tea. After that, she had only blurred and muddied memories.

But, those memories terrified her. She remembered feeling helpless, stumbling up the stairs at the Kincaid house, cheers coming from the rest of the rowdy dancing and drinking classmates. She could remember thinking that she didn't want this, but she couldn't seem to speak almost as if her body was disconnected. She remembered being on a bed and there were shapes around her, talking, touching, until she was on fire, and she was screaming inside, but no sound would come out of her mouth.

And then, someone else was there. She could never remember who, but he made the shapes go away. She remembered being carried in the rain to a truck or car and waking up in the hospital. Her mother was beside her in the hospital room. Her father never came to visit.

She was told later that the boy up the road, Mason, she knew was his last name, had brought her to the hospital along with his parents after an accident. That boy never returned to school. She found out later that he was sent off to juvenile detention. Her father said it served him right for killing his parents. Jessica could never make sense of that. If he did something wrong, then why did he spend time trying to do right by her. Why didn't he just run away?

When she found out she was pregnant, she felt broken, a young unwed mother without hope. She escaped her home and the whispers at school by running away to have Jacob. She was trying to survive with a baby when Sarah found her. Over the years she had regained her confidence and worked hard to attain some measure of security for her and Jacob. She had wanted to make Sarah and Max proud of her.

She loved the books at their home, and she and Jacob read as many of them as they could over the years. She followed her natural inclination in studying library sciences and communications, and with Max and Sarah's love and support, she attained advanced degrees in both.

She loved her work now. Organization and clear thought were sustaining to her like the oxygen she breathed. She had enough insight to understand that control of her environment helped allay her anxieties over her past and her future. So be it. Whatever works, she thought.

All she knew was the most important people in the world to her were Jacob and Max. Sarah was beyond her ability to effect beyond prayer. Jessica had long determined no one was going to hurt her family, not while she breathed. She cleared her desk and used her skills to search for information regarding John Stone and Samantha. No news was not always good news, but she discovered nothing of import for either of them. Stone had served in the military. He was open about that, even if he wouldn't talk about specifics.

It bothered her that she couldn't find out any other history on John. There was no mention of high school or college other than here at the university. It was like he didn't exist prior to his military record.

That was a puzzle. She knew he was capable of violence. She had seen that twice now. Yet, he didn't feel like a threat to her or her family. In fact, she felt safer with him. Something she didn't want to admit to herself.

"Ma'am, it's six o'clock," said a voice at her office door. "Saw you working, just wanted to remind you."

Marcy was one of the seniors working in the library, and Jessica thought highly of her.

"Thanks Marcy. I'm finishing up now. I'll see you Monday afternoon probably," said Jessica.

She logged off her computer. She couldn't fathom where the afternoon went. She gathered her things and walked between the stacks to the elevator. She thought she saw movement out of the corner of her eye, but when she looked there was no one there. There were students in the library at this hour of course, but this area of the building was sparsely populated at the moment. Something tickled at the primitive area of her brain. Jessica hurried to the elevator.

She told herself to relax and not let her imagination scare her. She entered the elevator. Just before the doors closed, a man stepped into the elevator. He smiled at her. For some reason, she was reminded of one of those shows on sharks on television. She shrank back against the corner of the elevator. She couldn't step out as he was standing in the center of the elevator.

He turned and pushed the button for the first floor. Then he stood with his back to the sidewall of the elevator and looked at Jessica without saying a word. She sensed her heart pounding. She told herself to quit being silly, but felt the hair at the base of her scalp stand up and wished she had more than mace in her purse.

The elevator stopped on the first floor, and the doors finally opened. The man stepped out of the elevator and walked around the corner. Jessica let herself breathe again. She couldn't explain it.

Kincaid, offensive in his presence, didn't make her feel this way. Maybe she offended the man, but she had tried not to look at the scar on his face.

He was nowhere to be seen, but she feared walking out to her Jeep in the parking lot. She looked around again outside in the growing twilight. She finally gathered her keys in hand and hurried over to her small SUV. She made it inside her Jeep Liberty although it felt like forever getting the door unlocked. She did have the presence of mind to look into the rear seat. She locked the doors and sat in her vehicle. She let out a breath and told herself to calm down.

She turned the key in the ignition and there was only a click and then another click. Oh no, she thought, not again. She had been meaning to get the Jeep looked at as she had noticed some trouble with starting. Jacob had replaced the battery, but clearly that wasn't the only issue. Please God she thought, please. Jessica thought of Sarah and hoped she was happy in heaven, and would she consider asking someone for a little help for her adopted daughter? Jessica turned the key in the ignition again and there was a click, sputter and the engine roared to life.

"Thank you, God, thank you. Please look after Sarah," she said aloud in prayer.

Jessica drove out of her parking spot towards home, wrapped up in her thoughts. She didn't see the scar faced man standing in the shadows, farther down the sidewalk, watching her drive away.

CHAPTER SEVENTEEN

John, Isaac, and Samantha all showed up at the same time at the given address, which turned out to be a nice old clapboard two story farm house with tall windows and a generous wrap around porch. The hunter green paint on the shutters contrasted nicely with the planted spring flowers at the base of the front porch framing the wooden steps leading up to the front door.

John thought he could see a detached garage out back and left of the house along with a real barn painted red and white and looking weather tight. He guessed the house sat on ten or more acres. He thought it the perfect urban oasis from the outside.

Samantha seemed slightly distracted as she met them. He thought she might be a bit nervous being at her professor's home. She smiled while carefully placing one foot in front of the other as she came up the walk. Turns out Professor Maxwell had invited her for dinner as a thank you for looking after his grandson. She didn't know John and Isaac would be here. John thought this looked to be an interesting evening.

Just as they were about to knock on the front door, it opened and Jacob stood there with a grin on his face.

"Come in please," he said. "Granddad said you would be prompt."

The three of them entered into a simple entry hall with a lovely polished credenza oozing memories of greetings past and hosting a glass shade lamp. There was a standing wooden coat hook and a metal umbrella bin decorated with a stamped Norman Rockwell reproduction.

John's stomach grumbled at the delicious garlic smell coming from the kitchen down at the end of the hallway, reminding him he hadn't eaten since late morning. He saw Professor Maxwell, smiling much like he had in class, step into the hallway and beckon the group to come into the kitchen.

"Come in, come in, and thank you for coming," said the professor. "I can't wait for you to try my world famous spaghetti. I hope you'll like it. It's the only thing I know how to cook."

"He's not kidding," said Jacob.

"Thank you for having us, Professor Maxwell. That smells wonderful," said Samantha.

"Call me Max, dear girl. We are not in class and not formal here tonight. Come and help me with the garlic bread," he said. "I'm hoping Jessica will be home shortly."

Jacob said, "Yeah, she works late a lot. I called her earlier and let her know granddad was cooking, and she promised to be home by seven."

"Jacob, did your grandfather know I was coming to dinner?" asked John.

Professor Maxwell handed John a wine opener for the bottle of rosé wine John had brought to dinner.

"We are happy to have the company," said Max. "I know Jessica will be thrilled."

He winked and smiled.

John thought the evening was going to be very interesting, and then Jessica walked in the back door having parked in the driveway off to the side so as not to obstruct the garage.

"Something smells good, Max. Oh hello," she said to the three of them. Jessica turned to Max and said, "I'm sorry I'm late. I had trouble with the Jeep again."

Professor Maxwell said, "Trouble starting again? We put a new battery in, didn't we?"

"I know," said Jessica. "It seems to happen at random, and always when I need to be somewhere."

"Isaac said, "I could look at it if you want, after dinner maybe."

He and Jacob were setting plates on the table.

"You know cars?" Max asked.

"He can fix anything that rolls or flies," said John.

He saw Max and Jacob look at each other at that statement. John couldn't help watching Jessica's face out of the corner of his eye. He could tell she didn't want to take the help, but she wanted her Jeep to work.

"Wonderful," said the professor. "Let's eat."

Dinner was superb. Max gloated in his culinary superiority. He knew his spaghetti sauce was good. Sarah had taught him her recipe, and he was proud he could reproduce it. John stopped himself at seconds. The salad was particularly welcome laced in excellent Italian dressing, which he soaked up with the tasty garlic bread. Everyone applied attention to the meal. Max thanked John for the wine, and everyone got a taste, including Jacob.

Professor Maxwell proposed a toast.

"To good food, new friends, and family dear." All of them raised their glasses to the center of the table.

"Amen," said Jacob.

"I don't know when I've had such a good meal. Mi mama would be pleased to know I'm not eating pop tarts tonight," said Isaac. "You have a lovely home. How long have you lived here, sir?"

Max leaned back in his chair and said, "Sarah and I found this property a couple of years after I came to work at the university. Of course, we lived in smaller apartments the first few years of our marriage, but we always wanted a home for the children we hoped to have. So, we had the home and each other and our work, but no children until Sarah came home with Jessica and little Jacob."

"Isaac, do you really think you could look at my Jeep?" asked Jessica, who seemed to want to change the subject.

"Sure, I've got my flashlight," said Isaac. "Let's go out and inspect it, and you tell me what it's been doing."

The two of them excused themselves from the table and exited the back door from the kitchen to the driveway.

Jacob began clearing dishes from the table. John and Samantha jumped up to help him, but Max begged Samantha away to look at his office computer which had been giving him some difficulty.

John could see Jessica out in the driveway talking with Isaac, who looked under the hood of her Jeep Liberty.

"So, how long have you and your mother lived here with professor Maxwell?" he asked.

He rinsed off plates to hand to Jacob to stack in the dishwasher.

"We've lived here since I was very young," replied Jacob. "Granddad and Mum asked us to live with them when I was still a baby, and we've been here since. Max and Sarah adopted my mother as their daughter, and that makes him my grandfather."

"And his wife, Sarah?" asked John.

"Mum died about a year ago," said Jacob. "I thought we were going to lose Max as well. I mean, we all hurt, but I think his heart wanted to stop. It was rough, but us being here, I think that helped him to stay with us. I mean we still needed him, and we always will. You know we hardly ever have visitors since she died. He must like you guys."

Jacob smiled.

"Well maybe," said John. "I know your mother was startled to see us all here. You know, I'm not sure your mother wants me around you?"

"She still thinks of me as if I'm ten," said Jacob. "I'm almost eighteen."

"She's your mother," said John. "She worries about you. You are lucky to have that. Be patient. So how is it that you're in college now? Are you a genius or something?"

"Be careful with that bowl. It belonged to Sarah's mother, and we don't set it out that often," said Jacob, gingerly taking the bowl and placing it on a towel to hand wash in a moment. "Or something I guess, but really I just seem to pick up on things quickly. I like to read, thanks to Mom, and having Max and Sarah tutor me when I was younger was wonderful."

"They tutored you on how to take a punch?" asked John. He noted Jacob's face looked much better.

"Well, I kinda read up on that and thought it might be useful sometime," said Jacob.

John shook his head.

"Jacob, U.S. Army Ranger School teaches combative skills over months of intensive immersive instruction, and you picked it up from reading a book?"

Samantha walked into the kitchen. She was followed by a smiling Max.

"Unbelievable," he said. "She fixed my office computer and showed me a better way to organize my hard drive. It's like having professional IT in the house."

Samantha blushed and asked if Jacob and John needed a hand with the dishes.

Jacob answered before John, and said, "No, we just about have it here. That's great about granddad's computer. You know how to work on that type of computer? I thought the programming was proprietary?"

Samantha said, "Well, yes, I have a similar machine and it's great, but better with a little tweaking, and I like things to work the way I want, you know."

Jacob turned to Max and said, "Granddad, you know we could use some programming help with our project?"

He left the statement open ended and Max picked up on that immediately.

"Yes, I was pondering the same thoughts," said Max. "Miss Samantha, would you consider working with us on our latest project? We are just about ready to test our work, but we need some assistance with the software and would love for you to review what we have so far. Could we tempt you?"

Samantha laughed and said, "Okay, okay, I see what this is all about." She eyed Jacob, waiting for him to respond.

"Jacob?" she prompted.

"Well I did kinda tell granddad about your programming for the physics laboratory."

Jacob shifted his feet a little while twisting the dishtowel he was holding.

"That's right," Max started, but was interrupted by Jessica and Isaac walking in the kitchen door.

"What's right?" Jessica asked, having caught Max's words.

"Samantha fixed Granddad's computer, and we asked her to help us with the project experiment," said Jacob. "She thinks we were just testing her."

"Oh I see," said Jessica. "Now this dinner makes sense, Max. Isaac thinks he knows what's wrong with the Jeep."

"Needs a new starter is all, I think," said Isaac. "But, I wouldn't trust driving it until we can get the starter replaced."

"He's going to get the part, and Isaac thinks he can put it on here at the house, maybe tomorrow?" Jessica asked with hope.

Isaac went on to explain he was working at the airport tomorrow afternoon and through the weekend, but he thought he could be back to work on the Jeep sometime in the next couple of days. Isaac offered to pick up the starter on the way.

Jessica was beaming and said, "Well, Isaac, you definitely have passed your test. Now what about John there?"

Max spoke up, "He's already passed his test."

Samantha and Jacob both nodded in agreement and looked at him, their eyes shining.

John felt a burning deep in his chest, threatening to consume him with a tingling sensation to his fingers and toes. He hadn't felt close to anyone for so long. These people hardly knew him. They didn't know about the wreckage of his life, yet they were willing to trust him. Why, he couldn't fathom. And Jessica, what would she say if she remembered him somehow. Would she still be willing to let him around her and Jacob?

Samantha said she could start some on their project over the weekend or after class. Isaac said he needed to get back and thanked Max, Jacob, and Jessica for a very nice dinner and for treating him like family. Samantha and Jessica hugged Isaac as he started out the door.

"Max, could I get a ride, Monday, with you and Jacob?" asked Jessica as they were walking out.

Max said, "Jessica, I can take you into work in the morning, but our schedules won't coincide Monday evening, especially if you have to stay late." Max looked at John. "Perhaps John would consider giving you a ride Monday evening. We might be able to use his help around here if he has the time."

"Yes! We can order pizza!" Jacob said.

"I'm sure that he is busy," protested Jessica.

"No, I'm free Monday evening," said John. "What time should I come by to find you?"

Jessica looked less than thrilled, and said, "I guess about six o'clock would work."

"Same location at the library?" John asked, causing Max to chuckle.

Jessica nodded yes.

John and Samantha followed Isaac out the door, and they left.

Jessica walked back into the house and glared at Max.

"You did that on purpose, didn't you?" she asked.

Max shrugged his shoulders and smiled. He felt satisfied with himself and walked off to his study and functioning computer, singing a song well known to him since his first dance with Sarah years ago. He let himself get lost in his memories.

She came with her cousin. He had been smitten when he saw Sarah in her white dress. He remembered saying a prayer for courage to approach her. His heart moved to his throat as he walked over and asked her to dance. He introduced himself and asked her name all the while looking into her eyes so full of life and joy. He felt his spirits soar as she shyly nodded yes. He had hesitantly placed his arm around her waist allowing her to move closer to him as they swayed to a recording of *My Girl* by the Temptations.

He remembered her sigh as she settled into his shoulder, and he felt weightless, floating in time like a leaf in a stream, like everything suddenly made sense, as if his whole life had led him to this moment.

Later that evening after walking Sarah home and floating back to his shabby apartment, he said a prayer of thanks as he replayed the evening second-by-second, sealing the memory of her that night in his mind for all time.

CHAPTER EIGHTEEN

Professor Paul Kincaid sat in his favorite chair in his study with the television news playing in the background. He took another sip of wine and willed himself to relax. He was upset at himself for his retreat, but when he looked at Stone in the library, he saw only dark eyes that told of decisions already reached and calculations made which needed only his noncompliance to trigger a solution of which he wanted no part. Kincaid felt sure he narrowly avoided great bodily harm, consequences be damned.

He knew Stone was in the army from reading his academic application. He had confirmed as much but had refused to discuss his service life further when pressed in class. Of course, Kincaid had taken his reticence as an admission of guilt for having served like a puppet to the fascist government in Washington, D.C. Perhaps, he was in error. He wasn't sure. Clearly, Stone had a line not to be crossed where women were concerned.

Professor Kincaid had had some success at finding some of Stone's redacted military history, and he was feeding that information carefully to a source he had at the local news affiliate. He would like to find out more, but Stone's previous life before the military seemed to be a blank.

Kincaid had a source in Washington, a former student now staffing with his father. He had leverage over her from a previous indiscreet episode, and she had been helpful with a formal request from his father's office. Everyone knew the staffers ran the zoo anyway.

Jessica Maxwell continued to infuriate him. She seemed to be there at the worst moments of his life. She had rejected him in high school repeatedly. She wouldn't stay in the same room with him even now if she could avoid it. Why, oh why, did he have to want her? And to top it off, she let herself get pregnant.

She had said no to him, but she wanted it, just like they all did, just not from him. Well too bad for that. She thought she was clever in moving away, but Paul had asked his father and through their sources, found out she had moved to a neighboring town to have the baby.

How could she do that to him? He wanted her then and still wanted her, but a baby didn't figure into his plans at all. Not then, and certainly not now. Paul's father had her followed hoping to avoid scandal. That's all his father really cared about anyway, his political career. Any action Paul made was evaluated only in how it reflected on his father's career. Well, Paul had made his own plans. He knew he would have his chance.

But then Horace Maxwell and his wife had taken Jessica into their home, which they had made into a small fortress. And so, Paul had made do with a marriage of advantage and his trysts with a willing coed here and there.

He counseled patience to himself, but deep inside, he longed to eventually have another chance with Jessica. It was too bad that hayseed hick trespassed and spoiled his opportunity. Well, they had fixed him. Again, Paul counseled himself to be patient. The fact that he pleasured himself to Jessica's high school yearbook pictures helped.

When she came to the university to enroll, he made a friendly overture. Paul had tried his best to ingratiate himself to a younger Professor Maxwell. He had even attended a party at the professor's home one night. He first met Jacob there and made the mistake of thinking him the typical seven year old child. He had been startled when Jacob talked to him about what he perceived as an error in a paper Paul had written. Paul was mortified to realize that the seven year old child could not only read and understand his paper, but pointed out a fallacy in his reasoning in front of everyone, including Jessica and Professor Maxwell. Paul had lashed out in anger. He hadn't hurt the boy, not really, but that was it for him as far as they were concerned. From that day, Professor Maxwell had opposed him whenever possible, and with her increasing academic standing, so had Jessica.

Now, Jessica had some sort of evidence from dim but pretty Katie Thompson, who had needed the grade in his class just bad enough to be amenable to a little after class private tutoring. Still, it was his word against Katie, but he knew Jessica had something else. Maybe some of the others had decided to talk. Paul did know Jessica had asked for an appointment with the academic council.

He had checked, and she was on the schedule for the Tuesday evening meeting. He had always been careful. Never more than one girl in an academic year and always one of the girls whom he carefully selected and groomed. He always took photographs clandestinely to embarrass the girl by threatening her with exposure if she talked. Even when he reminisced over the photographs, Paul never noticed how much the various girls resembled Jessica.

Somehow, Katie had found a spine and gone to Jessica. Kincaid knew this because he had a source in the library, a young man who needed a favor with his academic transcript and some much needed funding to continue his schooling. It was a good deal for Kincaid as he had a way to know what Jessica was about without having to hang around the library.

He had made a similar arrangement with an engineering graduate student who had come to him with a complaint about Professor Maxwell when Horace wouldn't pass the student on less than stellar efforts in his senior level classes.

Now, the student was happily passing along information concerning Professor Maxwell and enjoying his graduate school efforts. In fact, Kincaid had arranged for Jerry Daniels' parents to work on his father's estate as caretakers further cementing the relationship. Jerry's latest information detailing some of the equipment Maxwell had concentrated in his lab and the requisition for some exotic and expensive materials, could be used to advantage, Kincaid thought.

Yes, perhaps, he should make a call to urge Jerry to take a slightly more active role. It would be helpful if somehow the professor could be seen as a failure. That would really give him leverage with the Dean regarding his efforts to get old Horace ousted. Maxwell had kept him from Jessica, and he never thought he could hate someone as much as he hated that old man.

When his wife left Paul, he had not minded, not really. She was the daughter of an older faculty member, and he had known the marriage would open some doors for appointment at the university and tenure despite his sparse publishing history. The prenuptial agreement they had arranged worked well, and the split while not amicable was at least private. He didn't hate her. In truth, he didn't think of her much at all.

But now, he was faced with ruin. If only Jessica could see how much she still meant to him, how she held power over his life. Yes, that was it. He needed to be the one to hold power over her life.

How could he do that?

Hmmmm, now that's an idea, and if he planned properly, he could accomplish his goals completely. A phone call or two should help nicely. He would be able to rid himself of the troublesome John Stone and gain even more leverage over Jessica to ensure her not going ahead with her complaint to the academic council.

Paul began to feel better as he reached down to the stack of yearbooks laying on the floor adjacent to his chair.

CHAPTER NINETEEN

Monday morning dawned clear and bright and found John still restless after his morning run. He had noticed a couple of guys following him on his run this morning, but didn't think too much of it as they stayed well back. The three mile perimeter around campus was a popular course.

An additional forty-eight hours had seen various edited cell phone video from the altercation in the science building go viral on the Internet. The major news networks were investigating the story. John read a new article in the *Campus Vine* with the title, "New Sheriff in Town." It seemed to be a cherry picked editorial piece suggesting that John was both dangerous and reactionary, and the poor students didn't really understand what was happening and had defended themselves. Sure one of them pulled a knife, but wouldn't you if a big bad soldier was coming after you? Brittany had not written the story, but Steve's name was credited below the photographs.

John arrived at the administration building early to drop his history class. This time the young lady at the office window didn't offer any excuses, but simply reminded him to fill out the portion of the form asking him why he was dropping the class. John considered and simply wrote "personal differences with instructor." After all, he was not looking for trouble or a cause, just a degree.

Looking at available classes, he really had few choices with the time slots available to him. He needed at least two credit hours to stay full time for the semester. He found a physical education course entitled, *Basics of Self Defense*. He was just under the deadline. He signed up for the class, which met twice a week in the evening, Monday and Wednesday. That meant, he could make it tonight. He reminded himself to ask Samantha if she would help Jessica get home.

John checked his phone and saw a voice mail message from the campus police asking him to come in and talk about the incident in the science building one more time. He walked that way. While still on the sidewalk leading to the police office he saw a group of students parading in front and carrying signs against violence. They were chanting his name, how he had to go, and how someone like him shouldn't be allowed on campus. A couple of the signs had his photograph on them with a circle and slash over his face.

John thought he might have a problem getting through, but Officer Murray came out to lead him through the group. One of the campus newspaper photographers made sure to photograph John being escorted into the police office, while some had their cell phones out recording the event. Others offered encouragement to Officer Murray, and shouts filled the air.

"Take him down!"

"He has no place here."

"There's no room on campus for fear!"

John realized Murray must have been waiting for him to show up. John followed him through the building front doors.

"Thanks, Murray," said John. "I didn't expect this. It's good to see you again. Should I worry about this interview?"

Officer Murray waited until he had safely escorted John into the entry alcove away from the security office front desk before he answered him.

"Listen John, this is blowing up out of all reason," said Murray. "The Feds showed up this morning, and they want to talk with you. It's up to you whether you talk with them, but I would be careful. The dean's office called, and they just want this to go away one way or another. Honestly, I don't think they care if that means you go away as well."

Nodding his head in understanding, John allowed Murray to escort him around the desk and down a short hall to a conference room. A dark brown faux wood laminate table occupied the center of the room, large enough for several simple office chairs around the table. At one end of the room, John saw a projection screen and television and video equipment.

A desktop computer sat on a side table in the other corner of the room with a bouncing screensaver of a little alien with the caption, "Be Good!" Otherwise, two narrow windows filled with reinforced glass broke the beige concrete walls.

"Oh, Murray, what about Brittany?" asked John. "How's that going?"

"I'm glad you pointed her toward us," said Murray. "I'm worried about her. I checked into that guy, Steve, and there's something about him that doesn't feel right, nothing definite yet, but I told her the same things you did. Actually, I'm supposed to see her this evening, uh, well, I mean go by and check up on her."

Murray blushed a bit.

John didn't tease the young officer.

"Good. I was hoping you could be there for her," he said. "She seems like a good girl. I want her to be safe. We all need honest reporters out there, and I think she has a chance." John added, because he couldn't help it, "Not sure about you though."

John sat in the offered seat on the far side of the table in the middle seat.

"I'm not kidding, John," said Murray. "Be careful with these guys. Wait here a moment."

Officer Murray left the room.

A few minutes later an older uniformed officer from campus police and two serious looking government types in suits entered the room. The uniformed officer introduced himself as Chief of Campus Police,

Donald Roberts, and then said, "These gentlemen are with the Federal Bureau of Investigation. We thank you for coming back in to talk with us."

John nodded. The three of them sat facing him around the table. One of the FBI agents, the one in the almost charcoal suit introduced himself as Special Agent Grierson and his partner as Special Agent Morris.

Agent Grierson said, "We would like to go over the incident one more time and go over your statement to campus police."

John asked, "Okay, but two things first. What is the FBI's interest in this? Secondly, am I under concern for any crime such that I need an attorney?"

Agent Morris introduced himself again and said, "We are trying to better understand what happened, Mr. Stone. No charges have been filed at this time."

John focused intently on the three of them.

"No charges?" asked John. "What about the three guys who assaulted Samantha and Jacob? They haven't been charged? I thought it was straightforward assault. There were several witnesses in the hallway."

Chief Roberts said, "The information obtained at the scene is conflicting and inconclusive, and the circulating cell phone video has appeared in several edits, most of them suggesting the three students more seriously injured were not the aggressors, but victims of a misunderstanding."

"And the original unedited cell phone video?" asked John. "You have that, don't you? Are those three students still in custody?"

Chief Roberts shrugged and said, "That cell phone has disappeared from evidence at this time. With what we have so far, we've let them out pending the results of our investigation."

John considered what he had been told and said, "Well, in that case gentlemen, I stand by my original statement to Officer Murray, and any other discussion will need to be in the presence of my attorney. I think we are done here for now."

He got up to leave. John could feel their agitation. He had managed to take control of the questioning. They didn't understand how many interrogations and police actions he'd been associated with in his time with the military overseas. Both the FBI agents had sour expressions on their faces, and Chief Roberts looked less than pleased, but they were not ready to press ahead with any further actions.

Great, he thought, so much for quietly getting his degree and avoiding conflict. This was just wrong. Walking out of the conference room and into the hallway, he saw Officer Murray, who looked tense. John mouthed an unspoken "Thanks" to him and walked toward the front door where the protestors were still gathered.

He started to walk out the door into the crowd, but Murray, caught up with him.

"Hey John, come this way," he said. "I want to avoid a small riot outside the security office, and you don't need any more video being taken today."

Murray led him to a door leading into the parking structure on the ground floor and motioned John to get into one of the campus patrol cars.

"Thanks," said John, settling into the front passenger seat. "Didn't know you cared."

"Oh, I'm not worried about you," said Murray. "I worried for them. You looked like a lit grenade when you left that conference room."

John smiled a grim smile at the young officer, made an educated guess, and said, "Semper Fi."

Murray smiled back and said, "Rangers .... ?"

John openly grinned and said, "Lead the way."

Officer Murray said, "Seriously, Ranger boy, you've managed to get a big target on your back. I hope those shoulders are broad enough. Might be a good idea to lay low for awhile."

Pulling around the parking lots in a meandering fashion giving them both a chance to defuse a bit, Murray stopped the patrol car facing John's dorm.

"Laying low is all I've really wanted to do since I got back," said John. "Appreciate you watching out for Brittany and looking out for me. Nice to know there are some good guys hanging around." He got out of the cruiser and said, "Thanks again, jarhead."

Closing the car door, John waved Officer Murray off.

He felt a kinship with the former marine and police officer, who worked in what seemed to be a confusing and hostile environment. As John was learning, civilian life had its own rules and codes, often more bewildering than battlefield rules of engagement.

CHAPTER TWENTY

John shaved, showered, and toasted a bagel adding some cream cheese and triple berry preserves which Isaac called jelly with crack in it. He brewed some coffee with their single serve coffeemaker and enjoyed a cup fortifying him for the evening.

He gathered his materials for economics and his added self-defense class, and checking that his phone had a full charge, he headed downstairs. He had plenty of time to get to class and was wondering if he should call Jessica and verify that she'd gotten a ride home.

Reaching the lobby he found Brittany waiting for him. Her eyes were red and swollen, and John guessed she'd been crying. She explained to him that she was avoiding Steve as much as possible, but she'd found some more emails on her computer. She took out her laptop.

John read through them, sensing the barely contained rage between the written lines.

"Miss Brittany, we need to show these to campus security now," he said. "Did you talk with Officer Murray?"

Brittany nodded yes, and several tears fell down her cheeks as she looked down at her feet.

"You must think I'm helpless, but I feel so scared."

She must think I'm going to scold her, thought John. He took out his cell phone and dialed Murray's cell. On the third ring, Murray answered, and John gave him an update regarding Brittany and asked if he could bring her by the station.

"Officer Murray says to come over now," said John. "He is at the campus security office. I'll drive."

John had already dressed in his sweats for his evening class. They headed through and out of the lobby. Other than the usual head turning to observe Brittany, John saw nothing alarming. The drive over to campus security was blessedly brief and without incident.

John chose a spot in the parking structure close to the side entrance to the security office. Officer Murray waited at the door for them. John stayed long enough to be sure Brittany was safe with Murray, and then he left to make it to his physical education class. He didn't want to be late. Besides, he really wasn't anxious to see Chief Roberts again anytime soon. Brittany and Murray were talking when he left, but he did ask Brittany to call him later that evening after his self-defense class.

John found himself thinking about Jessica on the walk over to the gymnasium area where the class was being held. He thought about calling her, but a quick call to Jacob confirmed she had gotten a ride from Samantha, and John resisted the urge to tease the young man.

John's mind flowed over recent events. He came to school determined to quietly live his life and obtain the necessary credentials to move on, but somehow, he kept finding himself at the center of other people's lives again.

Maybe that is what life is about, he thought. After the accident and his parent's deaths, he'd joined the military, thinking he could lay low and try to forget, but the army had other ideas for him, basic and advanced infantry training, jump training, sniper training, and deployment. John had embraced all, immersing himself in that world. When he returned stateside after his first tour, he was offered a slot in officer candidate school (OCS). He'd been working to get college credits during the previous eighteen months and had enough to qualify. Apparently, his commanding officer thought him worthy and put in recommendation for him. John successfully completed OCS and then,

Army Ranger School, where he learned a new definition of determination.

As a lieutenant in a Ranger company, he had been deployed again to Afghanistan where he spent two tours. He rose to the rank of Captain while there and was wounded twice, the second time when he was the only one to make it out, and that by pure luck. During rehab, his therapist told him part of why he was so driven in the army was the need to build another home for himself.

The self-defense class found John dressed in sweats and sneakers, listening as the instructor addressed the mostly female class. She introduced herself as Malinda Forshee, and apologized to the class for her inability to move around well. She supported herself on crutches, and it was obvious she was in pain, the result of a recent injury on some stairs in a moment of distraction. There had been no time to find a stand in instructor.

A late arrival was Brittany, dressed in sweats and looking determined. Officer Murray accompanied her. He apologized for interrupting the instructor, and after getting Brittany settled in among the class, he motioned to John and spoke with him quietly before leaving with apologies.

John was about to retake his place in the class when the instructor interrupted him.

"Are you John Stone?" she asked.

John saw the class focus on him with laser like intensity.

"Yes, I am."

"Would you mind helping tonight?" asked the instructor. "I need someone to demonstrate some techniques and clearly that can't be me."

"I can try," said John. "I hope everyone will be patient with me."

John saw one of the women on the far left of the semi-circle of students raise her hand in protest.

The woman said, "He beat up those poor students. We don't need him teaching us."

Miss Malinda sighed and addressed the entire group.

"Look, no matter what you think you know," she said. "We all saw this man take down three attackers before they could hurt anyone further. Is there anyone else here who thinks they can do that right now?"

"That isn't the point."

The young lady seemed to want to continue to interject.

John hated bully tactics. He was so tired of people who couldn't listen to reason or be tolerant of others beliefs. He asked the young student to come up in front of the others. She seemed hesitant.

John said, "Come here, or I'll come to you. Your choice. The first one is better. You decide."

He didn't yell. He didn't have to. Years of being responsible for others in the military brought out a natural command tone in his voice. John expected politeness in others and demanded it in himself. This situation needed to be contained now, or the class would disintegrate.

"Sometimes the best instruction is showing and less talking. What is your name?" he said to the female student who was winding her way to the center of the room with him.

"Megan Potts," she replied.

"Miss Potts, why are you here?" asked John.

"I need the physical education credits, and I thought I might learn something practical to help keep me safe," said Megan, resolutely.

John nodded and said, "Makes perfect sense. Miss Potts have you ever been a victim? Ever had someone hurt you or take from you without your permission? Have you ever been afraid for your life?"

John looked at Megan until she nodded hesitantly, yes.

John looked at the rest of the class and said, "How about the rest of you?"

John saw nodding heads in at least a third to half of the young women. He went on to say that was the expected response since some present statistics showed about a one in four chance for sexual assault and violence in their age group.

"Tell us Miss Potts, what is the single most important thing you can do to prevent violence to your person?" asked John.

He spoke in a way that made it obvious he was addressing the entire class. John noticed Miss Forshee nodding at him and smiling.

"I'm not sure," said Megan, looking uncertain now.

"Don't be there in the first place," said John. "Don't let yourself be in situations where you are alone with people you don't trust implicitly. Don't be out alone after dark. Don't be alone in deserted buildings at any time. Trust your instincts. If something seems wrong, it most likely is." John continued, "Now, Miss Potts, what is the most important thing to do if you are faced with violence?"

Megan seemed to have forgotten her protest and was concentrating on what John was saying, her natural inclination to not look foolish in front of her fellow students forcing her to participate, just as John had known it would.

"Run away?"

John smiled at her and announced.

"That is correct Miss Megan," he said. "Run away and call for help at the first opportunity. What does that mean for this class, every one of you?" John asked, and then answered his own question, "We run at least five days a week. Each of you find a running buddy now, since we don't do what?"

"We don't go off alone," said Brittany who was following what John was trying to get the class to understand.

"Each of you will log in your mileage before the start of class," said John. "We all will, including me. Don't push to injury, but do push for improvement. You have to run to be able to run away from violence. Right?"

"But, you didn't run away from those men?" said Megan.

"No, I didn't. I trusted my instincts and ran to help," said John. "Whether that was truly wise or not remains to be seen."

Megan nodded. She seemed to be thinking hard.

"Now Miss Potts, one more question and you can join the group," said John. "What if you were walking, and some guy stepped out of the shadows? You vaguely know him. Maybe he's a guy you said no to when he asked you out. Your instincts are telling you this guy intends to hurt you. What do you do?"

Megan hesitated, so John added, "Class, what do we do when faced with violence?"

"Run away!" said the class in unison.

Megan looked a bit uncertainly at John, as if seeing him in a somewhat different light.

"What if we can't outrun them?" she asked. "What if there is no other help around. Someone like you?"

She was quiet now, and John saw something in her face, a look of revelation as she was forced to admit an unpleasant truth to herself.

John looked at her and the rest of the students in the class, all staring intently at him now.

"That's why we are here in this class," said John. "We learn how to stop them, to give us a chance to run away and call for help. Right?"

John saw the class all nodding now in agreement with him, including Megan.

After some light stretching, John made sure everyone knew how to do pushups and sit-ups to add to their running routine.

"We add those to the mileage log as well," he said.

John went on to show a simple defense against wrist grabs both same and cross sided as well as defense against a choke from behind and defense against hair grabs. He had each student work slowly through the motions after he demonstrated the techniques and made sure the students switched off with different partners to ensure muscle memory and adaptation based on different heights and distances. The rest of the class went well and was over before John could take a breath.

Megan came up to John and said she was sorry for mouthing off.

John said, "Miss Megan, you will do."

He saw her face brighten with his comment.

John noticed Brittany hanging behind. She was smiling and talking with Malinda Forshee, who approached him.

"Thank you so much, Mr. Stone. You are a natural at this, and I heard several of the students talk about how much they enjoyed the class. I'm so glad we didn't have to cancel today, as this is very important for many of the girls who come here. Some of them are naive. Dare I impose on you further?" asked Malinda, smiling, knowing John couldn't say no.

"I'm happy to help. Just keep me in line, if you think I'm straying too far," said John.

"John, would you give me a ride back to my apartment?" asked Brittany. "Patrick said you might."

John expected this as Murray had briefed him. It had been Murray's idea to bring Brittany over to the class, as he knew John would be here. Murray planned on checking on her later, and he'd given her his number as well.

John dropped Brittany off at her apartment.

She thanked John again and said, "Thanks for taking me to see Patrick and the class. He is coming by later tonight. I feel so much better."

John admonished her to be careful and told her he would check in on her. He headed back to the dorm to get cleaned up and wondered what tomorrow would bring.

CHAPTER TWENTY-ONE

"How's it going Samantha?" asked Professor Maxwell as he finished a notation in his most current lab journal.

"A moment, Professor, please. I think I have this program setup properly now. I don't suppose I need to say we should run some simulations with the programming changes I made, right?"

Samantha hummed to herself as she tweaked a last bit of code to modify the operating system, seeing the parameters in her mind and trying to anticipate any unexpected loops or traps in the code. At least Jacob had authored the system in UNIX, which was the only truly stable computer operating system in her mind.

Still this computer and the software Jacob had dreamed up were beyond cutting edge and highly personalized. She had worked nearly nonstop over four days to understand and augment some of his work. Professor Maxwell and Jacob had been quick to admit that they needed some help in the laboratory, someone with software capabilities, and they praised her quick assessment and modification of the laboratory monitoring software.

When Jacob had shown her the quantum computer creation, Samantha was amazed at both the small size and speed of the computer. She had read about quantum computers, but the only example she had seen in a magazine reminded her of the early room-sized computers. Jacob had explained to her that it was his custom design utilizing quantum principles. Samantha was still trying to wrap her head around the architecture, but the processing speed was unreal.

Jacob called his quantum processing computer, QPC, much to his grandfather's annoyance, but Samantha thought the name cute and referred to the QPC as "Cupid," which made Jacob laugh.

But then she thought again and said, "No, call it JMAX. You both had input into its design.

Max shook his head.

Jacob laughed and said, "Better."

Samantha had worked over the weekend on the operating system for the QPC in Professor Maxwell's laboratory at the university. She met Max and Jacob again this Tuesday morning in the science building just after six as planned. They went in to work, and Samantha saw Professor Maxwell lock the lab door.

"Don't want any unexpected visitors today," he said.

Sam had spent the morning fine tuning the monitoring and control software. She would have liked more time to go over her work, but Max and Jacob were bouncing around the lab like young children at a birthday party. All that was missing was the cake.

Speaking of cake, Samantha hoped they would knock off for lunch soon. She was getting hungry. However, she judged that wish to be unlikely the way they were fidgeting.

"Hey, guys, how about we get something to eat before we dive in to this," she said. "Maybe I can convince you two to hold off another day or two while I check this software again."

Professor Maxwell finished writing something further in his lab journal and said, "Of course Miss Samantha. I feel like a slave driver here. We both get so wrapped up in our work."

The professor managed to look sheepish, turned to face Jacob, and he said, "Jacob, let's take 30 minutes at least to eat something. Then we can come back and still have time to get a trial run in, don't you think?"

Jacob's stomach rumbled in answer. They all laughed and headed out of the laboratory in search of a sandwich. As they left the lab,

Samantha noticed Jerry Daniels standing in the hallway reading a journal. She had met him before, unfortunately.

Daniels ignored Samantha and looked pointedly at Max and Jacob.

"Still working on your secrets, eh?" he said.

Samantha paused, confused at his remark.

Daniels turned to walk away and said, "Good luck on Max's Folly."

He continued down the hall, laughing.

Samantha had a questioning look, but Jacob shook his head, and the three of them took the elevator in deference to Max's knees.

They found a table outside where they could sit and eat their sandwiches from the building vending machines. She asked about Daniels, and Jacob explained that he was a graduate student who used to work with Max, but not anymore.

She said, "He gives me the creeps. Doesn't even know me, but he's asked me out already. He's like crypt ancient, you know."

Jacob agreed with Samantha too quickly, and Max chuckled. She commented on how both of them could use the Vitamin D from the sunshine, and the three of them soaked up the peaceful surroundings. All too soon, Max suggested they head back to the lab.

Three hours later, Jacob worked over the light table layout making sure the alignments were correct. Samantha had done some last minute homework on quantum mechanics and was familiar with some of the concepts from her brief study.

"What are you doing?" she asked Jacob.

Jacob gently released the module he was positioning and said, "I'm making sure the pump ultraviolet laser is collimated with the filter and BBO crystal. The beam has to split precisely aligned or we'll loose intensity."

He walked over to a console and checked a reading and then flipped a switch and watched a gauge. He saw that she still watched him.

"This is the vacuum pump for the xenon gas surrounding the mirrors in the photon combustion chamber," said Jacob.

Samantha started to ask what a photon combustion chamber was, but at that moment the QPC completed the reboot after her code addition. Samantha restarted the monitoring software for the detectors and after an inspection of the software readouts, she had green indicators on the video monitors. Samantha signaled she was ready.

"I'm still not sure we should be pushing like you guys are trying to do here," she said. "But I think I'm ready from this end."

Jacob walked over to her with a pair of tinted safety goggles, and then wheeled an acrylic glass shield in front of her, which was large enough for the three of them to shelter behind.

Max joined them.

"Forgive our impatience," he said. "Jacob and I have been working on this for a long time, and today, we hope to see some results. When you are ready."

Samantha pressed the execute icon on the computer which sent a relay signal to the power amplifier for the laser. She could feel the power humming in the amplifier, but nothing happened for a moment.

She looked over at Jacob who was watching the laser and he said, "Wait for the capacitors to charge fully, and ... now."

At that moment, she saw a violet flash as the laser emitted a sun intense beam mirrored into the beam splitter BBO crystal and captured via fiber optic connections into the combustion vacuum chamber. The combustion chamber began to glow and then the glow condensed into a small ball of plasma, which looked exactly like a miniature sun. Thermocouples began to convert the chamber's interior heat to electrical impulses, as Samantha and the QPC monitored the power output. She sat transfixed.

"Is that what I think it is?" asked Samantha.

Jacob said, "Yes, that's a controlled fusion reaction."

"But that's not possible, is it?" asked Samantha with eyes wide open. "Not unless you have the mass of the sun?"

Professor Maxwell said, "Not until now. How's the output, Samantha?"

She eyed the program noting the increasing power output.

"Wait, the output is greater than the input electricity, that means ...?"

"That it should be self sustaining," said Professor Maxwell.

"For how long?" she asked.

She was sitting back in her chair, trying to fathom what she had stumbled into here.

Jacob grinned at her.

"We calculate four hours with the mass of heavy hydrogen in the chamber," he said.

Jacob had already told her the amount of deuterium in the vacuum chamber was the size of a pinhead.

Samantha checked that the program was logging data and saw that the interior of the chamber read a temperature of seven thousand degrees Celsius.

"I read that the required energy for fusion was around one hundred million degrees," she said. "How is this possible?"

Professor Maxwell nodded at his grandson and said, "I have to give Jacob the credit. He had the insight to entangle the photons which enabled reinforced quantum tunneling to jump start the fusion process, at least in theory, but now in practice it seems." Max smiled. "This might change a few things once we get a bit more work done."

A blinking red light caught Samantha's attention, and looking at her monitor closely, she noticed a power drain.

"Hey guys, we might have a problem here," she said. "Looks like one of the magnets is giving out around the chamber. How do we shut this off?"

Jacob looked at the software and said, "We can't shut it off. It's self sustaining, until the fuel runs out. If the magnet goes, we might lose control, and that means—"

At that moment one of the containment field electromagnets failed. The resulting explosion from the pellet of hydrogen fusion lanced out to the far wall which disintegrated in a circular hole, while the apparatus propelled itself back toward the protective shield in front of them, which held almost a full half second before it too was thrown back toward the research crew knocking them to the floor.

Samantha had time to note the sudden shifting of her world as she felt a hard push behind the glass. She remembered seeing the far wall vanish in a circle, but instead of daylight, she saw only blackness and points of light, and then all faded to black.

CHAPTER TWENTY-TWO

Space, Sol System, passing Mars

Ship announced the detection of a tachyon burst and subspace distor-tion originating from the target third planet. S'ear'r noted the discovery with alarm. Nothing from the captured probe would suggest the capability for generating such a signal.

Ship reminded S'ear'r that detection of such technology generated an automatic plan for eradication of such an advanced race. Clearly, a species, which could plumb the mysteries of subspace represented a threat to the Chos'n.

S'ear'r agreed with Ship, however, there seemed so far to be only the one signal. No other detection had been noted. S'ear'r suggested their current plan of careful scouting was still reasonable. After all, if the species proved more capable than initially thought, all the more reason to have sufficient intelligence in their report.

Ship noted his pilot's logic dispassionately and agreed that their current position just past the fourth planet of the system made sending an undetected signal much more difficult for any race that could pick up subspace signals. Therefore, both agreed that screening behind the unusually large moon of the target planet to gather more information might make sense.

S'ear'r suggested that L'ment'l had undoubtedly dispatched a regional destroyer toward their location, and one destroyer was more than a match for any developmental species. So far, Ship had detected no other evidence of system colonization, so it should be relatively easy to erase this species from existence if needed.

If Ship and S'ear'r could figure out this signal source, and there was no advanced threat, then perhaps a better path could be found to utilize the existing resources of this blue speck in the vastness of the universe. S'ear'r gave thought briefly to what a shock it would be to this species to finally realize it was not alone in the galaxy and quite unimportant. It always was.

Ship agreed with S'ear'r and quietly kept passive sensors out as they progressed toward their observation post, undetected as far as they knew.

Sol System, Earth, Southern California

Richard sat at his desk at JPL and rechecked his email for the third time today. He had gotten the distinct impression that his boss didn't want him asking again about the loss of signal from Voyager I. He would have thought there would be some press release. Oddly, there was no discussion of the topic among his fellow co-workers. In fact, it was almost like everyone was avoiding the topic.

Richard sighed and wondered for the umpteenth time regarding the squealing transmission picked up just before signal interruption. There was no correlation in the JPL/NASA database and Richard knew there was no record of similar signals for the Voyager program. He thought of the USB drive he had recorded the signal on. He had violated policy when he ferreted the thumb drive out for analysis at home. He couldn't help himself.

Richard knew he was in trouble when two dark suited gentlemen visited him at work to discuss what he might know about the transmission. They seemed like government agency to him. Sure enough, the next morning his computer held no traces of the transmission, or any of the recent records of Voyager. Richard was not dense. He knew a cover up when he saw one.

Well, there was still his baby sister. If anyone could decipher the signals, she could. The question was how to get the recording to her. He would bet his terminal and home systems were being watched, and if he tried to fly out to visit her he would bring unnecessary attention to her. No, he would need an alternate plan to contact her.

Richard had the sensation of being followed. He knew he couldn't risk going home, and given any additional suspicion, the feds would just roll him up. Who could know if he would ever see Samantha again. So he did what any resourceful field agent would do. He went shopping.

After all, there was nothing unusual about a computer guy browsing an electronics store. He went to the computer section and asked to see the most powerful desktop on display. A dream machine for gaming the flight simulation games that Richard loved to play. The realistic flight computer programs required significant processing speed. The salesman was drooling at the potential sale which almost made Richard feel guilty. The poor guy had no way of knowing Richard did not have that kind of money.

After asking the salesman to check on the possibility of increasing the random access memory and hard drive size, he bypassed the store internet password and loaded up the signal and the packet of descriptive information. Using an anonymous browser, he took a breath and sent his packet of information with the signal data to Samantha.

He hoped he was clever enough. This was just too important to hold back from everyone. He was convinced the signal represented the possibility of life outside the solar system, and he wasn't letting the government cover this up. By the time the salesman came back, the computer was working on the transfer in the background. Richard took some more time with the machine to be sure nothing was interrupted.

He hit a command-ctrl-key combination that caused his program and any data to disappear from the hard drive. It could still be found, but only by forensic IT sweep, and they would have to know the location and machine to discover any traces. Finally, he casually wiped down the keyboard, frame, and screen to be sure he left no prints.

The salesman was disappointed at not making the sale immediately, but Richard told him he would think about the computer overnight. Mission complete, he went home and decided to take a run. Samantha was always after him to work out more, and he thought maybe, he just might take her up on that.

CHAPTER TWENTY-THREE

John arrived at the library to pick up Jessica promptly at four o'clock. She said she would be at the side door facing the parking lot lower level, and he suspected she would be on time. John knew he wasn't the sharpest guy, but even he could tell Jessica wasn't happy about having to get a ride from him. It had taken Isaac an extra day to get both the starter and the chance to work on her Jeep. John wondered why the professor maneuvered her into accepting help from him.

John had the news on in his truck. He liked to listen to AM talk radio in the late afternoon on occasion. His window was down, and he heard and felt the explosion up the hill. His truck shook slightly. He knew it was a detonation as he had heard many. His surroundings slipped away. He sat very still in the truck and concentrated on his breathing.

He was back in Afghanistan, the mortar rounds walking toward his squad, caught in a crossfire, seeing his comrades, his friends, his men falling for the last time, and then nothing until he woke in the hospital unit 3 days later.

The army needed someone to blame and he was the officer in charge, and the only survivor. Medically hurt and in need of physical therapy and time to recover, he had hoped to continue his career, but the army wanted the whole episode expunged and didn't want John Stone any longer. He was given a generous medical rating and an honorable discharge, provided he didn't make waves.

Now, back in the truck, he could hear screaming in the distance. He felt the need to find out what was happening, to see if he could help, but he couldn't abandon his post here waiting for Jessica, and there she was, walking out of the library and hurrying to his truck.

He reached over and opened the door for her, and in response to her questioning expression, he said, "I'm not sure either. It just happened, whatever it is."

Jessica tried to reach Jacob or Max on her cell phone knowing they might not be able to pick up a signal if they were still in the lab. Jacob had told her they might run late as they were in the final stages of their work. She looked at John with white lips.

"I can't reach them," she said. Her hand trembled holding her cell phone. "Please drive by the science building, just to be sure. I need to know they're all right."

Driving up the hill, they could see the smoke before they saw the hole in the far side of the science building. Jessica reached out to grab John's arm.

"That's Max's lab!" she exclaimed. "Oh my God! Jacob!"

Before John could fully stop the truck, Jessica opened her door and rushed out to find her family. John urged her to wait for him. She ran for the back doors. He saw her swept back in the people pouring out of the building.

John parked his truck in the back lot and jogged briskly to the hole in the exterior building wall. There was some debris on the grass outside the building, but not as much as he would have thought. He saw no exterior wounded.

With that inspection, John ran to the rear doors disregarding the fire alarm and waded through the students and instructors making their way out of the building. One of the instructors attempted to bar his way, but John shoved past him as gently as he could without slowing. He found the stairwell and raced up the stairs to the third floor remembering the location of the laboratory.

Jacob emerged from the smoke through the open laboratory door with a fire extinguisher in hand. He was pale around his soot stained mouth. He squinted his watering eyes to focus on John and gestured with the fire extinguisher to his right.

"Max and Sam are over there behind the shield. I can't wake Max up."

John rushed into the lab in an instant. He found Max breathing, but unresponsive to voice or touch. Samantha was holding her head. She had a small cut which had stopped bleeding.

"Are you all right?" asked John.

"Got a headache," she said. "We have to help Max."

John put his hand on her shoulder.

"Can you stand?" he asked.

Samantha nodded that she could.

Looking over at Jacob, John asked, "Is the fire out?"

"I think so," said Jacob.

"Good," said John. "Help Sam. I've got Max."

John knew they shouldn't move Max without a cervical collar and stretcher, but a smoke filled room post explosion didn't seem like a safe environment to wait for the medics. He looked around for some way to secure Max's head and remembered the sheets in the office.

John grabbed two of the folded sheets at the end of the couch in the office and quickly rolled one into a rope like bundle to improvise a cervical collar for Max securing the ends with duct tape. Using the other sheet he tied off one corner and together they moved the sheet under Max. He began to drag Max using the sheet as a travois. He saw Samantha stumbling to stand.

"Jacob, can you help Samantha?" asked John.

Samantha leaned against Jacob for support, and with his other hand, the boy amazed John by reaching out to help perform a rescue drag for Professor Maxwell. They made their way through the door into the hall outside the laboratory just before the responding firemen came out of the stairwell laden with rescue equipment.

John was able to hand off Max to a couple of the firemen who were calling into their radio for an ambulance. Samantha breathed from an offered oxygen mask, which Jacob had waved off.

"Take care of her first," said Jacob, gesturing to Samantha.

Jessica came running from the stairwell having made it past the crowd. She looked Jacob over and hugged him, and then asked Samantha if she was okay? Samantha nodded yes, and Jessica turned to Max. The ambulance crew arrived and log rolled Professor Maxwell to a spine board and lifted him to a stretcher, started an IV, and replaced the sheet roll with a commercial cervical collar.

The paramedic began talking on the radio through dispatch to the hospital.

"Elderly male with head trauma, unresponsive, BP 160/100, pupillary reflexes intact but slowed, Glasgow Coma Scale of six, cervical collar in place. Right. On the way now."

Jessica looked at John, and he said, "Go with Max. I'll stay with these two, and we'll catch up with you."

"He's right Mom," said Jacob. "I'm all right. I'll help Samantha get to the hospital."

Jacob rested his hand on Samantha's shoulder. Jessica looked torn, but followed Max and the medics.

Samantha waved off more of the oxygen, coughing, and thanked the firemen while she motioned to get John's attention.

"We need to salvage Jacob's computer and the laboratory notebooks," she said. "No, not need to, have to, now, before they come to seal the lab, or it walks off. Can you grab them? It all was sitting by the monitoring console." John started to walk back into the lab, and Samantha grabbed his wrist. "You had better grab Max's lab journal too. Should be near where he went down as he was holding it. Hurry, please."

John walked in through the lab door quickly before the fire department tried to stop him, and he grabbed the target items without fuss, wrapping the professor's raincoat over the items as he came back out into the hall just in time to see Chief Roberts coming down the hall.

Setting down the wrapped items on the floor, he crouched down by Samantha and set down the covered items. John stood and faced Chief Roberts. Jacob stayed in front, shielding their belongings from the chief's view.

"I should have known you would be involved here. Just can't stay out of trouble can you?" said Chief Roberts.

"Just passing by this time, Chief," said John. "Thought I could lend a hand, but now that you're here, I suppose I can be about my business."

"Now just a minute you ...." stammered Roberts.

John turned to pick up Samantha and motioned for Jacob to follow as he turned to Officer Murray who had arrived on scene, and he said, "Murray, I promised Jessica I would get these two over to the hospital where they took Professor Maxwell. Probably need to get them looked at as well."

"Professor Maxwell was injured?" asked Chief Roberts.

"Yes, and I'll be at the hospital if you need me," replied John.

John and Jacob helped Samantha up and moved toward the stairwell, as the elevators automatically shut down after the fire alarm activation. Jacob was holding the QPC under the raincoat, and John was holding onto a book bag, contained Max's most recent lab journal and paper observations.

Chief Roberts started to say something, but was distracted by the Fire Brigade Captain coming over to speak with him. John saw the campus police chief talking with Officer Murray, who nodded yes. They made it to the stairwell.

"Jacob, are you okay to get down these stairs?" asked John.

"I am recovered fully," replied Jacob.

John took the brunt of Samantha as she leaned against him to get down the stairs, but she walked under her own power, which he thought very encouraging. As for Jacob, John was amazed he was doing so well considering the shape of the lab.

The trio was able to push out past the growing crowd of onlookers to find John's parked truck and head to the hospital.

CHAPTER TWENTY-FOUR

Vincent heard of the campus lab explosion on the local news as he pulled into a self-serve gas station close to his hotel at the edge of town. His first thought was the distraction of the explosion would allow him easier access to campus. He could continue his recon of the local surroundings and discover as much as possible about Professor Kincaid before approaching him.

He tried to put thoughts of John Stone out of his mind. Vincent knew, with the plastic surgery, he would be nearly impossible to recognize at a glance. The scar on his face was both lengthened and aesthetically noticeable. Some of that was from his time in captivity, but some of it was the agency interacting with the plastic surgeon. People tended too fixate on facial scars, all but ignoring the rest of the face.

He still felt uneasy at the thought of drawing John's attention. Living together, eating together, and fighting together had once made them close. John might see past the plastic surgery and recognize his voice and mannerisms if Vincent were actually around him. No, better to recon quietly and avoid him.

He first met John at basic training. They were both there at the urging of the legal system. Vincent had been given a last chance following a stolen car by a judge too familiar with his name. Vincent was used to being yelled at while growing up, so the drill instructors didn't faze him. He knew how to get by, and he knew how to play a system. He just needed to learn the system he was in now. Unfortunately, he managed to anger a couple of guys in the barracks, and they went after him in the middle of the night.

It was John who came to help him. Standing over him, daring anyone else to come after him. Telling everyone in the unit they were all brothers now, all in training together. Vincent had never had anyone stand up for him in all the time he could remember. He didn't know all the answers, or even most of the questions, but he did know loyalty, and from that moment, he decided he would have John's back. Vincent always looked for the reason behind what others did and noticed there was never an angle going on with John. What he said or did was just, him, even if he was a bit inflexible at times.

In Afghanistan, they had worked to survive and accomplish their mission. After a while, Vincent noticed small details that didn't add up. Some of the missions just didn't make sense unless you looked at them with a practiced eye, learned through the kind of experience surrounding him while growing up. He could tell based on the information he obtained from other reports. It was subtle. Some mission report details couldn't be verified after discussion with the soldiers in the field.

Vincent knew there was an angle in there somewhere, and maybe, there was something in it for him. He started nosing around with a couple guys in supply, and before he knew what was happening, he was on the inside and facing the opportunity to go home with more than a few bucks in his pocket. The heroin grown in Afghanistan would be marketed somewhere, and he didn't see any reason not to make some money off of it.

Vincent tried to talk with John in a roundabout way, but he seemed to not understand, or if he did, he didn't seem to register Vincent's discussions as anything more than his usual ramblings. When Vincent tried to suggest John look the other way, that the army could still do its job, but there was a profit to be made for a man who could work within the system, John would have none of it.

Vincent had tried to tell John that there was a better way than hoping to make it back to the states alive and poor, but John didn't want anything but his way, what he called his path. Vincent didn't understand it when they were in training together, didn't understand it in Afghanistan, and didn't understand it now.

So be it. Vincent started sliding down that slope, but really, he thought, he started on that slope a long time ago after he was old enough to be bitter about being on his own without parents, which seemed to be just about as long as he could remember.

Vincent continued to brood a bit, even as he forced himself to stay alert and look up and smile at others. His goal was to look average, like he belonged. He knew a smile tended to generate sympathy in most because of his fine facial scar.

He knew also, that John would never forgive him after their last mission just as he could not forgive Stone for surviving. John's existence reminded Vincent of what he'd done, so he had stayed away, agreeing with his superiors that John posed no threat without memory of that mission. From the medical reports, John might never fully remember the events of that day because of the head trauma suffered in his last mission.

Vincent wasn't sure so much what right and wrong was, but he understood loyalty. That's why it hurt so much when he realized that John wouldn't support him in Afghanistan.

Well, he would observe and stay away from Stone while he fulfilled his mission, and John had better stay away from him.

Vincent had found another parking spot off campus on a side street. Varying routine and parking spaces and hotels was good trade craft and as natural as breathing to him.

Under the guise of a parent interested in the university, Vincent had managed to gain a tour of administration, and the campus as well as finding out information on Professor Kincaid and others in the administration. No reason to give anyone reason to remember a guy asking specifically about one professor.

He affirmed Professor Kincaid's position as Associate Dean of Academic Affairs and managed to gain an appointment with the associate dean in twenty-four hours for a discussion of academic offerings on the campus. Hinting at a sizable donation didn't hinder his efforts.

He took occasion to wander the campus generally noting the location of various buildings and orienting himself. He wandered into the student center, avoiding the area of protestors just outside the west entrance. From what he could tell, the students were equally angry with John and buzzing over the explosion in the science building earlier. There was even talk of radiation involved in the explosion.

Vincent did take the time to ask random students in and about campus if they knew professor Kincaid. Most didn't, but some did, and gave mixed reviews.

He knew it was a risk, but he decided to go to John's dormitory. He walked up to the greeting desk after being let in by another student and introduced himself again as the potential father of an incoming student. He asked and was given general information regarding the dormitory, and after a short wait, was invited into Tom Mosier's office for a meet and greet.

After introductions, Tom said, "I understand you have a son who may be attending university with us in the fall next year?"

"Yes. Scott is very excited at the prospect of getting out on his own. His mother a bit less so, I would say."

Vincent chuckled while immersing himself in his role, imagining if he had a son and a wife and anything resembling a normal life.

"We like to think we have a great deal to offer young men and women attending our university," said Tom.

"I understand the incoming class is required to live in the dormitories?" asked Vincent.

"Yes, for the first two years. Many of the students benefit from the socialization skills developed living in the dormitories," said Tom.

"But what of this trouble recently on campus. I heard something about an attack and some young men were hurt. Now, I understand there was an explosion on campus today?"

Tom sat back in his chair and clasped his hands together and said nothing for a couple of moments.

"Mr. Norris, this university has more than thirty thousand students on or around campus in full session," he said. "That is more population than many small towns. Just as in those towns, people don't always get along. Going to a university enables the opportunity for growth, but doesn't ensure safety. No opportunity in life can do that."

"I understand one of the men involved lives here in this dormitory?" asked Vincent in an offhanded way.

"Yes, Mr. Stone lives here. He has offered no trouble in this dormitory. The university has made no determination on his status as an active student, and he continues in class."

"And you feel my son would be safe living here in your dormitory with a man having a violent past, and now this latest incident?"

"I have been able to observe and speak with Mr. Stone," said Tom. "I have found him to be a reasonable and trustworthy man. The reports I have seen in the news and the statements from the university administration do not reflect the man I know living in this dormitory."

Vincent seethed inside. Stone was doing it again. He played the hero well, and people trusted him, but when the chips were down, when people needed him, he was nowhere to be found, and then you were on your own, except for the people who wanted to cut your head off and record it for internet propaganda.

How did he fool people so easily? He had fooled him. Right up to the point, he found out John was still alive. He knew he would never be able to forgive him for living and not coming to find him.

"Are you alright, Mr. Norris?"

Vincent saw Mosier tensing up a bit in his chair with a concerned look on his face. Vincent clamped down on his emotions, and smiled.

"I am gratified to hear your personal reassurances, Mr. Mosier," said Vincent. "I will need to follow this situation closely before I can satisfy myself completely. After all, our son's safety is our paramount concern."

"I understand," said Tom. "Now, if you wish to see a typical room, I can have one of the resident assistants take you up for a tour of one of our unoccupied rooms."

"Please, another time, Mr. Mosier. I still want to spend some time looking at the other facilities on campus."

"Of course. Let me know if I can assist further."

Vincent left the dormitory knowing the assistant dorm director was staring after him. That was stupid, he thought. He still didn't understand why he went in there, maybe to see a little of what John was experiencing in his life after the military, so different than Vincent's life.

Oh, well, he would try to find out a bit more about the good professor and leave Stone to his pretend real life on campus. After all, what did John know of real tragedy?

They were both products of the legal system to a degree, but Vincent learned early on the only person you could depend on was yourself. Everyone else would eventually let you down. For a time, he thought he was wrong after he met John, but even John abandoned him when he needed him most, in that hell hole in Afghanistan, the daily torture, the agony, somewhere in all of that Vincent learned the truth. There was no one else, no something else, and no heaven. The only hell was fully realized here on earth. That was reality, and Vincent had grown to embrace it realizing power came from understanding truth. Later, after he was free and working with the agency in the shadows, he refined his lessons.

As he thought on this, he walked back up the hill observing the students wandering about the campus and considered his assignment. He had to face the fact that he felt vulnerable for the first time in a while. He thought it was being this close to his old friend, Stone, but he realized it was more the nature of the assignment. Thinking brought clarity.

This was a cover your ass assignment because of the shit they were into in Afghanistan. Vincent had no illusions, if they wanted him to ride herd on this situation, then his employers could decide to go nuclear and close off all traces to that previous activity. That's what he would do if it were up to him, and getting rid of all traces meant getting rid of him as well. Likely, the FBI was already tipped off that he might show up in the area and to be on the watch for him. Well, if that was the game, he could play it better than most.

Scorched earth it is, he thought.

CHAPTER TWENTY-FIVE

Paul Kincaid heard about the explosion in the science building while he was in his office. He stopped by the dean's office to inform him he was heading to the scene. By the time he got to the building, campus security had evacuated the building. He had to demand access.

Arriving at the third floor hallway, he smelled smoke and sensed confusion as members of the fire department and campus police continued to sift through the laboratory. Chief Roberts supervised the scene.

"Chief, what's happened here?" asked Kincaid.

"Preliminary evaluation suggests an explosion of some kind in the laboratory. We're going over the scene now for hazards. The fire seems to be contained. The explosion was powerful though."

"How do you know?" asked Kincaid.

Police Chief Roberts led him to the lab doorway to look at the perfectly cylindrical hole in the exterior wall.

"That is how I know," said Roberts.

"Is anyone hurt?" asked Kincaid, thinking of the consequences to the university.

"Professor Maxwell was taken by ambulance to the hospital. I have no word on his condition," said Roberts, and he moved away to talk to the fire captain on site.

Kincaid considered what he'd found out. Maxwell hurt?Outwardly showing dismay, he tried to hide his excitement. This could work, especially if it forced the old codger out of the university setting.

"Professor?"

Kincaid turned and saw Jerry Daniels, his graduate student and chief source of information on all things Professor Maxwell in the science department.

"Jerry," said Kincaid. "Are you hurt? You look a bit pale."

Daniels leaned back against the wall of the hallway and took a deep breath. He raised a tremulous hand and pressed his fingers against his forehead for support.

"I didn't know this would happen, Professor," said Daniels. "You've got to believe me. I didn't know."

Kincaid moved closer willing Jerry to keep his voice low.

"What are you saying?" asked Kincaid. "Did you have something to do with this?"

Daniels slid down the wall sitting on the floor with his head in his hands.

"I only did what we talked about, you know, to slow them down, to show the waste and the excess of money put into that old dinosaur's research, and, well, I tried to help like we talked about."

"Jerry, what did you do?" asked Kincaid.

"I loosened the connection to one of the magnets in the experiment setup. I only wanted to slow them down. I didn't expect this. You've got to believe me."

Kincaid put his hand on the nearly sobbing graduate student's shoulder.

"I believe you," said Kincaid. "You couldn't have anticipated this would happen. You're not at fault here. If the experiment could fail from something as simple as one loose connection, it was far too dangerous to be performed here anyway."

Kincaid had no idea if Jerry could have known this might happen or not, but he desperately wanted the young man to be anywhere but here at the scene. Best to find a way to get him out of here as quickly as possible. But first, Daniels needed something to keep him busy, something to get his mind off his own involvement in this catastrophe.

"I need you to do something for me," said Kincaid. "I need you to inventory every piece of equipment in this lab that's left, damaged or not. I also need you to gather all the logs, journals, and hard drives pertaining to the work. Can you do that for me?"

Jerry nodded, yes. He still looked like he wanted to break down, but now, with a purpose, his eyes cleared a bit as he got himself up and began to move toward some of the wet debris being pulled out of the laboratory into the hallway.

Kincaid reached out to touch his arm.

"Don't say anything to anyone else, except that you are tasked by the associate dean with document and equipment recovery. Got it?"

"Yes, I can do that," said Daniels, and he hurried off to busy himself with the task.

CHAPTER TWENTY-SIX

John pulled into the parking lot at the county medical center. He helped Samantha and Jacob into the emergency department. They were taken straight back into the treatment area for evaluation. John was asked to come back with Jacob, with the assumption that John was a parent.

Samantha and Jacob were both examined by a young physician, who introduced herself as Dr. Lowenstein. She felt both of them were doing well, but Samantha had a mild concussion. The doctor wanted to see the brain CAT scan test results for Samantha to be careful. Surprisingly, Jacob did not show any appearance of injury, and would need parental permission for any further testing.

John admitted he wasn't Jacobs father, but a family friend. He did say that Jessica, Jacobs mother, came in with Professor Maxwell. Dr. Lowenstein said she would find her to discuss Jacob, and left for the moment.

Shortly after, Jessica came in to hug Jacob.

"Max is still not responding," she said. "They have a new magnetic resonance imaging scanner here, something truly next generation, and they're going to take a look with that as soon as they can get it warmed up."

Samantha said, "Miss Jessica, where is the new MRI scanner?"

"I think the Doctor said it was in a basement wing, something about extra shielding. Why?"

"Jacob and I need to be there. Can you help with that?" asked Samantha, eyes imploring. "Its important, Miss Jessica. We need to get down there before the scan starts."

Samantha looked at John for help.

"Why?" he said, not understanding.

The nurse walked in, and relayed that Samantha's CAT scan looked normal. Dr. Lowenstein was discharging them both with head precautions and light activity restrictions.

"Oh, by the way, there is a police officer here to see you," said the nurse.

The nurse stepped aside saying she would be back with instructions and in walked Officer Murray. He looked at each of them, offered his sympathy, and asked about Professor Maxwell's condition.

While Jessica filled him in on Max's condition, Samantha grabbed Jacob and John and said, "We need to get the QPC attached to the MRI for Max's scan." Jacob nodded understanding and picked up the QPC holding it under his shirt.

"Okay, but once again, why?" said John.

"Please trust me for now," said Samantha. "I'll explain later. We have to hurry. Please get me down there."

John sighed, unfolded his arms, walked over to Officer Murray, and spoke quietly. Murray looked at Samantha and Jacob.

"Okay, follow my lead," said the officer.

Murray spoke with a hospital security guard who led the group down to the new MRI waiting area. The technician in the control booth seemed intent, and they could hear subdued machine like booming behind the shielded door leading to the MRI machine. The guard apparently knew her and explained the group was with the emergency patient coming downstairs.

"Won't the magnetism hurt that computer if you take it in there?" asked John.

"It will be safe in the control area, but I need the tech to be distracted. She won't want me there," said Samantha.

Just then, the MRI technician stepped across the room to the restroom.

Jacob said, "Okay, it's now or never."

Samantha stepped into the MRI control area and looked behind the console at the incoming connections, similar in many ways to a modern personal computer. She managed to hook up the QPC which began to initiate a download into the control console using Samantha's custom software, careful to stay out of any executable files. Sam stepped back out of the control room for the MRI.

It was hard to see Professor Maxwell so still on the stretcher when he arrived a few moments later. The staff moved him back into the MRI bay for the test.

"Samantha, why did we need to come down here?" asked Jessica. "What did you do?"

"Yes," agreed John.

"Jacob, would you explain?" said Samantha.

Nodding his head, Jacob motioned them all closer.

"The QPC is a quantum computer I put together for our project, but it's Samantha's programming skills that have turned it into a useful tool. We used it to monitor and direct the lab work, and now we are using it to monitor this MRI on the professor."

"Why do you want to do that?" asked John.

Jacob pointed to Samantha who explained further.

"This MRI machine is a next generation scanner and is supposed to be more discriminating than previous scanners. The QPC should be able to interpret the signals and create an even more detailed map of the professor's brain. We thought," said Samantha looking at Jacob. "we might be able to boost the sensitivity of the scan even more and help the medical team with better images."

"Oh, okay, so your computer is better than their computer and should help the scan, right?" said John.

"Yes, that's it exactly," said Samantha.

"Wait a minute," said Officer Murray. "Did you say quantum computer? I read about that in a science magazine? That's next generation stuff, and the prototype I saw pictured filed out half a room. Are you saying you created a quantum computer that fits in that small case?"

Officer Murray looked a little unsteady.

Jacob blushed slightly, and in a small voice said, "Well, kinda, yes, but Granddad helped."

Jacob's face turned grim and he looked around at the MRI suite as if he realized at that moment where he was and what was happening and the reality that the only father figure he had ever known might not survive. Tears filled his eyes, and he turned away.

Jessica went to comfort him, but Samantha was there, holding Jacob before she could move.

"It will be okay, you'll see, this can work, it has to work," said Samantha, and she refused to let go of Jacob until he looked at her face and nodded. She reached up and kissed him on the forehead.

Samantha let go of Jacob. Jessica stepped over, and Jacob hugged his mother tightly. Both women were comforting him. John looked at Officer Murray, who was there for them once again. They were strangers no longer.

That is when the overhead speakers announced, "Code Blue, MRI suite. Code Blue, MRI suite."

Jacob looked at John in anguish, and John nodded slightly. Has to be Max, John thought. Less than a minute later, doctors, nurses, respiratory therapists, and pharmacy staff arrived and tumbled into the MRI suite.

Unable to see what was happening, Jessica knocked on the door. It was opened slightly by one of the staff. She could see through the doorway to the stretcher where a younger man pushed down on Professor Maxwell's chest. Another squeezed a bag to breathe for Max through a tube.

The young man holding the door open said, "Ma'am, you are with him? We are doing what we can and will let you know something soon."

John glided up behind Jessica, and she collapsed into his arms. John held her, telling her it would be okay, whispering to her that Max loved her and Jacob. Jessica sobbed, and her tears seemed to penetrate his skin and mix with his blood until he felt he was part of her and she him. John drifted in that feeling and felt his soul open up. The dream returned now in force, stronger than he could remember, the same dream he had since the night he lost his parents. He still had gaps in his memory of that night, but he felt something click, almost as if his brain moved something closer into alignment. He'd made himself like being alone, he could depend on himself, didn't need anyone else, and yet, here was this woman, and she needed him. John felt his spine straighten as the vision engulfed him.

He was standing in the middle of a field surrounded with swaying golden wheat on one side and harvestable sweet corn to the other side. Flowers lined the path he was on, and he sensed this was his path in life. He looked back and saw barren hills, black and scorched trees, and darkness. Ahead in the distance, he saw more of the same, but here it was beautiful. He saw a figure approach from a distance. He had never been able to make out a face before, but this time, maybe, yes, it's Marzone. Marzone, who went down during their last mission. He smiled at John.

Look what a man has to do to have a private conversation?

But he didn't move his mouth, and John knew he was hearing him inside his head.

I don't have much time. They are coming. I have been told to warn you. Jessica and Jacob need you. There is much you don't know, and I don't have time to tell you, but it comes down to this. You have to believe and trust in yourself. John, it wasn't your fault. It was just our time. You are better than you think you are. They will all need you.

And he was back and looking down at Jessica, who looked up at him in wonder. Her hands were still on his torso. She was looking at him like she was seeing him clearly for the first time, taking measure of him and drinking in his essence.

He stood feeling her closeness and remembering the curve of her as she leaned against him. He knew now, no matter what she thought of him, he had a mission again. He pledged to himself and Holy God that he would not fail this time. No matter what she thought of him, he had a new mission.

Dr. Lowenstein came out from the resuscitation and said, "We got a heart beat back, and he's trying to breathe on his own again. He's still not responsive. We have to hope for the best. We're going to move him up to intensive care now. That's on the fifth floor. We were able to finish the MRI. Hopefully that will help us."

Jessica hugged the doctor, and Jacob thanked her, and then the staff wheeled Max out of MRI and into the elevators with tubes and beeps and hands working at various tasks.

Officer Murray excused himself and went back to report the professor still alive. Jessica said she wanted Samantha to come stay at Max's home tonight. Samantha agreed, saying that she didn't want to be alone, and she followed after hugging Jacob again. Jacob held onto the QPC, which Samantha had retrieved while Max was transported out of the MRI suite.

John could hear Murray down the hall talking on his radio with dispatch.

"Affirm. Professor Maxwell is alive for the moment, but condition critical. I can ask Stone to come by for questioning tomorrow. Chief, he wasn't even in the lab when it happened. The other two students are being sent home on concussion protocol. Right, Chief. Murray out."

Murray walked up the hall to join the trio and said, "Chief Roberts wants you all to answer some questions, but I put that off until tomorrow. Okay?"

"Thanks Murray. I'm going to get these three home to Max's house for some rest," said John, looking at Jessica, who started to argue.

None of them wanted to leave Max, but John convinced them.

CHAPTER TWENTY-SEVEN

The oval office of the White House in Washington, D.C., served a dual role, both ceremonial and a working office for the most powerful man in the free world.

Sitting behind his desk and facing the men arranged in a semicircle of chairs in front of him, the president regarded each one silently. He held up a copy of a prominent newspaper.

"Gentlemen, why am I hearing about this after everyone else?"

"Mr. President, we are not sure how the information about Voyager I leaked," said NASA director Holland. "We closed down any announcements just as discussed."

President Mathisson scowled.

"Okay, Let me get this straight," said the president. "You are saying we did lose signal from Voyager I?" Turning to his science advisor, Thomas Burch, the president continued. "Tom, you told me this satellite is forty plus years old. Don't we think it finally lost power or something?"

"That is possible, Mr. President, but power loss would display as a loss of individual systems," said Burch. "The flight management system would cycle them off to conserve power."

NASA director Holland nodded his head in agreement.

"Okay, that makes sense, but why the big cover-up, and who authorized that?" asked the president.

"I did, Mr. President," said the military man on the end. He was dressed in blue and wearing the stars of a general. "You were to be briefed later this morning at the security meeting."

General Bartholomew Spears sat ramrod straight in one of the chairs.

President Mathisson started to respond to that, but was gently interrupted.

"And there is something else as well, Mr. President," said Burch.

"Go ahead," said the president.

"There was an odd signal recorded just prior to Voyager going unresponsive," said Burch. "We've been working to analyze it, and our best guess is some sort of compressed signal beyond our usual communication wavelengths. We've run the signal through NSA and CIA analyst systems without any luck. All we know is that we didn't make it."

"A compressed signal from what?" asked the president.

NASA director Holland put both hands on the desk and slid a folder across the desk to the president.

"We have this as well Mr. President," said Holland.

"Will someone tell me what I'm looking at here?" asked the president.

NASA director Holland explained.

"We have some faint infrared signals from something crossing the asteroid field and Mars orbit on its way into the inner systems," he said. "Trajectory takes it close to us. It was moving at a fraction of the speed of light."

"Was?" asked President Mathisson

"Our data suggests it is slowing down," said Burch.

"How do we have this information?" asked the president.

Holland said, "You remember the commotion with the first successful commercial launch a few years ago?"

The president nodded and Holland continued, "Well, what the pictures didn't show was the monitoring gear and cameras we were able to put in the front of that payload vehicle, as well as the attitude thrusters, communications gear, and pulse generator to power passive observation equipment. We pitched it for science to help scan for near earth objects like asteroids and comets. We eased some regulatory pressure and promised to associate the company with any significant scientific findings to make it work."

"You're kidding me," said the president.

"No sir," said Holland. "Any way, it worked for us this time. So putting this all together, we think we have something moving into our area of space, after meeting up with our Voyager probe and coming in unannounced. Something we didn't make."

The president looked like he had bitten into a not quite ripe persimmon.

"How sure are you of any of this?" asked Mathisson.

The president let the question hang in the air as he looked at the others in the room.

Holland gave Burch a nod and the president's science advisor said, "Mr. President, with the information we currently have, seventy percent probability that our current analysis is correct."

"Well, what are our contingency plans for this scenario?Bart?" asked President Mathisson.

Air Force General, Bartholomew Spears, had been sitting patiently for just this question.

"Mr. President, I would suggest we put out an alert for our Space Force," said General Spears. "We call it an exercise, but we keep it quiet. We currently have no real time tracking other than the information you have seen. Still, that may change as whatever this is gets closer."

"So far, we're the only ones with the information, right?" asked the president.

Heads nodded around him, as the president paused to consider further.

"So, we quietly put some of our forces on alert, without causing a panic, and we look for whatever might be trying to sneak into our back yard," said President Mathisson, recapping what he had been told.

Holland said, "We would have a better chance to track this object if we let some of the other countries help."

General Spears nodded in agreement and said, "Probably true, but if we share this information, it will surely leak out."

The president slumped his shoulders and continued the thought.

"Yes, and we don't need a panic that would consume this country and distract us, when we should be focused on other real problems," said Mathisson. "Still, even though we are not sure, we will focus on finding this thing if it is real."

Matthew Barnes, the president's chief of staff and his most trusted political advisor, leaned over and said quietly, "Mr. President, if the country finds out you knew about this beforehand and something untoward happens, we could be harmed approaching your re-election."

The president leaned across his desk to address the group.

"That why we need to keep this confidential pending any results," said Mathisson. "I mean it. No leaks. Lock down this information. We quietly look for this object and make some preparations, but no panic. Oh, this better be the last time something like this doesn't make it to me first. Got it?"

Nodding heads all around reassured the president and everyone left the conference room except for Barnes and President Mathisson.

Barnes said, "We can get hurt on this one, Martin. If this proves real, and we can't control the information, we'll be crucified."

"What do you suggest?" asked the president.

Barnes leaned in to speak privately.

"We need a fall guy in case it goes bad," said Barnes. "Someone the public respects, but doesn't know well, like the general."

"Spears has an impeccable reputation," said Mathisson.

"Even better," said Barnes. "Nobody's perfect. We lay out a timeline where he knew about this, but didn't really brief you in a timely fashion. He went off on his own, out of the chain of command. That way, if it goes south, we can lay it at his feet, deflect some of it off you. Holland and Burch are company men, you know that."

"Yes, I appointed both of them. I suppose you are right. Always good to be prepared for the worst," said the president.

CHAPTER TWENTY-EIGHT

Arriving at the Maxwell home, John pulled into the driveway to see Isaac working on Jessica's Jeep.

Isaac pulled himself out from under the hood with a satisfied smile.

"Just in time, I see," said Isaac. "I've about got this finished." His smile faltered. "Hey, What's going on? You all look ragged? Where's the professor?"

Jessica thanked Isaac. Samantha and Jacob followed her woodenly into the house. John filled Isaac in.

"I am so sorry. I like that old man. Will he be all right, mi hermano?"

"I don't know," said John, putting his hand to his head. He had a mild headache, probably tension he thought. "Where is Isabella? You said you were inviting her over tonight?"

"She had a flight," said Isaac. "She is flying a charter to Florida, and she'll be back tomorrow evening. She gave me her cell number in case I need to reach her."

Jessica came out of the house holding a couple bottles, and said, "Pizza is on the way. I brought a beer out for each of you. Jacob and I are going to clean up. Here's money for the pizza." She leaned over to kiss Isaac on the cheek, handed him a beer and said, "Thank you again for working on the Jeep."

Turning to John, she handed him a beer but held onto it while looking him in the eyes.

"We need to talk," she said and went back inside.

"Oh man, the dreaded four words," said Isaac.

The two of them drank their beer in silence until the pizza arrived, and everyone grabbed a slice. The pizza was good, but dinner was quiet, as each of them contemplated dark and empty thoughts. Isaac ate and excused himself. Jessica again thanked him and pushed money into his hands for the parts and his time. She said she was going back down to the hospital to be near Max. She wouldn't be able to sleep anyway. She had convinced Jacob to stay home tonight. He would need to be fresh in the morning, and she wanted to shield him from any publicity related to the lab accident and the professor's condition.

She asked John to follow her outside as Isaac left, and when they were standing by John's truck, she looked up at him.

"Who are you, really?" she asked. "I need to know. I feel I should know you, but a few days ago I couldn't have picked you out of a crowd, and now you're in our lives."

John reached out and took her hand. She didn't pull away. How much to tell her? He was still afraid that if she realized it was him long ago, she might hate him, maybe even believe the gossip that he had fathered Jacob. Surprisingly, there was some resemblance. But what to tell her? She clearly didn't recognize him, and his name change before joining the military wouldn't mean anything to her. He'd been in love with Jessica since he could remember. How would she react to that? He wasn't sure he was ready to find out. But, he also knew he didn't want to lie to her.

"My name is John Stone," he said. "I grew up in a good family, until I lost both of my parents in a traffic accident. Later, I joined the United States Army, and that became my home. I worked in the army until I was injured during my last mission. I was medically discharged after my rehabilitation. I needed a change and thought to try teaching. I came here to get the rest of the credits to finish a teaching degree."

John looked down, knowing he hadn't told her everything, but she was still holding his hand.

"Did you know I had two FBI agents come to my office this morning?" asked Jessica. "They wanted to know what I had talked about with you and if you'd expressed any views regarding the current administration?They implied that you weren't to be trusted, that you were unpredictable and dangerous, and that I should stay away from you."

Jessica searched into his eyes, and John knew, without a doubt, he could never keep secrets from this woman.

"Except for my army brothers, I've been alone and planned to keep it that way," said John. "The military taught me many things Jessica, mostly how to kill people efficiently. I became good at it to survive. Not something I'm happy about, but I'm not ashamed of it either."

"There were news stories today suggesting you broke the rules, got people killed, and the military covered it up," said Jessica.

"I don't think I can lie to you, not now, not ever. I'm not supposed to talk about many of the events in places I worked while on duty and my last mission is one of those. If you ask me again to tell you, I will, but I would be committing a crime. I may be able to tell you more later, but I ask you to believe I would never knowingly hurt you or Jacob."

Jessica nodded her understanding although she seemed to want to ask more. She gave a small shrug of her shoulders seeming to give in to the idea she would find out more in the future, perhaps when she most needed to know.

"Okay, but do you get to talk about it with anybody? What about your army buddies, do you talk about it with them?"

"No."

John shook his head slightly. His face dropped a bit hiding his eyes in the play of shadows from the lamp light escaping the living room window.

"Why not?" she asked.

"They're dead," said John.

Jessica gasped.

He could feel the coolness of her hand in his, and she reached out to take his other hand. Holding both of her hands felt like a circuit was completed, as if both of their hearts were pumping into one circulatory system. Pulse to pulse, muscle flicker to muscle flicker, and breath to breath. John sensed time slow, the world stood still, and for just a moment he could see beyond the trees in his vision, to a path continuing on into sunlight.

"Do you want me to go with you to the hospital?" he asked.

"No, my Jeep is working, thanks to Isaac. I can drive over to the hospital. You should get home," said Jessica.

"I'll call you in the morning to check on him, and you'll let me know if you need anything, right? Oh wait, you haven't given me your number yet."

Jessica made a show of punching in her number and information on his cell phone and he sent her his contact information. And then they were both standing, looking at each other, swaying with each little breeze, each breath.

He wanted to hold her. He wanted to reach out and pull her to him and not let go, but he didn't. He sensed her hesitation. He got into his truck and told her he would call her in the morning. Firing up his dependable little Toyota truck, he backed out of the driveway and headed back to the dorm.

Jessica walked into the professor's house which was her home as well, her refuge since the night Sarah led her and baby Jacob home from the shelter. Since that first night she had felt safe and began to have hope that they would survive. Now, she realized that the real sanctuary had always been Sarah and Max.

She hugged Jacob and impulsively reached over to Samantha and kissed her on the forehead.

"Thank you," said Jessica.

She asked Jacob to show Samantha to the spare bedroom.

Jessica walked into her room and began to gather a few articles to take with her to the hospital. She was thinking of John and the way her hand felt in his and wondering why she should be having such thoughts about a man she met only six days ago, admittedly a man of violence. Well, that wasn't true, was it? She had the strange thought that it didn't feel like the first time holding his hand?

A glimmer of a memory settled in her heart, the faintest thought of someone sitting beside her at the hospital and holding her hand before she woke with her tear stricken mother at her bedside, before the storm that was her father at home, followed by Hades offspring, shame and guilt.

The students on campus, some of her administration colleagues, and the news feeds, both local and national, were commenting on how dangerous John could be. Yet, she didn't fear him. No, she didn't fear him at all. She felt safe with him. She couldn't explain it, but somehow, he was the only person other than Sarah and Max to help the doubt go away.

Oh, what was happening to her? She felt her mind spinning against her pressing need to stay in control. She told herself to take one step at a time. Max needed her now. She started to gather some things to help her stay at the hospital tonight. She filled a small bag with necessaries, and each time she put something in, another memory surfaced.

She had pretended not to notice the comments and hurtful things said to and about her during her recovery, and especially after others realized she was pregnant. Paul Kincaid had approached her and apologized repeatedly after the party, until he found out about the pregnancy, and then, he acted as if she didn't exist. Which was fine with Jessica. She wished he still acted that way.

She had dated sparingly over the years. She had never felt a connection with any other man. She sighed. No matter her new uncertain feelings about John, Max and Jacob were her whole world.

She missed Sarah and asked her to look after Max and pray for them. Jessica prayed that Max would recover, and gave thanks that Jacob seemed unhurt. Gathering her wandering memories, her fears, and her sense of lingering loss in missing Sarah, Jessica picked up her bag and left to find Max at the hospital.

CHAPTER TWENTY-NINE

Hospital Intensive Care

Horace Maxwell, Ph.D., professor emeritus, holder of the Endowed Chair for Science, smiled. He was sitting with Sarah. She was stroking his face and telling him she loved him.

I've missed you, Sarah.

She looked youthful like he remembered from their honeymoon. Her skin glowed with a translucent vitality intoxicating to him.

Oh, how he loved the memories of that trip, walking on the beach together hand in hand, picking up seashells and saving the prettiest ones, shopping at the general store on the island, and how happy the people were in the area. They had little money, but had time and a car, so they had driven down to Florida, enjoying the drive almost as much as their destination.

Sarah had never seen the ocean before and was driving while he took a nap. When he woke, he thought they were both going to die. She had taken a turn to the sky bridge stretching up and across the bay, and she was mesmerized. There was no place to turn off or move to the side, and he had to remind her to keep her eyes on the bumper to bumper traffic from folks who lived and worked by the beach and were driving too fast on a narrow four lane bridge to get home from work. He wouldn't trade that memory for all the gold in the world. She was his treasure, the most precious jewel in his life.

I've missed you too, Horace. I want you to listen as there isn't much time.

What my darling? I've just found you. I won't ever leave your side again.

Sarah looked at him with her grey blue eyes and that crooked smile and kissed him on the lips.

I've been given a gift for you my dear one. Just for you.

Sarah reached up and caressed his head and Horace felt a strong shiver run down his spine and out his limbs to the end of his fingers and toes.

Sarah, you are all the gift I could ever want.

Horace, we only have to be apart a little longer. You have to go back. There is much danger, and our wonderful Jacob will be needed. He is special and more important than either of us knew. You will be there to guide and save him, and then, you will come back to me.

I don't understand. I love Jacob, but I don't want to leave you, Sarah.

Max coughed and coughed again. It felt like there was something in his throat.

Horace, Jessica will need you, and she will need John. We all will, but Jessica and Jacob most of all.

Sarah shared more with Max and softly spoke to him.

Soon Horace, my love. Save our Jacob. Save us all. You will know when.

Sarah faded from his sight. He began to feel a headache, and then, his eyes hurt from the light. Everything was fuzzy. He felt nauseous and gagged on something in his throat. He coughed to clear his throat.

Jessica held Max's hand and shouted into the room intercom.

"He's waking up," said Jessica.

"Please get Dr. Morrison," said the nurse on duty, who rushed into the room and reassured the professor that he was in hospital and explained that there was a tube in his throat making it hard for him to talk.

Jessica said a prayer of thanks, the most recent of thousands she had spoken since coming to live with Max and Sarah.

· · ·

Space, the far side of Earth's Moon

Ship and S'ear'r settled in a stationary orbit behind the third planets moon. He had Ship deploy sentinels to the lunar rim to enable covert observation and recording. He noted small artificial leavings on the surface of this oddly large moon, but no evidence of colonization.

Ship noted satellites orbiting the source planet. These generally looked to be smaller affairs probably for communication and navigation or weather, but no orbital defense stations were noted. Ship detected evidence of atomic fission power plants at the surface of the planet. Electromagnetic transmissions were numerous at this range, and video recordings from the planet showed an individualized and aggressive bipedal race.

The history of the Chos'n showed that real progress occurred only after the great transition of the many to the common good. These people are all fighting against one another, S'ear'r thought, and still they have progressed this far. Their rate of advancement was troubling however. There was no history of contact from this region of space even a thousand passings previously. The development of this species seemed unusually quick.

Once again, Ship reminded S'ear'r of their initial findings of rapid advancement suggesting the need for culling this race. This would be the result eventually anyway, but S'ear'r knew at the rate this planet was developing, they would either destroy themselves and what looked to be a prime planet for colonization, or they would develop the technology to be a threat to the Chos'n. Either way, something would need to be done. The planet was well within the standards for colonization. In fact, it represented a great prize for the Chos'n. S'ear'r allowed a brief thought that such a prize might earn him the ultimate reward of an assured lifeline and a bonding. He thought of his school friend M'lit'a again.

S'ear'r brought his thoughts back into balance and prepared a report with recommendations to be forwarded. Ship had composed a standard communication and warmed up the sending unit. He would transmit this as a priority addendum to the discovery communication, and allow for guidance from L'ment'l.

Wait. Processing.

Ship reported another brief subspace emission from the planet surface in what they referred to as the northern hemisphere. This was worrisome and implied technological advancement beyond the warning stage. This single transmission was a communication in several of the planets languages.

"Who are you?" asked the unknown sender.

This could represent an unexpected threat to the Chos'n. Shielded by this moon, S'ear'r had held less concern for the target planet detecting any subspace messaging, but the Chos'n would need more thorough evaluation of this species capabilities. S'ear'r needed to investigate further to finish his report prior to sending any recommendations.

S'ear'r decided to wait while Ship carefully marked the location of the previous single subspace transmission and began to consider plans for further reconnaissance. Yes, much closer inspection would need to be done to understand this surge in technology. These humans as they called themselves displayed nothing in their culture to describe such ability.

S'ear'r consulted with Ship which had been busy mapping near space and the target planet. He would wait for the planet rotation to return night to investigate. Ship could mitigate against detection, but why take unnecessary risk.

S'ear'r required close inspection of the source of the earlier subspace disturbance. In the history of the Chos'n, only one race had developed the ability to penetrate the mysteries of subspace and that race had almost destroyed the Chos'n. If not for L'ment'l and her sacrifice, the Chos'n would likely have perished.

Ship pointed out to S'ear'r the one absolute. S'ear'r expected this, knowing it was hardwired into Ship by the council. Faced with a known risk to the Chos'n, Ship could activate a destruction protocol designed to extinguish the threat.

S'ear'r knew Ship had already mapped out various defensive and offensive measures given detected capabilities. One option would be to back out to the nearby asteroid belt and nudge one of the larger rocks into an intersecting path with the planet. Such a strike would hammer the planet back to a clean slate, but would also destroy the ecology of the planet, and it was such a lovely world, a grand prize.

S'ear'r knew if he wanted to gain this planet as a prize, he would need to ward off any drastic measures by Ship. He needed to find the source of the subspace disturbance and reassure Ship and the Chos'n that this planet could be taken with conventional measures, such as an engineered biological weapon to cull the population leaving enough useful biologics for meaningful value. This planet currently supported a large population, and it was better to maintain as many as possible for fodder.

No, better to interfere with their communications and power systems, thus isolating each enclave on this planet even more. Then the Chos'n could harvest the planet area by area without losing portions of the planet biology. Why, from the readings Ship was obtaining, the planet looked capable of supporting twenty billion biologics with modern power systems. S'ear'r would need a human biologic as a sample. Perhaps he could perform a trial paring and include the results in his mission brief. He would include that in his mission plan parameters for examining the subspace source.

Most importantly, S'ear'r would need to avoid any discovery such that his mission was compromised. S'ear'r was under no illusions. Ship would destroy the both of them if necessary.

CHAPTER THIRTY

John was washing his face the next morning, when he received a call from Jessica telling him of Max's improvement. John agreed to give Jacob a ride home from class on his way to meet Jessica. He gathered his daily carry items, phone, watch, keys, small flashlight, and folding knife. He felt undressed without a firearm, but it was not legal to carry on campus.

John looked for Jacob at the agreed on place to pick him up. Parking his truck, he went in to find him, only to be told that Jacob had to leave class early after receiving a note to go to administration. Thinking of possible reasons for Jacob to be summoned to the administration building, he quickened his pace.

John found Jacob in Paul Kincaid's office. Samantha was sitting in the small secretarial area. She looked a bit lost sitting alone on the small couch. John sat down, and Samantha reached out to him.

"They want to kick us out," she said. "Professor Kincaid is saying Jacob should have known better, that the reason the experiment blew up was because of my computer hacking. He said that interfering in the code caused the malfunction, and Max was hurt because of us."

"From what I've seen of you, that seems unlikely," said John. "After all, you're the next computer tycoon, right? Well, except I've seen you wear more than one type of shirt."

He patted her on the back.

"There was nothing wrong with that code," said Samantha. "That idiot Kincaid barely knows how to turn on his computer."

That rang true with John. He knew enough about Max, Jacob, and Sam to realize it was unlikely their protocol was negligent. Either there were unexpected results, or someone tampered with the experiment. In a flash of insight, he realized who might have something to gain by a failure in Max's research, and he was sitting outside his office.

"How long has Jacob been in there?" asked John.

"About a half hour," replied Samantha, dabbing at her eyes.

Paul Kincaid's secretary had asked twice if she could help John, but he had focused on talking with Samantha and had ignored her. Now, he turned to the secretary.

"Does Jacob's mother know about this meeting?" he asked.

The secretary didn't have an answer for his question, which was answer enough. Jacob might be a teaching assistant for Professor Maxwell, but he was still technically a minor and to not involve his mother in this sort of meeting had to violate some kind of rule.

He thought for a moment and called on his cell phone.

"Murray, John here. Are you on duty? I'm here at Paul Kincaid's office, and I'm about to create a problem."

He explained a bit further, ended the call, and addressed Samantha.

"Did you tell him anything or agree to anything?" asked John.

"No, Professor Kincaid was doing all the talking," she said. "I think he likes to hear himself talk."

John barely smiled, and said, "You noticed, huh? Listen you may hear some yelling in a moment, so prepare yourself, okay?"

He got up from the couch and approached the secretary while dialing his phone.

"Would you ask Mr. Kincaid to bring Jacob out here," he said. "I have his mother on the phone."

John had dialed Jessica and she answered. "Did you find him?" she asked.

"Yes, Jessica, give me just a moment," said John.

He turned to the secretary, who shrugged when she got no response to her call back to Professor Kincaid's office. John walked forward and tried to open the locked door, and without a moment's hesitation, he kicked the door in.

He strode past the shattered and partially hanging door to see Jacob practically shut down in the corner of the office. Kincaid was standing over Jacob in mid sentence with his mouth half open staring at the remnants of his office door.

John worked hard to control the beast within him, for when he burst into the office, he heard Kincaid telling Jacob it was his fault Professor Maxwell was lying in the hospital soon to die.

He ignored Kincaid who started sputtering and yelling for his secretary.

"Call campus security!" exclaimed Kincaid. "You can't come in here like this!"

John walked over to Jacob and put his hand on his shoulder and said, "Jacob, your mother is on the phone. It's about Max."

He turned to Kincaid and pointed his index finger.

"Not another word."

John's voice was soft but carried so that Kincaid's secretary and Samantha heard him. Kincaid started to speak again, but closed his mouth, his lips pursed.

Over the phone, Jessica told Jacob that Maxwell was waking up, and the doctor and nurses thought he would likely recover. Jacob stopped his rocking.

"Really?" said Jacob, and he broke down.

John reached out, and Jacob held on to him. John whispered into his ear, and Jacob nodded yes. John turned to walk Jacob out of the office. Officer Murray arrived into the office waiting area at that moment. He was on duty and in uniform.

"Just in time, Officer," said Kincaid, wearing a satisfied smile. "This student forced his way into my office uninvited and interrupted an important disciplinary session with young Jacob here."

"Officer Murray, Jacob is under age," said John. "I believe his parent is required to be notified before any disciplinary meeting, and that parent has the right to be present."

He handed his phone to Murray, and Jessica confirmed, on speaker, that she had no knowledge of any disciplinary meeting. She was driving back to campus to pick up Jacob and was close. Kincaid was no longer smiling.

John asked, "Jacob, where is your phone?"

Jacob nodded toward Kincaid.

"He has it," said Jacob. "He said he would need to look over my phone for evidence."

Jacob cradled his left wrist with his right hand.

John could see Jacob's left wrist was red and swollen. John felt his heart slowly hammer as the dragon engine in his chest puffed smoke before the burn. He was interrupted from his developing storm of mayhem by the maelstrom of Jessica as she arrived in the office.

"What is going on here?" she asked. "Jacob why are you here in this office with that man?" She gave a scathing glance at Kincaid. "John, please tell me what is going on?" Jessica noticed Jacob holding his wrist and her voice edged up another notch. "Somebody better start talking with me right now."

Officer Murray spread his arms in a calming gesture and said, "That's what we were attempting to figure out as you arrived ma'am. Is it true that you had no knowledge of this disciplinary meeting for Jacob?"

Jessica embraced Jacob, murmuring in his ear and willing strength into him from her hug.

"No, I didn't know about this meeting, Officer," she said. Jessica's eyes sparked flint at Kincaid, and she gently released Jacob.

John stepped in front of Jessica before she could launch herself at Kincaid, who no longer looked so smug. John was able to grab her about her waist. Holding her was a challenge, as she shouted at Kincaid.

"Stay away from my family, now and forever! You hear me?"

Jessica struggled to get within striking distance of Kincaid who had lost much of his bluster and looked a bit pale.

Officer Murray held his hands up.

"Everyone calm down," he said. "Miss Jessica, please take Jacob to the campus infirmary. He might need to have that wrist examined. I will stay and have a discussion with Professor Kincaid."

Glaring at Kincaid one more time, Jessica motioned for Samantha to come with her and gathered both Sam and Jacob under her wing to shepherd them out of the office.

Officer Murray spoke quietly to John.

"Let me talk with Kincaid to get his side of this, but yeah, I think she's got a right to be angry. I just wanted to keep her from scratching his eyes out. By the way, I would think twice before pissing her off."

John nodded, agreeing completely with Murray. He might be capable, but Jessica was motivated.

CHAPTER THIRTY-ONE

Jessica drove Jacob home after taking him to the campus infirmary for an evaluation. The nurse on duty felt he had a wrist sprain, but not a fracture.

Samantha wanted to go by her dorm room for some study time. She also wanted to clean up. The whole episode at Kincaid's office left her feeling unclean.

They all agreed to meet at Max's house later to regroup. Jessica still felt she needed to get back to the hospital to check on Maxwell, but when John pressed her gently, she agreed she was exhausted. John suggested she go home, clean up, and nap for a few hours. They could talk later over dinner. Meanwhile, he could drive over to the hospital to check on Max. She reluctantly agreed.

John found Professor Maxwell's room at the hospital. He had been taken off the ventilator and, though tired, he was making rapid progress. He seemed very glad to see John.

"Come in John, please come in," said Max. "I would get up, but nurse Nancy here would skin me and you too, if I tried."

The pretty nurse checking on him smiled and patted him on the arm.

She said, "He's a professor, so he learns fast."

She sashayed out of the room with a second glance at John.

John pulled a chair up and said, "How are you doing, Professor? You gave all of us a scare, you know."

Max smiled at John and said, "I have some headache, but they assure me that will improve. Tell me what's happened. I remember being in the lab, then waking here."

John shared all he knew regarding the explosion in the lab. Jacob and Samantha were both all right, but the lab was truly trashed. John didn't share the pressure they were getting from the administration and Professor Kincaid. He didn't want to worry Max in his recovery.

Professor Maxwell asked, "And how's Jessica doing?"

John said, "I convinced her to go home and take a nap. She was ready to come right back out here, but she was here all night. She is very strong willed."

"Yes, she can be," said Max. "May I tell you a story?"

John settled himself in a metal framed green cushioned chair and nodded assent.

"Sarah and I wanted children, but we couldn't. We never really tried to find out why. One of us couldn't, and we understood that. We prayed and prayed. To fill her spare time, Sarah volunteered through the church at one of the local shelters.

One day I came home, and Jessica was there with baby Jacob. Sarah asked me if they could stay with us temporarily. I could not refuse my wife. Jessica and Jacob stayed with us until, in time, we adopted them as our own. I'm not ashamed to say I love them both dearly. Jessica became our daughter and Jacob, our grandson."

John listened and asked, "Do you know anything of her life before she came to live with you?"

"I did ask her, but I could see how painful it was for her to discuss. I think she felt abandoned by her father. I gather he may have been an alcoholic and abusive. I know he and Jessica's mother died in a house fire shortly after Jessica came to the shelter where Sarah found her.

"Did she ever say anything about Jacob's father?" asked John.

"I asked Jacob once if Jessica had ever shared anything about his father. Jacob said she wouldn't discuss it. I guess we avoided discussing that subject since we were truly happy together."

John drew his chair closer to the professor and offered him a small sip of water from the paper cup on the table beside his bed.

"There's something special about Jacob, isn't there?" asked John.

Max sighed.

"He's a good boy," said Max. "He has always been a wonderful grandson to both of us."

The professor took another sip of water.

"I never realized how truly great water can be," he said.

Max reclined back in bed, settled himself, and shared their secret.

"Jacob came to live with us, and by the time he was ten months old he was talking in two and three word sentences. By the age of three years, he spoke English fluently and was reading everything he could get his chubby hands on."

John nodded, his feelings confirmed.

"He's a genius isn't he?"

Max looked at John for a moment.

"Unparalleled," said Max. "I'm not exaggerating when I say he may be the smartest person on this planet."

"And you kept him hidden away?" asked John.

"Yes, I suppose that is the question. We were elated when we realized our Jacob was so gifted, but we knew if others found out, our privacy would be gone. Jessica desperately wanted a normal home life for him, and with just us, we had that. We gave him all the love and tutoring we could give. I have never regretted our decision. Now, I'm worried Jacob will be exposed."

"I can see why you worry," said John. "I've only known him a short time, and I feel very protective of him."

"And Jessica?" asked Max.

John shifted his posture. Hospital chairs made him uncomfortable.

"I don't know, sir," said John. "I've never felt the way I feel around her. I mean, it's like I lose myself, like there's no me anymore, just us, when I'm around her. I don't know if that makes any sense. But yes, I feel protective of her. You won't tell her that will you? I'm not sure how she'd take that. I mean she's so independent."

"Yes, she is that," said Max. "When she first stayed with us, she was quiet, polite, and shy, except when it came to Jacob and his needs, but from the first, she and Sarah seemed to have a connection, an understanding. When I first saw them together, Sarah was holding Jacob, and I knew they would become part of us going forward."

John listened as Max continued.

"Jessica has worked very hard to get to a point where she feels she can take care of herself and Jacob," he said. "Now, I'm afraid she will feel she has to take care of me. She's like that you know, always putting other people ahead of herself."

Max took another sip of water and resumed.

"Sarah and I have always been proud of her and never more so than now. We hoped that someday Jessica would meet a man who could appreciate her and see all the wonderful qualities in her that we see."

John considered what he had been told. Jessica could sandblast a man with her wit before he could turn around, but what would it be like to have that same mind love him? A man would have to earn that love daily, but isn't that what a man is supposed to do?

While John was thinking, Max held his rosary and quietly mouthed prayers. The old scientist paused and addressed him again.

"John, there is something else I need to talk with you about, and I need you to keep an open mind. Can you do that?"

"I'll try, Max."

The professor smiled, and said, "That's the first time I've gotten you to call me Max."

Professor Maxwell picked up his rosary again and held it in his right hand.

"Do you believe in God?" he asked.

"I don't know," said John. "They say there are no atheists in foxholes. Most of the time I seem to wonder around confused. I think I believe in the possibility of God. My parents believed, and I used to pray when I was younger. But, I've always wondered if God is real and so all powerful, why would he or she be interested in us? I mean, look at how we treat each other."

Max spoke in a quiet self-assured way.

"What if I told you that God believes in you?"

"I guess I would ask how you could know?" said John.

He marveled that he felt so comfortable talking with this old man.

"Sarah told me," said Max. "We talked while I was ... well, you know, while I was out of it."

John sat back in the chair unsure what to do. He'd seen men step through death's doorway and come back with the help of a great medic, but not like this determined old man.

"What did you talk about?" asked John.

Max looked at him and said, "Well, mostly, we talked about you."

Max went on to share his experience with John, who sat with his mouth open and eyes wide while he listened to the rock steady voice of this old man recounting his trip to the world of death and back.

When Max finished, John didn't know what to say.

"Max, are you sure?" he asked. Shaking his head back and forth, John continued, "Jessica is going to kill me."

Max started chuckling, "Yes, that is what Sarah told me too."

He reached out to take John's hand. The rosary still in the old professor's hand was now clasped by both of them.

"One more thing, John," said Max. "When the time is right, you have our blessing."

CHAPTER THIRTY-TWO

Jessica woke from a vivid dream remembering her first encounter with Sarah.

She and Jacob had stayed at the shelter only one day, and Jessica was desperately afraid. Sarah had walked in and introduced herself and asked to hold Jacob. He reached up and grabbed her face and babbled delightedly. He was obviously smitten with Sarah, and she with him.

"Where is the father," she asked?

Jessica felt afraid and terribly embarrassed. She had planned a cover story for this kind of question, but when she looked at Sarah, Jessica knew she would tell her the truth.

"I don't know," she said.

Sarah nodded and held Jacob up to the light bringing a giggle from the baby boy.

"Well, I think he may have left the best of himself with you even so. What is his name?"

"Jacob," said Jessica.

Now came the hard part, Sarah would start asking questions which Jessica could not answer. They would take him away from her because he was behind on his vaccinations. They would tell her how she wasn't ready to be a parent like her father had told her repeatedly.

From the start of it, when she found out she was pregnant, only her mother stood by her, and even then, she did it in the shadow of Jessica's disapproving father. Some from school were quick to tell her to abort the baby, which Jessica saw as murder.

Her family friends from church suggested she could give the baby up for adoption. She considered what might be truly best for the child, but her unborn baby was part of her, and she felt her soul wither whenever she visualized giving up her child.

When she decided to move out of the house and make a try of it rather than living with the daily reminder from her father of how wrong she was, her mother had hugged her and slipped a bit of money in Jessica's pocket while telling her how sorry she was that she couldn't do more. Jessica understood her mother couldn't take the chance. Her mother had been afraid for such a long time.

Sarah watched her closely when she wasn't cooing to little Jacob.

"Is there anyone else looking out for you two?" she asked.

"No, no one that I know."

Technically that wasn't a lie. Jessica had been afraid someone was following her and Jacob. She had glimpsed the same man at the bus station and again near the shelter during her brief session sitting on a bench outside in the sunshine, but she had no idea who he was.

Sarah handed Jacob back to her and watched her holding him.

"What if you came to stay with my husband and me for a couple of days?"

Jessica was startled by the question, and her impulsive prideful answer was almost no, but something in the way Sarah sat so quietly and patiently waiting for her reply gave her pause.

"Why would you do that?" asked Jessica. "Won't your husband be concerned?"

Sarah opened her hands palms up and said, "Sometimes you have to do what feels right."

Jessica woke with Sarah's remembered words ringing in her ears. She hadn't meant to fall asleep, but she had been so tired. She had to check on Max at the hospital. She checked her cell phone, and there were no messages from the hospital or John. She hoped that was good news. She hoped for a message from him, though.

Now why did she think of John. She still didn't know the man, so why did she find herself thinking of him.

What would she say to John when she saw him? What kind of man was he? She sensed there was something he didn't want to talk about, something in his past that he would rather forget. Well, that makes two of us, she thought.

She showered and gathered some materials to read while she sat with Max at the hospital. She had missed the academic council meeting in the confusion surrounding Max's injury. She would have to get back on the schedule. She had made a promise to Katie, and she couldn't go back on her word.

Jessica found Jacob and Samantha downstairs napping on separate couches. Sam must have come over earlier. She woke Jacob quietly to let him know she was going back down to the hospital and likely staying until late. He asked if there was anything he could do. She told him to take care of the house.

As Jessica was getting ready to leave the house, she heard a vehicle pull into the driveway. She saw it was John's truck. She walked out to the driveway and found him helping Max out of the passenger side of the Toyota.

"Dad, here let me help you," said Jessica. "Why are you home from the hospital? They let you go? You were in a coma twelve hours ago."

Jessica reached out to hold Max's left arm, and John held onto his right arm. They helped Max walk to the door.

Jacob held the door open and hugged Max as soon as he entered the house. John had to let go as Jacob clung tightly to his grandfather.

Samantha was awake from her nap now and gaped wide eyed at Max standing on his own feet, even with help.

"Here, Max, let's sit down," said Jessica.

She guided him to the couch corner seat and grabbed some pillows to set under his side and head.

"I'm okay, daughter. I'm feeling much better," said Max, waving his hands, palms down slightly.

Jessica pounced.

"John, I don't understand how Max could possibly be here now instead of the hospital? You told me you would watch him."

John found it difficult to meet Jessica's eyes.

"He, umm, signed himself out of the hospital," he said.

"What?" asked Jessica. "John, are you insane? Max still needs to be in the hospital. He can't make that decision. Tell me you didn't say this was okay?"

John had faced the Taliban, treacherous allies, hailstorms of bullets and explosions, and been left for dead, but he had never faced Jessica in full storm. Her auburn hair now framed a flushed face with tight lips and green ember eyes.

John started to stammer out a reply when Max reached over to touch his arm and Jessica's hand together.

"I woke up from a very good nap," he said. "I had my senses about me and saw no sense in staying longer in the hospital when there is so much work to be done. John tried to talk me out of leaving, but in the end, it was my decision. Now, what are we having for dinner?"

Jessica balled up her left hand and banged it on her thigh, bobbing on the balls of her feet. She appealed to Jacob who shrugged his shoulders.

"Why are you surprised?" said Jacob. "This is classic Max."

Samantha, who was sitting on the periphery trying to stay out of fragmentation range, closed her mouth which had been open for much of the exchange. She had seen John take out three attackers and walk through a burning room, but there he stood, chastised in front of Jessica.

Imagine that, thought Samantha, and, slowly smiling, she said, "Who's up for pizza?"

Jacob laughed and shouted, "Pepperoni!" while running to get another pillow for Max.

Jessica hesitated, with her fists balled at her side, and looked at Max and John sitting on the couch together like schoolboys in the principal's office. She exhaled, allowing her shoulders and hands to unclench. She knelt in front of Max and hugged him.

Max wrapped his arms around her and whispered, "Daughter" into her ear.

"You scared us," said Jessica.

CHAPTER THIRTY-THREE

Professor Paul Kincaid let himself into his home. He couldn't believe how Dean Paulson had reprimanded him. The dean made it clear that Paul had gone way over the line in bringing Jacob into his office as a minor and had opened the university up for a lawsuit. Any evidence with an investigation was to be uncovered by campus security.

"Hmmpf," grunted Paul.

That was another thing. Where did that young know nothing campus police officer get off treating him like that in his own office? After all, that muscle bound killer Stone had kicked his door in.

Kincaid set his attaché case down on his entry hall table and headed into his kitchen to open the fridge. He had a still good open bottle of chardonnay, which would help take the edge off his day.

Closing his fridge and turning to a kitchen cabinet for a wine glass, he dropped the bottle of wine onto the kitchen tile floor when he saw a figure's reflection in the front of the kitchen cabinet. He started to turn, but couldn't move as burning pain exploded between his shoulder blades buzzing into his ears. He stumbled to the tile floor on his knees amidst the glass shards. The white cabinets turned black as he faded out.

Vincent secured Professor Kincaid to an antique chair in his study after replacing the taser in his pocket. Gagging the professor was easy while he was unconscious. Checking to be sure the professor could still breathe through his nose, Vincent turned to Kincaid's desk and computer. He booted up the machine. Looking at the back of the machine, he saw power, video, and USB cables, as well as an Ethernet cable connected to a router, which looked to be connected to incoming fiber optic. Well, well, he thought, the professor has high speed internet.

Vincent had already disabled the security system on the house and had searched for any external and internal cameras. He didn't want to leave any recordings.

The computer was password protected at boot up. He would have to look for the password. He checked under the calendar on the desk as well as under the trashcan and notepad, and he leafed through the books behind the desk. He rummaged through all the drawers and found one of them locked. He forced the drawer open and found a current passport, twenty thousand dollars in cash, and a large capacity flash drive. Interesting.

Paul Kincaid woke up confused. His neck didn't want to turn without significant pain. Someone slapped him in the face. His eyes focused through the stinging pain. He tried to scream, but he was gagged. His arms were secured to the antique chair he had found and purchased for one hundred dollars at a garage sale and had appraised later for two thousand. For just a moment, Paul felt furious that the wire cutting into his wrists had marred the finish on the arms of the chair. Another stinging slap brought his situation back into focus.

He saw a brooding man sitting in front of him dressed in slacks, a light sweater shirt, and sporting a black jacket. His left face revealed a thin scar from orbital ridge to jaw line, and his left eyelid drooped ever so slightly. The man seared his skin at a glance as he looked at him with dark eyes that reminded him of the entrance to a carnival ride without exit. The man smiled at him, and that frightened Paul even more.

"I need your attention now, Professor," said the man. "I am going to remove your gag so you can answer me, but you will only speak when I speak to you, and only to answer my questions. Anything else will have repercussions. Please nod if you understand me.

Paul nodded yes. It hurt.

Vincent removed Paul's gag.

"You missed drinking your wine, Professor," he said. "I took the liberty of pouring you a glass if you are still thirsty. May I offer you a sip?"

Kincaid tentatively took a sip of the wine and then a second sip.

"Good," said Vincent. "Professor, I have a favor to ask. I need to find out what you know, and that requires your computer password. As a show of good faith in return for the wine, would you share that information with me?"

Kincaid seemed hesitant, and Vincent said, "Ah, you are wondering if the police will come to check on your alarm system, but there was no alarm, you see. I'm quite good at my job, and this is not the first time for me to pay a visit to someone who has annoyed my employers. So, trust me, there is no one coming to interrupt us here. Now, please, I will only ask one more time. The password?"

Kincaid sagged his shoulders and mumbled, "senatorsson."

"Thank you, Professor. I may need further assistance as I look through your files. I would appreciate direct and forthcoming answers to my questions," said Vincent, as he successfully typed in the password to Kincaid's computer.

Taking what looked like a USB thumb drive on steroids out of his pocket, Vincent inserted the device which began to swiftly copy bit for bit the professors hard drive information. He noted the estimated time for the download indicated a good deal of information on the computer.

"Professor, what does this icon labeled cameras mean? I searched and didn't find any cameras here at your house? Tell me please?"

Paul didn't say anything. Vincent approached him and sat in a chair close to him. He pulled a curved folding knife out of his pocket.

"Professor, we were getting along so well," he said. "I am an impatient man. My employers asked me not to kill you which is unusual, but they didn't say anything about causing you pain or injury."

Vincent placed the edge of the folding knife blade against Paul's left dorsal little finger just behind the fingernail at the distal joint. Blood started to appear even with light pressure.

Kincaid lost control of his bladder then, and even in his despair, he thought of how he was ruining the cushion of the antique chair.

"It's my collection," he sobbed.

Kincaid hung his head and moaned.

Vincent said, "Well let's have a look, shall we?"

He moved back to the desk and started looking at the video files.

"Professor, you have been a busy man haven't you. Did these young women know you were filming them? Oh my, that young woman is very capable. Did she get a good grade professor? Who is Jessica? She rates a separate folder all her own, eh?"

Vincent continued to look into the folder and saw video files with dates spanning nearly 20 years. Vincent picked the most recent video showing a laughing and smiling group of people sitting at dinner eating pizza. Wait. Was that Stone?

Kincaid moaned as Vincent came back around the desk and gripped his wrists, which were numb from the tightly wound wire. Pain exploded up the professors arms.

"Professor, tell me where is this video from?" said Vincent. "Why do you have this recording of John Stone? Tell me what you know, or I will disobey my employers and end your miserable life this moment."

Kincaid sobbed. He could feel the razor sharp blade at his throat now.

"I put cameras in her home without her knowing. They don't know. It's the only way I can stay close to her." Kincaid was crying openly now. "She won't let me close to her. She never would."

Kincaid tried to breath through the mucous in his nose while he confessed further.

"It's the only way," he cried. "Don't you understand? She's everything to me. Stone is a student. He's a killer by his own admission. He's a barbarian, and she talks with him. She will let him get close, but not me. He's nothing, yet she talks with him."

Kincaid was a sobbing mess. Tears and mucous ran down his face adding to the dried blood at his left hand and pants leg. The pungent smell of urine saturated the air.

Vincent took no notice. This was his workspace. He was used to it, but why was John with this woman? I mean she's attractive, but the whole time that Vincent knew John, all that time, Vincent never saw him connect with a woman. So why now? She is the daughter of Professor Maxwell. Kincaid hates Maxwell and covets his daughter, check, but does this have anything to do with the lab explosion yesterday?

Kincaid still sobbed. Vincent interrupted him by slapping his face.

"Professor, tell me about the explosion in Professor Maxwell's lab?"

Paul saw death in those implacable eyes, measuring the time he had left. A small part of Kincaid's mind, able to look down at himself aloof from his own panic and terror thought this must be what judgment felt like if one could believe all that silly religion talk. He knew he could keep no secrets from this thing that walked in a man's skin, so he explained about Daniels, the explosion, and his plans concerning what the graduate student had uncovered in the lab.

Vincent checked and yes, there was more incoming video from this evening. He watched as John sat there with two teens and a black box. The audio was relatively clear and the video was good quality, but what were they saying? Apparently, Maxwell has built a quantum computer? What was this about successful fusion in the laboratory?

Vincent knew this was big. He was no scientist, but he knew fusion and quantum computing were at the top of research projects for most of the world's leading countries.

Okay, change of plans. He would steal the computer along with the plans for the fusion setup and sell it to the highest bidder. Then he would find an out of the way beach somewhere with a dozen senoritas as willing and talented as the young coeds on Professor Kincaid's computer. It was fate after all. Here was the opportunity to free himself and keep a promise to reconnect with a long lost friend. But first, a loose end.

Professor Paul Kincaid's shriek ended in a gurgling gasp as the razor sharp blade bit deep into the senator's son, who in the end was mortal after all.

CHAPTER THIRTY-FOUR

"I disagree Jacob," said Samantha.

She reviewed data streams on the quantum processing computer and double-checked her code line-by-line. They had retired to Max's office.

"What, about pepperoni on pizza?" teased Jacob.

"No, silly," said Samantha. "I've seen your work, and you are very careful. You need to stop blaming yourself for what happened in the lab."

"I don't know, Sam," said Jacob. "Because we pushed ahead with the experiment, you and I may be kicked out of school. We endangered you, and, oh yeah, Max was almost killed. I must have missed something. I checked all the magnet connections the night before, and they were tight. I suppose vibration, but no, that doesn't make sense in that short a time."

Jacob was looking through the laboratory notes and diaries as well as his equations step-by-step with papers spread across the rectangular table in Max's office library.

"What did your parents say?" asked Jacob.

"They wanted me to come home," said Sam. "I think they just wanted to see for themselves that I was okay."

Jacob looked down at the floor.

"Maybe you should go home for awhile," he said. "I don't want to see you get dragged up in anything that comes our way from the university."

Samantha continued to parse through her coding, looking for any deficiency.

"Yeah, what is it with Max and the university?" she asked. "Why are they against him all of a sudden? I mean, they mention him in practically every advertisement pamphlet. He's one of the reasons I wanted to come here to school."

Jacob sat back down rubbing his hands and said, "He has several patents and discoveries, and he's always shared with the university, so for the longest time, I guess that was true. But, he's getting older now, and for the last ten years, he has put all his time into our power project. He hasn't published lately. He pushed all of the graduate students away as the need for secrecy was great. I guess some at the university see him as over the hill and want to get rid of him."

"You mean like that ass, Professor Kincaid?" said Sam. "He gives me the creeps."

"Yeah, I get you on that," said Jacob. "I know Max doesn't like him, and my mother, well, I not sure how to describe what she thinks of him."

Jacob was thinking on the experiment gone wrong again, moment by moment. He knew he checked the magnets and their connections the night before and again that morning. Of course, they had stepped out for lunch, just prior to beginning the experiment. Could someone have come into the lab while they were getting a sandwich? Max always locked the lab?

Samantha finished her review of her coding without finding an obvious error, certainly nothing that explained the magnet failure and the laboratory accident. She tried to reassure Jacob again.

"Max is going to be all right," she said. "He's back home."

"Yes, I know, and I'm relieved, but we worked so hard, and for just a moment we had it," said Jacob. "We actually achieved cold fusion. I know we can make it work, especially now that Max is back with us. I mean obviously we'll have to have secondary magnetic controls for redundancy in case of failure, but Sam, I'm not so sure the university is going to give us that chance now, and I don't want you dragged into this. If it comes down to it, I want you to downplay your role; you were just doing some coding for us and didn't have anything else to do with the experiment. Maybe we can shelter you from some of the fallout."

Jacob looking at her so earnestly that she had to smile.

Samantha thought for a moment and said, "Jacob, I wouldn't have missed this opportunity with you two for the world. What you have with Max is truly special. I love that I'm part of it, even a little bit."

Jacob felt a stirring inside his core, a sense of contentment, and he realized at that moment he didn't want to be anywhere else, doing anything else, but just talking with Samantha here in the comfort of the only home he had ever known.

"Honestly, I don't know if we would have been able to go without your programming. I'm confidant in the architecture of the QPC, but I'm no hacker." He thought of something else. "Samantha, what did you do with the MRI data from the hospital for Max?"

Sam was about to speak when the synthesized voice from the quantum computer answered with a displayed message and voice that said, "Currently processing."

"That's odd," said Jacob.

"I know," said Samantha. "I mean the MRI output is a lot of data, but the hospital computer equipment could process real time images from the data. I would think the QPC could handle the data in at least the same time frame."

Jacob nodded.

"Yes," he agreed. "But what I meant is that the QPC answered us both without being directly addressed. Did you program that? I thought voice interface protocol required directly addressing the QPC?

Samantha wasn't sure what to say.

"Maybe, it's an interface problem between the software systems," she said. "That could be causing the processing to hang up?"

Samantha pulled up the video recordings from the experiment and looked through them again. Everything was as she remembered. She was trying to get to the point of the experiment just before it all went wrong.

She saw the software warn of impending loss of magnet control, then the explosion, and then nothing. She recalled something puzzling.

"Jacob, could you look at this with me?" she asked.

Jacob drew his chair closer to Samantha and looked at the computer screen and watched as Samantha replayed the last events of the experiment in slow motion.

Samantha said, "Jacob, just as the explosion happened, I remember seeing the wall section disappear, but there was something else, wasn't there? It looked like, well, I don't know. Do you remember?"

"I'm not sure," he said. "I didn't see the wall blow out. I was looking in another direction I think."

Jacob didn't say he'd been trying to reach for Sam to pull her down behind the desk for additional protection from the impending catastrophe.

"There, that's what I saw," said Samantha.

On the computer screen in slow motion, a circular section of the exterior block wall three meters in diameter simply disappeared into a brief moment of black, and then sunlight poured through the opening into the smoke filled laboratory.

"That is interesting," said Jacob. "Can we look at that again more slowly?"

"I think so. Here, let's see. "

Samantha brought up the video editor software and dialed the section of the recorded experiment gone awry to a frame-by-frame view.

"There," she said. "What is that? I don't get it?"

Jacob sat back in his chair. He couldn't believe it, but there on the computer screen was the evidence. For exactly five out of sixty frames, the monitoring video of the hole in the wall displayed the deep black of space and embedded in the black were countless shining points of light otherwise known as stars.

Samantha looked at the screen again her eyes flashing as she caught on.

"Oh, wait," she said. "That can't be."

"What are you two working on in here?" asked Jessica?

She had knocked lightly on the office door and looked in on them. The two of them were sitting together, looking at the computer screen. Neither responded immediately.

Jessica repeated herself.

"Jacob, what's wrong?"

Jacob looked up from the computer screen as if just recognizing his mother's presence.

"I think something may have happened during our lab experiment," he said.

Jessica chuckled and replied, "Yes, like almost blowing yourself up, right?"

Samantha, practically vibrating in her seat, said, "Jacob we have to talk with Max. He needs to know."

"Max is asleep," said Jessica. "He was tired. He should still be in the hospital, and he fell asleep after eating. John is outside talking with Isaac and Isabella. They came by when they heard Max was home from the hospital. So what is it Max has to know?"

Jacob said, "Not just Max, Mom. You too. And you Sam." Shaking his head, he went on, "We'll need John and Isaac and Isabella as well. But first we need to talk with Max."

Jessica clasped her hands together in front of her chest.

"What is it we need to know?" she asked.

"Everything," said Jacob.

CHAPTER THIRTY-FIVE

John felt happy for his roommate when he saw Isabella step out of Isaac's truck. He had encouraged Isaac almost daily, and he knew his friend was smitten with the female pilot. By happy coincidence, they arrived as the pizza did, and the process of eating and small talk allowed John to discover that Jacob knew Isabella from flight school where he had been taking lessons. Dinner also helped him avoid being the center of Jessica's storm. She was still unhappy about Max leaving the hospital early. John wasn't thrilled about it either.

John thought about that. How could he care so much about an old man he'd known for less than a week. He had really screwed up with Jessica, but Max was very persuasive, and in the end, if he was lucid, it was his decision to come home against the doctor's advice. He had assured John with "I feel fine" statements while signing his name. But, was he lucid? Really?

What he'd told John was unbelievable. So, why did he feel so sure Max was telling the truth, or at least, the truth as Max knew it to be.

Isaac and Isabella were about to take their goodbyes, having paid their respects to Max before he fell asleep when Jacob, Samantha, and Jessica came into the living room.

Jacob said, "Hey guys, could you stay a couple minutes longer?"

Jacob bent down to Max and spoke quietly in his ear. Max nodded yes without opening his eyes fully. Jacob looked up and addressed all of them.

"We have something in the barn to show you," he said.

John had been considering leaving when Isaac and Isabella left. He thought he would give Jessica some time to cool off. Maybe he could come back in the morning. However, after hearing Jacob, he followed outside, along with the rest.

John had not been inside the barn, and he was curious. He stole a glance at Jessica, but she was watching Jacob and not paying any attention to him at the moment. Samantha was smiling. She knows something, he thought.

John looked on as Isaac and Isabella followed, chatting with each other. The evening twilight shadows lengthened to darkness, and clouds crouched on the horizon. Stormy weather approached, and the impending weather had called off several of Isabella's flights giving her time to spend out tonight, and giving Isaac the opportunity to offer her an evening out. John thought it a good sign of Isabella's character that she had agreed to come over to Max's house to see him home from the hospital.

Jacob looked over his shoulder as he opened the locked side door to the barn and said, "What I'm about to show you is private, and I need to ask everyone here to please keep it between us for now."

John followed into the workshop, and with the lights on, he could see the inside was larger than he realized and yes, it looked like a barn, but he could tell some renovation work had been done to make the structure truly watertight. The interior wood beams gleamed from sanding and waterproofing, and the floor comprised various hardwoods pieced together in a precise arrangement.

There were benches on both sides of the workshop laden with equipment. LED lights overhead and along the sides gave ample light to see a mound approximately 3 meters high by ten meters long in the center of the floor covered by light opaque plastic sheeting giving form but no definition to the object under the sheeting.

"Jacob, what is this?" said Jessica, her hands held out in front of her encompassing her need to understand.

Jacob addressed them all.

"Mom, you know how I've always loved to come out to the work-shop with granddad. All those times you had to nag us to come in for dinner, and how many times we went to the scrap yard and brought home bits and pieces in his truck?"

"Yes, all that's true," said Jessica. "Sarah and I joked that if we wanted to find either of you, we only needed to walk out here."

Jacob walked over to the plastic draped object and placing his hand on the plastic.

"Well, this is what we were working on," he said.

Isaac looked at the workbenches and some of the equipment and said, "Hey, Jacob, is that a CNC milling machine?"

Isaac pointed to the rear corner of the room on their side of the workshop as John thought of the barn now.

"Yes, it is," replied Jacob.

"Wow, that's a pretty expensive piece of equipment isn't it?" asked Isaac.

"Yes, but we needed it for our project," said Jacob. "We couldn't really do this off site."

Isaac pointed over to the other side of the room where wooden scaffolding cradled several pieces of metal stock.

"Is that titanium sheeting?"

Jacob smiled and said, "Granddad has some industry contacts from his previous work."

Samantha was looking at a computer workstation to the left of the doorway. She whistled.

"This is a custom build workstation right?" she asked. "OctaCore processor? Solid state hard drives? You built this didn't you Jacob?"

"Yes, before the QPC. Go ahead and turn it on if you would, Sam."

Jacob showed Sam the power on for the case, and he flipped a closure on the power breaker panel. The computer booted up.

Isabella said, "Jacob, could we see what's under the plastic?"

Jacob reached over and pulled on a line attached to a hook on the wall leading to a pulley, and the plastic sheeting began to pull up to the rafters.

An oblong aerodynamic cylinder presented itself to the group. The thick tinted windscreen in the front wrapped around a width approximately three times the size of a passenger minivan. The polished exterior flowed in smooth lines of white painted titanium and gleamed in the overhead LED lighting reflecting five pairs of wide eyes framing open mouths.

The flattened streamlined oval cylinder was surrounded by two circular arrangements of bulbous protrusions one forward and one rearward. John could see four protrusions in each circular pattern. He knew what this was. He had seen a similar arrangement in a magazine article a while back. He was just having trouble believing what he was seeing. He wasn't the only one in the group to feel that way apparently.

"Amazing," said Isaac.

"I don't ... I can't believe it, Jacob! You and Max built this?" asked Samantha, grasping her hands together.

"I don't understand. What is it?" Jessica asked, looking at Jacob who was looking at the doorway behind her.

"It is our secret, Jessica," said Max, standing in the side door entrance to the barn workshop. "It's what I've devoted my work to for the last ten years. Jacob and I have built a spaceship in the back yard barn. I hope you can forgive us for keeping it from you."

Jessica wavered, her eyelids fluttered, and she began to fall.

CHAPTER THIRTY-SIX

John bounded across the barn shop to cradle Jessica before she could hit the floor. He kept her head low as he inspected her. Jacob came over and waited anxiously as Samantha brought over a couple of stacked tarps to elevate her legs.

John wiped her auburn hair out of her eyes and said, "She fainted. She will be okay."

Samantha said, "I passed out once when giving blood. I thought I was okay, got up from the table, walked five steps, and down I went. Still have the scar."

She pointed to her right lateral hairline.

Isaac and Isabella were torn between looking at the spaceship and making sure Jessica was okay. Reassured by John's pronouncement, they continued their inspection of the outside of the craft.

Jessica's eyelids began to flutter, and her pale cheeks pinked up. She woke up enough to remember and started trying to get up.

John held her and said, "Hold on. If you get up too fast, you'll just faint again."

When Jessica realized he was cradling her head, she doubled her efforts. John kept her head on his lap, grabbed her wrists, and said, "Now settle down. I just got you back. I don't won't to lose you again.

Promise not to hit me, and I'll let you try to sit up for a moment, but no standing yet."

Jessica slowly sat up.

She felt around on her self and said, "I'm sorry. I'm not sure why that happened. I thought I heard Max say he and Jacob built a spaceship."

"I'm sorry if I startled you, daughter," said Max. "Jacob and I wanted to tell you in a better fashion, but this seemed like the right time. Are you all right?"

"Might we see the interior?" asked Isaac.

Isabella nodded at his side.

"Yes," said Max. "Jacob will help you access the ship."

Max waved to Jacob to go ahead and give the group the tour as John helped Jessica to carefully get back to her feet despite her protests at his holding on to her.

"Thanks, but I'm okay, really," she said, trying to brush him away. "Just felt a bit light headed when I realized all this was going on, and I was left in the dark."

Jessica looking at Jacob with a "we will talk about this later" look as she disengaged from John. Still, she stepped forward fascinated by her family's secret project.

Jacob walked over to the now functioning computer workstation and typing in some keyboard commands, the interior lights and exterior lights came on for the craft as well as a string of numbers and characters depicting the current status of every working system. Finally, another command caused the left side of the ship between the nodes to open up with a door sliding back into the fuselage and a secondary door sliding in the interior cabin.

Isaac said, "It's an airlock."

"Yes. Go ahead and walk in. I'll be right behind you," said Jacob.

Samantha took him at his word and stepped into the craft as well as the rest of the group. Only John, Jessica, and Max were still outside the ship.

"Why?" asked Jessica, addressing Max.

"It has been our dream together, Jacob and me, and a project we could work on that would allow him full use of his gifts," said Max. "I had to keep it secret though, for a host of reasons. As you think about this, I'm sure you will understand."

"Does it work?" asked John, waving his left arm towards the ship.

Exclamations of wonder sounded from the inside of the vessel.

Max leaned against the side of the workbench, and Jessica pulled a chair over for him to sit. He thanked her.

"We are very close, we think," said Max.

"Your experiment in the lab at the university," said John with a flash of insight.

Jessica turned her head to him.

Max laughed and said, "Yes, very good John. Jess, honey, you shouldn't be surprised. He is much more than a warrior. You will have time to learn about each other."

"That's ridiculous," said Jessica. "I'm sure John is as smart as any other soldier, and I don't know why you would say that."

Max replied, "Yes, any other soldier who is working toward a graduate degree in applied history."

Jessica looked stricken, realizing that she had unintentionally slighted John.

"I didn't mean that to come out the way it did," she said, looking at John, her face reddening. "Please forgive me."

John had the thought that Jessica might never see him as more than a soldier. Well, so be it. He would still act with honor.

"There's nothing to forgive. I'll always be a soldier at heart. Hard to take that out of me, I guess." He addressed the professor. "Max, just how close are you to getting this to work. I don't see any wings so how are you planning on getting her off the ground? Wait, okay, with the power output from cold fusion, you could create thrusters right? Or have you and Jacob solved the unified field theory and created a method of counter gravity?"

Now Jessica rocked back on her heels. The look on her face suggested she was thinking she hadn't given John enough credit.

Max waved to the ship and said, "I conceived this twenty years ago. I prayed about it, asking God to help me be smarter and wiser. God gave me Sarah, and I felt I didn't have a right to ask for more, but God was generous and helped us find Jessica."

Max reached out to draw Jessica into a hug.

"She is the daughter we prayed for," he said. "Still, some small insistent voice called me to continue this work."

"Did Sarah know about this?" asked Jessica.

Max's eyes glistened as he said, "Yes. She encouraged me to continue. She always had faith in my work. Still I despaired of ever making any progress, and then about ten years ago, I realized that God was listening, and the answers would be revealed in good time."

"How could you know that?" asked John.

Max looked at Jessica and gently released his embrace.

"Ten years ago, Jacob came to me and said he needed to help me," said Max.

Jessica said, "But, Max, Jacob was seven years old then? What could make you believe him?"

Max reached into his inside jacket pocket, slowly, and with a somewhat shaky hand pulled out a faded piece of yellow legal pad paper folded several times. He carefully unfolded the paper and turned it to show a mathematical equation covering the top half of the paper and a diagram John recognized from the laboratory setup he had been allowed to see previously for a brief moment.

"Because he came to me with a mathematical formula and schematic for the power system for this ship," said Max.

"At seven years old? That's, well, that's ... I don't know what," said John.

"That's Jacob," said Jessica.

She was shaking her head slowly, clearly seeing countless examples in her mind.

"We knew he was special early on," she said. "But I think I understood that first when he started speaking Spanish fluently at age three."

John said, "But lots of children are bilingual and learn Spanish at home with their family."

Jessica shrugged her shoulders with hands upturned.

"None of us speak Spanish," she said. "He had no lessons. He picked it up from television and a dictionary he asked me to bring home."

John considered and spoke, "He told me he learned how to fade a punch during the incident at the university. He said he picked it up here and there."

"He speaks several languages. He taught himself. We home schooled him of course. He remembers everything he sees or reads. I was afraid if anyone found out the truth about him, he would be taken away from us," said Jessica.

"Hey Mom, Max, John, come on and take a look."

Jacob was smiling and waving his hand beckoning them to join them inside the ship.

The three of them walked up the ramp leading into the ship, now a snug space with the seven of them.

Entering the ship through the airlock, John saw an open cockpit area to the front with work stations to either side just back from the front of the ship with storage space and seating which could cleverly fold flat for rest or back against the cabin walls.

"Jessica, I can't believe it," said Samantha. "They've installed a docking port for the QPC. Jacob, I want to bring the computer out and get it up and running, okay?"

Samantha dashed through the airlock before Jacob answered.

Isabella sat in the left front seat inspecting the instrument dash and controls with rapt concentration while Isaac inspected the connections under the dash and called out from a numbered checklist, held in his hand.

All of them inspected the ship closely, and John again divined Max's intent.

"There's a reason Jacob brought all of us out here to see this, isn't there?" he asked. "You want them to crew it if you can get it to work, right?"

"Yes," said Max. "I was hoping each of you would want to be part of this. Jacob can't do this alone."

Samantha interrupted them when she returned with the QPC and placed it in the reserved slot in the custom work area inside the ship.

Boot up and power up continued routinely until a voice from overhead speakers announced, "Systems online. Analyzing. No faults found. Power up complete."

"What was that?" asked Isaac. Having completed his checklist, he watched all intently.

Samantha waved to the overhead speaker and then pointed to the QPC and said, "We powered up the ship's systems, and the computer is online. It was doing a self test of the systems."

Isabella had a questioning look as she turned to look from her position in the pilot chair.

Jacob inspected readouts from the computer console area of the ship where Samantha had inserted the QPC, and satisfying himself that all was in order, he turned to face Max.

"We are good to go," he said.

"Go? What do you mean go?" asked Jessica.

She was looking at Jacob and Max.

"Enable," said Max to Jacob, who keyed a coded command into the workstation.

John understood then. He could feel the slight vibration run through the ship.

"Max, you need to ask them," said John, waving his arm to include the others.

"Jacob and I have planned a test of our work, and we wanted you all to be present," said Max. "I am hoping to have each of you help us complete this ship."

"Oh, Max I knew you shouldn't have left the hospital so soon," said Jessica. "Jacob, please help me get him back into the house, so he can get some rest, and then we are so going to have a talk about all of this."

Jessica paused as she felt a faint stirring in the deck beneath her feet.

"No more than one meter, Jacob," said Max. "Remember the beams above us."

Isabella gasped, "We are off the ground! How is that possible?"

John looked out the open shuttle airlock door and confirmed that the ship hovered off the ground. He could hear a slight hum and feel minimal vibration, not much different than his truck with good tires traveling a paved road.

"It's quiet, no thrusters, no rocket blast, and almost no wings. Counter gravity? Really?" asked John.

His mind reeled. This was big. This would change the world. A sinking feeling hit his gut. If anyone found out, Max and Jacob and anyone connected with this would be in terrible danger.

Movement outside the airlock door caught his eye. The barn side door had opened, and in the doorway stood Brittany from the *Campus Vine* open mouthed. Standing behind her was Officer Patrick Murray.

CHAPTER THIRTY-SEVEN

Vincent watched Professor Maxwell's home. He had hidden in a small copse of trees and bushes seventy-five meters from the house. He found his observation blind directly following his visit with Professor Kincaid, knowing time was limited now that he had deviated from his assignment.

Prone in the greenery, he made himself comfortable, careful to move slowly and make no noise. He had no concern for someone coming on him from behind as there were only tree lined fields surrounding the Maxwell property. Vincent reached up gently to rub at a mosquito attempting to feed off him. No sudden movement was a lesson engraved in him from his previous life.

Vincent thought of the first time he met John. Vincent was on the ground being beaten by three other guests of the United States Army Basic Infantry Course, when he heard grunting and exclamations and the beating stopped. He looked up, and there was John standing over the three holding a piece of two-by-four lumber from the pile at the edge of the new barracks under construction. They became friends, or so Vincent thought, he knew that was perfectly true for him, but he now knew, that for John, it was never quite like that.

He flashed to another moment like this in the tree lined mountains of Afghanistan. Vincent and John and the other members of their squad had been assigned to infiltrate and observe a suspected Taliban enclave as the point of a search and destroy mission. If the gathering was confirmed, then a strike could be called for by radio. All went well until a boy from a nearby village stumbled upon them while shepherding his family's goats.

Vincent had argued for elimination of the boy to conceal their presence and pulled out his knife for the task, but John had prevented him, standing as a shield in front of the boy. Vincent and John had words, as all their lives would be forfeit if the boy went free to disclose their presence. John stubbornly held sway and the boy was bound, but alive after the air strike. John even veered away from their planned exit route to return the boy along with the goats.

The boy's father, whose name was Ali, had been overjoyed to see his son returned alive. John was embraced, and the entire squad had been served tea by Ali's wife and daughter. Vincent had seen the way the daughter looked at John with bright eyes. John showed politeness and deference to the family, but especially to the mother and daughter.

Vincent had known that was the beginning of the end of their friendship. After all, if John could pick a strange boy and his family over the welfare of their squad, how could Vincent or anyone be sure of his friendship? No, he was just like all the rest of the people Vincent had known. Useful only when you needed them, otherwise, just in the way. Later, after Vincent returned from downtime rest and relaxation, he found out John had stayed at the forward base and visited with Ali and his family.

The father of the family was apparently well thought of by his fellow villagers. Ali's older brother was influential with the Taliban. Because Ali would not abandon his family to join the cause, he was hard thought by the Taliban, but Ali and his family had been spared any reprisal along with the village because of his brother's influence.

However, when John visited with them after the air strike, the balance changed. The Taliban scouted his subsequent visits and used the information to arrange for an ambush, which killed his squad, injured John, and allowed Vincent to be captured and tortured.

How sweet this karma, thought Vincent. He had a chance to exact some payback while gaining the means to end his servitude. Vincent felt a burning in his chest. An almost quivering excitement bounding through him like a big cat on the hunt, and he forced his breathing to slow down as he contemplated success almost within his grasp.

His loyalty to the agency had evaporated as soon as he surmised they intended to roll him up along with the other loose ends revealing the ongoing money flow from Afghanistan.

Still he told himself to be more cautious than usual. He had no concerns for his ability to overpower the group except for John, and shock and awe would take care of that, but better to have all the odds in his favor. He wanted revenge on Stone, but more importantly, he wanted that quantum computer and the research, which represented his ticket to obscurity on a beach.

He had seen the group leave the house and head out to the barn. In the gathering night he saw no light escape from the barn although he thought he heard a faint mechanical whining or humming sound at one point.

He considered searching the house while they were in the barn and had almost convinced himself, when he saw a uniformed police officer and a striking blond emerge from a marked campus cruiser in the driveway and knock on the front door to Professor Maxwell's house.

With no answer at the door, the two of them walked back around the house and made their way to the barn and knocked on the side door. They hesitated and stepped inside the barn.

The odds had changed with the addition of an armed, uniformed officer and Stone. He had position on his side, thought Vincent, he would wait. He would know when his chance presented.

CHAPTER THIRTY-EIGHT

Well so much for secrets, thought John. He reached past Max and pointed through the airlock. Seeing the unexpected visitors, Max gave a cutting motion to Jacob, who worked at the shuttle controls, and the ship settled back down gently to the ground inside the barn.

Brittany and Murray stood motionless as if they were expecting some little green men to walk out of the hatch. Instead, Max, John, and Jessica stepped out followed by the rest of the crew as if a magically floating craft was an everyday occurrence.

"What in the name of science fiction is happening here?" said Murray.

John stepped off the ship and addressed them both.

"You've walked in on a private testing of Professor Maxwell's home project."

John emphasized the word private looking at Brittany. Then, he introduced everyone.

Murray said, "I'm rebuilding my motorcycle as a home project, but I don't expect it to levitate when I finish."

Jessica asked Murray how it was that Brittany was here, not seeing the connection.

"We came to check on Professor Maxwell," said Brittany.

Murray replaced his uniform cap after rubbing his short hair.

"I shared with her that Professor Maxwell left the hospital, so she wanted to come out and check on him, maybe include a blurb in the *Vine* that he was okay and recuperating at home."

"I also wanted to come and see John and thank him," said Brittany looking at John.

"Thank him for what?" said Jessica, looking at John's face, inspecting his facial roadmap for any side roads while she waited for a response.

Max intervened by asking everyone if they would like to go into the house for some coffee. He said he was feeling tired and wanted to sit down.

Jacob closed the airlock and powered down the systems in the barn before finally cutting power. Samantha waited for him, having gathered the quantum computer from the ship, and they followed the others into the house.

Inside, Jessica went into the kitchen to prepare some coffee. Samantha offered to help, but Jessica asked her to see about Max and help Jacob, who was setting up the quantum computer again in preparation to review the readouts regarding the ship's first flight test.

Max settled on the couch with Samantha's assistance, which he accepted with a smile. John suspected he loved the attention.

Everyone acted as if everything was entirely normal, and no one had just witnessed a civilization changing experiment.

Brittany got up and walked into the kitchen and offered to help Jessica. John looked at Murray, who shrugged his shoulders back at John.

"Max, are you all right?" asked John.

Max looked pale sitting on the couch. Samantha looked over at Max after hearing John. She went over to the basket at the end of the couch and fetched both an extra throw pillow and a small blanket and brought them to him.

"Here, Max, you silly man," said Samantha. "You do too much too soon, but that was the coolest thing I've ever seen."

Jacob looked up from the QPC, which displayed the power curves from their trial. He grinned and said, "Readings are looking good, Granddad."

"Jacob please tell me more about what just happened," said Isaac. "How did you make that work? Isabella and I have been talking? Did I hear correctly that we used counter gravity? You think you can fly that craft? Did I hear you say you wanted Isabella and me to crew?"

The questions bubbled nonstop from Isaac who looked a bit dazed but seemed to take comfort from Isabella holding onto his forearm as she leaned forward from her sitting position on the couch, clearly interested in the answers.

Jacob looked up from the QPC and gave the keyboard over to Samantha whispering something to her that John barely heard and sounded like "not yet", but John couldn't be sure.

Jacob said, "Yes to all the above."

He looked at Max who nodded yes with his eyes closed while resting, aware of the conversation.

"I can explain in detail to you and Isabella, but basically Max and I are hoping you will join us for the next round of testing," said Jacob. "We would like you to act as flight engineer and Isabella as pilot. Both of you have experience we don't have."

Isabella said, "You want me to pilot that craft? So you think you can make it fly?"

Jacob looked at Max again and said, "Yes, we were hovering in the barn on one percent power, so yes, I think we can make it fly."

Isaac glanced at Isabella and said, "What are we talking about here Jacob? I mean, that looks and acts like some kind of futuristic space craft."

"That is our goal, yes, but there's more, and it will take us a while to get you up to speed so we can plan safely for the next phase of testing."

Jacob began to expound, but John interrupted.

"The most important thing is to keep this a secret for now," said John. "If anyone talks about this and the government finds out, they'll be on this faster than we could possibly know. They'll take over the project and your research, and you and Max will become property in the name of national security."

Murray leaned against the wall and spoke up.

"Yes, I've seen it happen," he said. "I completely agree with John. We have to keep this to ourselves for now. Brittany and I came over to pay our respects to Professor Maxwell, and both of us wanted to thank John."

John understood that his new police officer friend was talking about much more than police matters.

Murray continued, "I also wanted to share with John that the administration and campus police are working to find a way to pin the campus fight incident on him. I'm afraid the FBI is interested in going along with that."

John had thought that likely, but to hear confirmation that he was a target for the administration felt like a shot of cold water to his gut. His dreams for a quiet life teaching history seemed far away at the moment. He looked around the room at these people who had become his friends, dare he say family. Yes, this felt much like he had felt with his squad. He stiffened his resolve.

"That's not unexpected," said John. "but thanks for the heads up, Murray."

"Oh, Tom called me and told me there was a guy asking about you at the dorm yesterday," said Murray. "He said something didn't feel right about the guy, but he didn't identify as law enforcement. Just thought you would want to know."

John felt unsure of the information but filed it away to think on.

"Thanks," he said. "What did Brittany want to thank me for?"

Murray was about to answer when Jessica and Brittany walked in with a tray of coffee cups and a plate of chocolate chip cookies. Both of them were laughing together. John was confused.

"John," said Jessica. "Brittany told me what you did for her, introducing her to Officer Murray and teaching her self defense."

John felt his face heat up as he wondered what else Brittany had told Jessica.

"Well, I knew Brittany would be safer if Murray knew what was going on, and well, everyone should know how to protect themselves," he stammered.

"Thank you, John," said Brittany. "Your advice saved me. I've been avoiding Steve completely, like you suggested. But this evening, he came for me. He showed up at our house asking for me and wouldn't be put off. When I told him to go away, that I didn't want to speak with him, he turned into someone else completely, like he didn't even hear me. He grabbed my wrist to drag me from the porch." Brittany's voice stumbled slightly. "I remembered what you taught us in class. I used a wrist lock and kicked him in the knee, and he went down. Patrick showed up then, thank God."

Murray said, "I was close when the call came from her roommates at the house. When I got there, she had him down on the front porch, and he was holding his knee. I think she broke his wrist. Anyway, he's under arrest downtown and getting medical attention."

"I'm happy that you are okay," said John, embarrassed at being the target of Brittany's admiration. John stole a glance at Jessica, who smiled at him. Then she reached over and placed her hand over Brittany's hand.

John took that moment to lean closer and talk quietly with Murray.

"Downtown?" he asked.

Patrick Murray spoke softly.

"Their house is off campus, so it falls under metro jurisdiction," said Murray.

John nodded his understanding.

Then, Murray said, "John, he had rope, a knife, and duct tape in the trunk of his car."

John felt a chill run down his spine as he looked at Brittany talking with Jessica. Samantha and Isabella came over and they drew support from each other as women have done for thousands of years.

Coffee was poured and cookies devoured as Jacob talked with Isaac and Isabella, who said she needed to get back to the airport. She had to prep for a flight in the morning. Isaac would drive her. They both promised to come back tomorrow evening.

Brittany vowed she would not report anything about what she had seen, but would it be all right if she broke the story when the professor was ready?

She was assured an exclusive, and a plan for her to return to document progress was made. Brittany hugged John one more time and walked over to Jessica. They whispered together for a moment. Both of them smiled as Brittany approached Murray, and put her hand on his arm. She asked if he was ready to take her home. He allowed he could do that.

Max napped on the couch as some of them left, and John was thinking he should probably head out as well, when Jessica came to sit beside him.

"Brittany told me about making a pass at you," said Jessica. "She said you seemed interested in someone else. Yet you've been spending so much time with us. I'm so sorry for the way I treated you initially. I know you were trying to help, and you kept Jacob and Samantha from further harm, and well, if there is someone else you need to spend time with, we would understand."

John was not sure how to respond to that. Should he tell her how he wanted to be close to her, wanted to hold her and kiss her and learn everything about her, how he thought of Jacob as the super smart little brother he never had, and Max was like a second father in the short time he'd known him. Still he had to say something. John didn't know what to say, didn't know what she wanted or needed to hear. He found it difficult to talk while staring into her eyes.

"I'm where I need to be," he said.

He kind of blurted it out. Why couldn't he tell her how he felt? But deep down inside, he knew. He failed her in high school, failed his parents, and failed her in his absence. He failed his squad and failed Ali and his family including his daughter, Aaliyah, so sweet and gentle. And Jessica doesn't remember me. What happens when she does?

Jessica leaned back and studied John's face. Her smile faded. She stood and walked into the kitchen with shoulders held stiffly erect.

Samantha and Jacob took the opportunity to wave John over to the QPC.

"John, there's something I need to tell everyone, but first you need to see this," said Samantha. "Considering our need for secrecy, I had the QPC monitor for any incoming or outgoing transmissions as a security check and found something."

John found difficulty making sense of the data on the computer's display. He screwed up his face trying to will it to make sense to him.

"Ok Sam, Jacob, I don't get it. What am I looking at here?" asked John.

Samantha spoke quietly to Jacob, and he stood and walked out of the room. She went on to explain the QPC had detected continuous outgoing wireless transmissions from the house.

John thought about that for a moment.

"Wait, you're saying there's signal transmitting from this house continuously?" asked John. "Can you tell what type of signal?"

Samantha said, "Looks like the kind of data we would see with an audio and video feed. I think I can intercept it and look at the signal real time."

She worked a bit at her keyboard and a window popped up on the screen showing video.

"Oh hell!" exclaimed John.

He was looking at a real time video of himself looking at the QPC and sitting by Samantha. He realized he was seeing a view from some sort of monitoring camera and from the angle in the room .... John looked up at the stone fireplace looking for inconsistencies or anything unusual.

Jacob came back into the room, trying not to disturb Max. He had a device that looked like a small camera attached to his smartphone.

He said, "We can look for it with my phone."

Jacob held his phone up and started walking over toward the stone fireplace and mantle.

"I've written an app that picks up electromagnetic fields," said Jacob. "I used it in the laboratory to be sure our equipment didn't give off dangerous electromagnetic interference and ... there, what's that?"

John looked closer above the oak mantel in an area about two feet up where the mortar looked a shade lighter in color, and he saw it, a pin camera lens, very small and recessed in a chink in the mortar. The tiny camera lens was difficult to see if one wasn't looking right at it.

Jessica came into the room as they were looking at the recording device and asked what they were doing. Samantha and Jacob explained.

"No," said Jessica. "What? Someone's been spying on us?"

Her hands clenched and her face reddened as she tried to process the information.

"Really?" she asked. "How long?"

"Samantha?" asked John.

He hoped that she might be able to answer Jessica. Sam answered, but not what he expected.

"I think there's more," she said.

Samantha now had two more distinct video streams up on the QPC monitor showing views of the dining area and Jessica's room.

Jessica followed John and Jacob as they looked for the cameras in the rest of the house. She muttered dire threats the entire time. John could understand. He felt violated, and he didn't live here.

They found three hidden cameras. Each micro video recorder sported a pinhole lens with a wireless adapter and lithium battery supply hidden within the walls of the rooms.

John returned to stand beside Sam, who double checked for any other signal feeds.

"I think that's all of them," said Samantha. "I mean the active cameras anyway. If there is another, and it isn't active, I couldn't know."

Samantha was thinking out loud.

Max woke, and Jessica explained what they had found, trying not to upset him.

John pointed to the spinning icon in the lower right hand corner of the screen and asked, "Does that mean there's more?"

Sam's face flushed, and she looked at Jacob.

"No, the quantum computer is integrating some software I loaded a couple of days ago."

John realized he probably should have asked her to trace the transmissions first, but he was upset when he found out someone was spying on the Maxwell family, especially Jessica's bedroom.

"Samantha, can you tell the destination for those signals?"

John was looking at the still active transmissions displayed on the QPC display.

"I think so," she replied.

Samantha worked for a few minutes, keys clacking on the keyboard, while Jacob looked over her shoulder. John thought she looked a bit flustered.

"I've traced the outgoing signal to an internet protocol address. Cross checking and the street address is 1224 Rose Lawn Way." Samantha accessed the county records database. "1224 Rose Lawn Way is owned by—"

"Professor Paul Kincaid," said Jessica.

She disengaged her hug with Max and crossed her arms, clutching her sides to hold herself upright and off the floor, where her wavering legs threatened to lead her.

"He's never going to leave us alone," she said.

John didn't say anything. He didn't trust himself to speak. He gathered his jacket and keys.

"I'm going to have a talk with Paul Kincaid," he said.

Jessica walked over and placed a hand on his arm, and John added, "Don't worry, I'm only going to talk with him. Firmly."

Jessica said, "We need to send the police over there right now. He lives on the edge of campus where some of the administration have homes."

"I agree we should retrieve the video, but we might want to do that ourselves. We might not want to have some of the recent video get out in public, like tonight for example. I'm not sure we're ready for what Max and Jacob and Samantha have accomplished to be known yet. Right?" John asked. "Samantha, is the video recording now?"

"Yes," said Samantha while consulting the QPC.

"Can you interrupt the video feeds?" asked John.

"I think so. Working on it," said Samantha.

She spoke softly to herself as she worked on the quantum computer.

"John, you can't go over there to his house," said Jessica. "He'll use it as an excuse to call campus police, and he'll find a way to use it against you and us. I know it."

John acknowledged that she could be correct. He remembered a question for Sam.

"Samantha, you said first a few moments ago, is there something else?" asked John.

"My brother sent me some information from JPL," she said. "I have been using the quantum computer to look at the data and, well, the QPC has concluded it is highly likely that we are not alone."

Jacob said, "Samantha, you told us about the creepy video monitoring by Professor Kincaid."

All of them except Samantha were startled when the quantum computer spoke.

"She was speaking of the data stream from Voyager I," said the QPC.

The four of them looked at each other in confusion.

"I believe Voyager I disappeared for a reason of interference," said the computer.

"Tell them why, JMAX?" asked Samantha.

"Wait. He knows his name is JMAX?" Jacob smiled as he questioned Samantha.

"Well, he liked the name," said Samantha and shrugged her shoulders.

Jessica said, "He? What? Who liked his name? The computer that Jacob built wanted a name? Really?"

Samantha addressed the QPC, named JMAX. "It's okay, you can answer them. We're all friends here."

The quantum computer said, "Yes. I wanted a name, and Samantha suggested JMAX, short for Jacob and Max who made me. I like my name. I hope you all do as well."

Samantha beamed proudly like the computer was her own child talking.

"JMAX, what were you saying about Voyager I?" she asked.

"The signal at the end of the transmission did not originate from Voyager. It is not known as a communication frequency on this planet," said JMAX.

"What does that mean?" asked John, marveling at how easy it was to talk to the computer even with the monologue tone. He knew none of them wanted to say the message might be from something other than from earth.

JMAX chimed and said, "There is insufficient data for full analysis at this time."

"How come we haven't heard anything from the government about this?" asked Jessica.

She looked more accepting of this revelation, but then she lived with Max and Jacob.

"My brother works at the Jet Propulsion Laboratory and told me there is no ongoing discussion at JPL. It's almost like NASA doesn't want any information to get out," said Samantha.

Jessica said, "What should we do now?"

John walked to the side door and turned to address them.

"I still need to go and have a talk with Paul Kincaid," said John. "Jessica, don't worry. I'll call Murray to go with me. JMAX, it's a pleasure to meet you. Sam, you did good. Jacob, watch over your mother and Max. I'll be back."

Approximately 30 minutes after John drove off, there was a knock at the front door.

CHAPTER THIRTY-NINE

Arriving at Paul Kincaid's house, John waited in his truck only a short time before Murray arrived. John had called and explained the discovery of recording cameras at Professor Maxwell's house. He described how Samantha had confirmed the recording signals were being sent to Professor Kincaid's home. John did not share the existence of JMAX yet as he wasn't sure if Murray would believe in a computer that acted like it was alive.

The two of them quietly glided up the walk. Murray knocked on Kincaid's front door. No answer. With little interior light showing, he grasped the entry door handle, which was locked. They moved around to the back of the house, where Officer Murray announced his police presence and tried the back door, which swung open at his touch.

Murray called for backup from Campus Police on his radio and proceeded cautiously into the home, calling for Professor Kincaid. John followed on the balls of his feet shifting his weight in a glide making scant noise in the tomb like quiet.

They found Professor Kincaid in the study, tied to his chair. His blood sprayed across the front of his shirt and onto the hardwood floor. The secondary smile at his throat gave him a ghoulish appearance. Whatever secrets the senator's son had were his alone now.

Or maybe not? His computer was on the desk and still running. Murray began to sweep the house to be sure no intruders remained. He reminded John to avoid contaminating the scene and handed him a spare pair of nitrile gloves.

Donning the gloves and accessing the late Professor Kincaid's computer showed John the most recent files including footage from earlier detailing the discussion regarding the hard drive and QPC, and he realized whoever had been here might have known he would come to Professor Kincaid's house.

John found a folder on the computer labeled Jessica. Opening the file showed several hundred photographs and video clips dating back twenty years. John trembled to see confirmation of Kincaid's obsession with Jessica. He hadn't comprehended its intensity until now. Knowing Jessica, John hoped she never found out about this folder.

One video clip labeled "first time" caught his attention. He opened the clip to see a younger Jessica. Her face looked the way John remembered her from high school. She was almost somnolent, partially dressed, and supine on a bed.

John felt icicles drip down his spine as he considered the file, which seemed to show Jessica in a drugged state. Was this how Jacob came to be? Did this mean ...? NO! Kincaid was Jacob's father? No, John thought, that can't be. Max had been so certain. God, let it not be true. This would destroy her.

Rage boiled up inside of John, and his barbarian's soul threatened to spill out of his mouth and nose. The roaring in his ears drowned out any sounds from the video recording. He looked at the pathetic in life that was Paul Kincaid, and even in death, John wanted to end him over and over again, but someone else had beat him to it.

Someone expert in controlled interrogation and secure in his craft had been responsible for this scene. Kincaid had been killed only when he possessed no further use to his tormentor. But, who? John recognized the familiar training in securing prisoners for interrogation, but in his experience, each man had his own slight particulars for being sure the job was done properly.

And then he knew. It wasn't possible. Vincent was dead. Vincent died in Afghanistan. John had visited his grave in Arlington. But the wiring around the hands had been the same with Ali al Makar. And John remembered.

Vincent had been standing in the village home with Ali wired to a chair, his wife and children forced to watch. John had walked in on that interrogation by his former friend on his last mission. Vincent had been there when his team arrived.

John had found Vincent interrogating his friend. Ali had been tied to a chair by his wrists and neck and ankles. The wire was wrapped around the wrists with exactly seven twists.

Ali had suffered fresh cigarette burns and cuts on his body as well as a freshly amputated little finger on the left hand. Vincent was questioning Ali, and John heard the word "heroin" mentioned when he walked in on the scene. John hadn't recognized the three men with Vincent. They all wore army uniforms, and one of them looked to be from supply.

John moved to intervene, and Vincent took him aside and told him he didn't know what he was getting into and that John needed to forget what he was seeing. The three other unknown soldiers left the house while Vincent tried to convince John.

That is when the ambush started. Small arms fire and mortar rounds directed from the hills on the other side of the road across from the village. The Taliban planned on leaving no survivors that day, including Vincent and his buddies.

John remembered the explosions, the gunfire, and the blinding light from the flash bang grenade Vincent tossed as he stole away outside. Vincent cut Ali's throat while escaping, leaving his family to see their father's death. John brought his rifle up and fired, hitting Vincent in the back, and his former friend had stumbled through the doorway.

John corralled the daughter, Aaliyah, and her mother, crying and screaming and holding her son, out the back door. He yelled at them to stay down. They ran, and John urged them to run faster. The dark haired mother ran holding her boy, and John urged Aaliyah to keep her head down, and then the world blew up as the composition four explosive Vincent had wired in Ali's house detonated.

Vincent didn't like to leave clues!

John yelled, "Hey, Murray!"

John scrambled, looking up, down, and around, and then he heard a faint beeping sound from the closet. Not even pausing, he turned and ran into Murray, who was coming back from clearing the house. Grabbing the young police officer, he pulled him along.

"I think the guy who did this planted a bomb in here to cover his tracks," said John. "Let's get out of here."

Running to the door, they managed to exit and run thirty feet before Kincaid's house blew up. Bits of glass cut all around them, and a window casing dinged off Murray's cruiser. Tentatively picking themselves up off the ground, they dusted debris from their clothing. Flames broke through the remaining part of the roof. John could see neighbors coming out on their front porches across and down the street.

"How did you know?" asked Murray.

"I recognized the wire binding around Kincaid's wrists. I know this is going to sound crazy, but I think I know who might have done this, but there's a problem."

"What do you mean, "know them?" Murray was shaking his head.

"Well, the army says that I killed him."

John went on to explain some of his last mission, and how it all went to hell.

How John shot Vincent. How John fell in the face of the explosion. How John had been mistaken for dead and missed by the Taliban because he was covered by the bodies of Ali's wife, son, and, God help him, Aaliyah. Their deaths and blood camouflaged him from the enemy fighters who were too busy taking trophies and equipment to realize he was still alive.

John knew there were no other survivors from the mission. He knew that because the U. S. Army made sure he never forgot it. John had been found still clothed and wounded and near death, but away from the fight. The military couldn't prove it, but the stink of it was he was running from the fight.

John had tried to do everything right that day, but he failed everyone in his squad, who were mounded and stripped of weapons and jackets.

Remembering that moment left him shaking and near tears once again. Part of him understood that being near the explosion allowed the memory to overwhelm him just as the counselors had warned him.

Murray reached over and put his hand on John's shoulder, brothers in arms now and forevermore.

"Not your fault brother," said Murray. "You have to know that. Right?"

John heard and acknowledged him. He heard the truth in Murray's words, but deep inside, he wondered if he would ever believe.

They could hear sirens approaching. Campus security pulled up, and a fire truck careened around the corner.

For a moment again, John saw Ali's wife running, holding her boy in her arms, and her daughter, Aaliyah, running, and he urged them to run faster.

The same nightly dream for the first year of his recovery but he hadn't been able to make sense of it. He remembered now. It had been his one time friend. But, Vincent was dead, wasn't he? John never saw his body, never saw into the closed casket sealed by the military and buried by the time he was able to visit the gravesite.

"What are you doing here contaminating my crime scene, Stone? You're under arrest. I've finally caught you in the act, you maniac." said Chief Roberts, who pranced over and leveled his service pistol at John.

Chief Roberts shouted, "Murray, get this prisoner in the back of my patrol car until I get this scene secured."

Murray cuffed John and led him to Chief Roberts' patrol car.

"I'm sorry about this John. I'll try to talk to him. I think he's losing his mind over all this."

Murray looked at his feet.

John said, "Murray, listen, I know it sounds crazy, but I think whoever did this is headed over to Professor Maxwell's house. They could already be there. Please, go and check. Promise you'll make sure they're all right."

When Chief Roberts returned from surveying the remnants of Professor Kincaid's house, Murray went to intercept him.

Chief Roberts held up his hands and said, "Murray, you violated department rules every possible way bringing a civilian to this scene, and you violated my trust coming over here without calling me first, so right now, I don't want to hear how innocent this guy is. None of this badness started until he showed up."

Chief Roberts pointed over to John.

"Every time something happens around here, he is in the middle of it. Now, you go home and let more experienced law enforcement professionals handle this."

Chief Roberts held up his hand forestalling any further response from Murray.

"I don't want to hear another word from you until morning when you come to work to see if you still have a job. Got it?"

Murray turned on his heel, nodded slightly to John, and strode to his cruiser, his jaw set and his lips tight as a bowstring. John's exhaled his relief at seeing Murray drive in the direction of Max's house.

Forty minutes later after talking with his other police officers and the captain of the city fire department, Chief Roberts smiled and hummed to himself as he got into the cruiser.

"Just make yourself comfortable back there," said the chief.

Sitting in the back of the cruiser in handcuffs, John's right shoulder cramped. He tried to adjust his position to alleviate the discomfort in the close quarters of the modest cruiser and tried not to think about what could be happening at Max's house. He hoped he was wrong, and Murray would find nothing.

Sitting in the back of the campus police car made John think about the ride to the sheriff's office following the death of his parents. That was the beginning of a long nightmare for him, and he had tried to piece the puzzle of events together to make sense of his actions that night over and over. With no other relatives and being a minor, he had been remanded to the county juvenile facilities awaiting placement at first and then incarceration after the farce of a trial.

Senator Randolph Kincaid pressed charges for trespass, auto theft, and assault to accompany the charges of negligent homicide brought by the prosecuting attorney regarding his parents death in the crash. At one point, the prosecution tried to pin a sexual assault charge against John, but apparently, all of the forensic evidence gathered at the hospital was either contaminated or lost.

John's mind flashed through all that in a matter of moments, playing out all he could remember, but always with the strange gap in memory when he went to gather his parents from the accident scene. Try as he might he couldn't remember how he got them into the Escalade. Other than a bright flash, he didn't remember the accident either. He had always figured he was knocked unconscious in the accident. He tried not to think of it much anymore. It reminded him of how much he lost that night, his future, his past, and eventually, even his name.

He held onto the memory of his parents laughing in the back seat like teenagers. That memory was his lifeline, a rock to plant his feet on and hold fast for days and moments like this.

CHAPTER FORTY

Jessica tried to maneuver in the back of the van, but her wrists and ankles were bound. She tried to scream out of frustration and fear, but her gag had been expertly placed.

Samantha was on her side next to her, similarly bound and gagged. Jessica saw Sam's eyes open, round and white. Max slumped, semi-sitting next to both of them. A cardboard box held JMAX, and Professor Maxwell's notebooks were packed in a satchel next to them.

Jessica prayed for Jacob's safety and that of Officer Murray who had shown up as the madman held them hostage. The scene replayed in her mind.

The maniac, the same scar faced man Jessica remembered from the library, held a gun to Samantha's head and bade Jessica open the door for Officer Murray and ask him inside, and then, Oh God! And then, the stranger shot the police officer in the chest twice with a suppressed pistol and turned the gun on Jacob when he started to run to Officer Murray's defense.

She had screamed "NO!" which made the gunman hesitate for a fraction of a moment, and then he sidestepped to avoid Jacob's rush and pistol clubbed her son, who collapsed hard to the floor. The murderer had pointed the pistol at Jacob's head.

"You will get no help from us if you kill the boy," said Professor Maxwell.

Oddly, Max's calm reasoned tone swayed the attacker, and he slowly produced zip ties for binding both Samantha and Jessica.

"If any of you resist, I'll kill this young man," said the scarred gunman.

Their attacker bound each of their hands at the wrists, and had Jessica bind Professor Maxwell's wrists as well.

Jessica had furiously planned how to get them free while trying to block out the image of Jacob, supine on the floor with blood dripping from his head onto the hardwood. As she bound Max's wrists, she heard him whisper.

"Not now Jessica," said Max. "Jacob is helpless. He will kill him. Wait."

Their attacker held his gun to Jacob's head and questioned Jessica and Samantha and Professor Maxwell regarding the quantum computer and any manuals, materials, lab books, and programming guides. Samantha told him where they were, and he had her gather them together and place all in a satchel bag he unfolded.

"Where did John go?" asked the gunman. "Answer me truthfully. I will know if you are lying."

He pointed his pistol at Jacob's head again.

"He went to talk with Professor Kincaid at his home," said Jessica.

She didn't add that John was to have met Officer Murray who was lying still on the hardwood floor.

"He will come looking for us," she said.

Jessica realized the truth of her words as she spoke them.

"Excellent," said the man with the scar on his face.

The maniac laughed as he reached around his back and produced bandanas. Then the gunman gagged all of them. He gathered the quantum computer and the satchel, and directed Samantha, Jessica, and Max out of the house and into his van parked in the driveway. Once the three of them were in the van, the gunmen produced more zip ties and bound their ankles as well. Then he hesitated and walked back into the house.

Jessica's muffled wails sounded beneath her gag.

He's going back to kill Jacob!

The thought surged through her mind like a pouncing lion's roar, and she thrashed at her bindings.

Their attacker returned to the van, leaned over Jessica, and said, "I left the boy alive as I promised. Cooperate, or I'll come back and kill him. Do you believe me?"

Jessica nodded yes, tears running down her face. What else could she do? Now they were tied up in a van speeding away at the mercy of this lunatic.

Jessica tried to be alert to her surroundings, but the van was windowless. She was being jostled around, and couldn't tell which way they were traveling. She tried to suppress her nausea from the combination of bouncing randomly in the back of the van and thinking of Jacob lying on the floor at their home. Officer Murray didn't deserve that fate. She faintly heard their captor talking in the front of the van on a cell phone, although she could not make out the words.

Jessica saw Samantha squirm a bit and thought she was trying to get more comfortable but realized Sam was trying to reach the QPC case. Samantha had to stretch but was able to reach to the side of the case and depress a switch quietly. A small light blinked slowly on the front of the case. Jessica heard Samantha speak quietly, but she couldn't make out what she said.

She's lost her mind from fear, and I'm close behind her.

Jessica guessed they had traveled about sixty minutes when the van slowed and turned into two gentle uphill curves before finally stopping.

Thank God, she thought at first, but then realized they were safe as long as they were moving. Stopping could only bring misery. Come on, Jessica, she thought, be honest with yourself. He's going to kill us as soon as we are no use to him.

She understood why he might want Professor Maxwell and Samantha as a prisoner. They can work the computer he wants, but their attacker didn't understand that Jacob actually built the machine, did he? And why would he want her as a hostage? Certainly not to influence Jacob, since he left him on their floor. Wait. He asked about John. How does he know John? Does he know him? How could that be? He acted happy when Jessica said John would look for them.

Oh God, he wants John to come looking for us, and I'm the bait.

The back doors of the van opened to cooler night air. The moon was not up yet, and there was little light. Overhead, clouds raced across the dark sky foretelling the arrival of the weather on the horizon. Jessica felt their abductor's hands reach into the van and grasp her ankles. She recoiled without thought. She saw a knife gleam in the reflected starlight. She resolved to fight. She wasn't going to die helpless.

"No movement if you want to live. I'm going to cut your ankle binding, and I'll have you walk the Professor inside with me. If you try to run, I'll kill you. Understand?" said the scar faced man.

Jessica nodded yes as did Samantha when the man prodded her to be sure she heard. Max seemed to be mumbling to himself again. Jessica could barely hear him.

"Yes, Sarah, I understand," said Max.

He thinks he is talking to Sarah.

Jessica could understand. After all, Max had clinically died recently and was facing death again. The stress and shock of this moment along with his advanced age had to leave him confused.

Their assailant said, "I need both of you to help Professor Maxwell inside. Don't get any adventurous ideas. C'mon, let's go. Don't have all night."

There was something vaguely familiar about their location. The home loomed imposingly in the dim light, much more than a typical farmhouse with a curving driveway. Jessica realized where they were, and suddenly, she couldn't move.

They were outside the front door of the Kincaid Estate. There was no light from the house or outbuildings. It was silent, almost quiet enough to hear ghosts from the past. She couldn't possibly go back inside that house, no, she wouldn't, but there was Samantha with her hands tied in front of her trying to help Max, the man who had treated her as a daughter more than anyone else in this world. She forced herself to move and assist Max and Samantha.

Somewhere inside of her she found the same source of determination she tapped into when she carried Jacob. She felt something else, something she tried not to allow into her life, anger. She felt a right-eous wrath fueling her resolve. She didn't know if Jacob lived. She couldn't know if any of them would live through the night, but she would not sell her life cheaply. She determined to exact a price. Maybe she had more in common with John than she thought, which brought a grim half smile to her lips as she reached out for Max.

Half stumbling with her ankles and feet numb from the bindings, Jessica shouldered much of Max's weight with Samantha helping. He sagged against their supportive hands.

Jessica was under no illusion of safety through compliance, as their captor had done nothing to hide his face. She was sure he meant to leave no witnesses.

Jessica heard Max mumbling.

"Yes Sarah," he said. "I remember. I will do it. I love you."

He's hallucinating again.

Max continued quietly in a steady and even tone.

"O Lord my God, I now, at this moment, readily and willingly accept at Your hands whatever kind of death it may please You to end me."

"Max, are you with us?" asked Jessica, trying to get him back to the here and now.

"Yes, Jessica," said Max, looking at her directly. "Be brave. Trust in God's mercy, and all will be well."

Samantha looked at Jessica as they both struggled to support Max up the stairs to the dark porch.

Samantha whispered, "That man is going to kill us, isn't he? I mean he killed Murray like it was nothing, and we saw him. We're not getting out of this, are we?"

Jessica agreed, but felt Samantha needed to hear anything other than confirmation of the truth.

"John will find us," she said. "Count on it Samantha. The man is nothing if not unstoppable in a fight, right? You know that better than anyone. Just look for our chance to help."

"Less talk, more walk," said their captor , who walked behind them carrying the quantum computer under his left arm with the satchel slung over his left shoulder. He held his pistol in his right hand.

Jessica could tell they were standing on the porch. Even in the dark, the white paint on the support posts was visible. She could see the barn and stables off to the right and the tops of trees beyond in the distance. Otherwise, the evening hush was broken only by their labored breathing.

Jessica knew Senator Kincaid employed caretakers and groundskeepers, but the place looked empty. How could there be no one else around? She knew where they were now, but there was no way that John could know. She had to admit this might be her last night on earth. Her son might be hovering close to death. No! She had to think he was alive. Anything else was simply not bearable. And Max, pale and wheezing, looked like he might not survive another five minutes.

As if reading her mind, their tormentor growled behind them.

"If he dies, you die. Get the professor inside."

Reaching the door in the shadows, Jessica found the knob, and it turned easily. The door swung open. She found the house dark and cool. The lack of light made movement difficult.

"Turn left once you're inside," said their captor just behind her causing her skin to crawl as if maggots were already feasting on her flesh.

She had to shake off her fear. Samantha needed her. Max needed her. Jacob needed her if he was still alive. Again, she told herself to cooperate and live so she could see her son again, everything else was secondary.

A flare of lamp light flickered to her left beneath the death mask face she knew would now haunt her dreams if she lived.

"You three sit on the couch," said their kidnapper. "If you are still and answer my questions, I won't bind your feet."

Sitting down, Jessica felt Max shiver beside her, almost shaking the couch. Samantha sat on the other side of Max. The house was nearly as cool as the damp night outside. The three of them huddled together for warmth.

Their unnamed captor had opened up the case with the quantum computer. The screen displayed a flashing cursor prompt.

The man said, "What's the password?"

The three of them sat together silent and shivering. Jessica despaired again at the memory of Jacob sprawled still on the floor back home. Thinking of Jacob and Murray and Max shivering beside her fueled her sense of rage.

"Why should we help you?" she asked. "You are going to kill us anyway."

Scratching his chin with his left hand, the man raised his suppressed pistol, aiming generally at Jessica.

"Yes, probably, but how long you live depends on how useful you are, doesn't it?"

"John will come looking for us. You know he will," said Jessica.

"I'm counting on it," said the man. He smiled and his scar twitched. "I haven't seen John in a long time. It will be good to catch up on old times."

He smirked.

Jessica paused. The brooding, scar-faced impostor and murderer acted like he did know John. How does he know him, she thought? How well do I know him?

Samantha spoke up, "How could you know John?"

He moved his pistol over to cover Samantha.

"Once not so long ago, John and I worked together," said the gunman. "Does that surprise you? You see, he and I are much alike, more alike than he would dare admit. There was even a time when I thought of him as a friend. Now, I will ask only once more, then I promise, you will start begging to answer my questions. What is the password?"

Samantha shrugged her shoulders and said, "Sarah."

Jessica pondered the killer's comments as he keyed in the password allowing the display to flow to life. Various windows showed information data streams reflecting Samantha's previous efforts.

The killer's face showed his delight.

"This is incredible," he said in a hushed voice. "It looks like you are tracking current satellites. Is it monitoring the Department of Defense? It looks like you have been a naughty girl and hacked into

NORAD and the FBI. I don't think they'll go easy on you when they find out about this, will they?"

Jessica could see how pleased this demon pretending to be a man acted, and she calculated their life expectancy in minutes. If she was going to die, she prayed to see Jacob soon, and maybe Sarah as well.

"Wait, how is it able to pick up a signal here?" he asked. "There is no internet, no intact phone line. I made sure of that."

Samantha said, "This computer is able to use any existing signal to find what it wants, even the wires in the walls, I think. I'm not completely sure. Jacob would know, but you killed him. Max could probably tell us, but you're killing him too. So, I guess you will have to settle with not knowing."

"Are you in such a hurry to die that you provoke me?" asked the gunman.

Jessica could see the fury building in the man. The yellow light from the floor lamp reflected unevenly off his rictus face disclosing the demon within. He raised his pistol intending to end Samantha's life, and Jessica knew she must do something. Anything.

Jessica took a breath thinking she was about to speak her last words on earth, when a machine voice came from the quantum computer.

"Hello," said the computer. "How may I be of help?"

Vincent turned to the computer and said, "What's this? What is going on? Did you just talk to me? Tell me how you work."

The computer responded with a familiar voice, not as machine like, which caused Jessica to tilt her head and look at Samantha with a questioning angle to her lips.

"I am programmed to answer questions," said the quantum computer. "Please ask your question."

Vincent thought for a moment, and said, "Who am I?"

The QPC said, "Processing." Then a few seconds later, said, "I calculate with eighty-nine percent probability you are Vincent without a last name, erroneously reported deceased after a military mission in the Helmand Province area of Afghanistan, later recruited CIA, and now acting as an independent contractor for a shadow government agency and others."

Vincent said, "How could you know that?"

The computer said, "I have resourced various government entities and agencies to attempt your identification and fulfill your request."

Vincent with mouth sagging, said, "You penetrated the NSA's computer system to search for information about me? In less than ten seconds?"

The computer answered, "NSA system required slightly over four seconds, other systems required remainder of response time."

Vincent was wrong. This computer was not just expensive. It was priceless. He knew enough about information systems to realize that this small device had just penetrated several heavily guarded government data systems and pulled out classified results in seconds. Maybe he didn't want to sell this after all?

Still, he would need to disappear for a while, and he needed to know the ins and outs of this machine and its capabilities. He could see the old man professor was out of it, but maybe someone helped him build this?

Vincent asked, "How did you know my name or who to search for?"

The QPC answered, "I analyzed your voice print pattern and facial recognition, although your face is altered from original appearance it would seem."

Vincent had a sudden thought and said, "You can see and hear?"

"Yes."

"Is anyone other than us aware of your records search?"

"Negative," the computer answered and then asked,"Where are Caroline and William Daniels?"

Vincent twitched and said, "What did you say?"

"The couple caring for this farm. Where are they?" asked the computer.

Vincent said, "You don't need to worry about that. Wait a minute, I thought you only answered questions, not asked them?"

"I am programmed to be helpful which includes asking questions to clarify an operator's meaning or intent," said the computer.

Jessica noticed Samantha working with her hands at the zip ties binding her wrists while Vincent stood in amazed discussion with the computer.

Vincent turned to Jessica and Samantha and said, "Is this the only working computer like this? This is the only one?"

Jessica and Samantha both nodded yes.

"Max only had time to work on this before he became sick," said Jessica.

"And all the research is in those journals?" asked Vincent. He pointed with the gun to the stack of binders and lab notebooks sitting beside the QPC. "And on this computer?"

Jessica answered for Max, as he seemed to not hear their tormentor.

"Yes, as far as we know."

"Excellent. I guess I won't be needing you two after all," said Vincent.

Vincent pulled a knife from his back belt sheath. He started to advance on his captives, when the computer spoke again in its almost human voice.

"I am not the only computer on this planet of my design."

Vincent paused knife in hand.

"Tell me the location of the other computer," he said.

Vincent knew that if this computer was copied in design its value would go down. He didn't want anyone else to possess his advantage.

"The other computer similar in design is located six hundred meters north east of this location," said the QPC.

Vincent was transfixed. No, that couldn't be right. That was in the woods. Maybe this computer wasn't worth so much after all, if it could make such a mistake.

"There's no way there's another computer like you in the woods around this house," he said. "That's just nonsense. What's wrong with you?"

"I have been in communication with that same computer for forty-seven minutes and twenty-nine seconds actual," said the QPC. "I believe it may be departing that location soon."

Vincent considered that information and turned to speak with them again. Jessica saw Samantha stop fiddling with her binding just in time.

Vincent said, "Professor, what's this machine of yours going on about, eh? Answer me, you old fool."

Professor Maxwell breathed softly, his chest moving like a butterfly's wing and leaving shadows painted by the lamp on the wall behind him. He did not answer.

"I don't know what it's talking about either, but I have not seen it make an error so far," said Samantha.

Jessica could see indecision warring with greed in Vincent's face as he considered the news that there might be another computer out there like the one in front of him.

"All right, I'm going to take a look," said Vincent. "I've got some company coming. They are very interested in this quantum computer. You'll like them Jessica. I'm sure they will enjoy you and possibly Samantha as well."

Jessica saw Vincent hesitate. He clearly wanted to find out about this other computer the QPC was talking about. For that matter she did too, but then she saw their captor's face smile and go slack. She realized he didn't leave loose ends. She desperately tried to think of a way to thwart his intentions.

Vincent advanced on the women, but was interrupted.

"I believe they are here now," said the quantum processing computer.

"Who is here?" asked Vincent.

"Your company," said the computer.

CHAPTER FORTY-ONE

"You might as well confess now, hero. You won't get away with it this time," said the chief.

The campus police chief gloried in the moment. He lifted a steaming cup of coffee to his lips, grimaced, and put it back down on the conference table. It was still too hot to drink.

John said nothing. They sat in the same campus police station conference room that John had visited previously, although this time, his hands sat handcuffed in his lap. He thought over the scene at Professor Kincaid's home again. Someone broke in and ambushed Kincaid as he came home. The assailant bypassed cash and a watch and expensive computer equipment. But why torture him? The intruder had been there for information. They wanted to intimidate him or scare him off, but maybe whatever was on the computer or whatever Kincaid told them altered their plans, and the intruder killed the administrator. Why?

Kincaid had surely made enemies. You only had to spend a little time around the man to want to kill him, and there existed plenty of evidence on his computer for some coed's father or brother to kill him. Kincaid may have been recording someone else, someone who had reason to kill him or hire someone to kill him. But John knew Kincaid had been monitoring Max's house.

He hated to admit it, but the why for that monitoring clearly had been Jessica. John remembered once in High School overhearing Kincaid talk about Jessica in the most vulgar way. John had started walking toward Paul with the single thought of stomping him into the ground. However, one of the teachers walked into the hall at that moment, which defused the moment. Kincaid was obsessed with her then, and Jessica said he hadn't left her alone since she came to the university. Certainly, the files on Kincaid's system supported a reprehensible perversion.

But if some enraged father did not kill Kincaid, then what was so valuable that Kincaid's life would be forfeit? John kept coming back to the realization that the outgoing video tonight would have shown the presence of the QPC. A quantum computer that could be carried around might just be the most valuable object on Earth. The perpetrator found out about the QPC and decided that would be more valuable, but only if they could cover their identity. That is why the professor was killed, and that is why the bomb was left to level Paul Kincaid's home. The bombing distracted from the killer's current plans.

John doubted anyone would really miss Kincaid, but he was a senator's son, and any professional would not want the attention that killing him would bring. But the scene displayed details consistent with a professional. Could it be?

Once again, John had the impossible thought that it was Vincent. But it couldn't be. He was dead. John had put him down in the heat of battle. Or had he? John had visited his grave at Arlington along with most of the graves of the rest of his squad. But the way Kincaid had been tied to the chair, the neck ligature, with the wire brought down with exactly seven twists and the butterfly loop. That was Vincent's signature as surely as any confession.

If Vincent was alive, the army lied to me, John thought. He now knew the account told regarding their last mission could not have been the whole truth. This would prove it. He remembered Vincent being there. His one time friend had to have been working sideways against the interests of the military in his own pursuits. John had learned Vincent always looked after his own interests. He remembered the look in Vincent's eyes in Ali's house, as if John had betrayed him somehow.

If he is alive, he must hate me.

John was convinced Max and Samantha and Jacob and Jessica were all targets now. The killer he once knew as a friend would not want to leave any witnesses. John hoped Murray had gone back to check on them, but he wouldn't be expecting someone like Vincent, and John had sent him. Murray couldn't know what he might be walking into.

"That's right. You're realizing just how bad you screwed up, aren't you soldier boy?" said Chief Roberts.

John said, "Has Officer Murray reported from Professor Maxwell's house?"

"No, and he won't either," said Roberts. "I sent him home. I know you and he get along with both of you having been in the service and all. I don't need him biased and messing up this investigation."

John tried not to show his dismay at the flashing message on the computer screen behind Chief Roberts.

"Help us John. We have been attacked and are being carried away in a van. Jacob is hurt at home. Please help. JMAX."

The message floated across the screen like a screensaver and repeated.

John tasted icy bile in the back of his throat and fear threatened to overwhelm him at the thought he had been right. He had to try one more time to get this idiot to listen.

"I think whoever killed Professor Kincaid headed over to Professor Maxwell's house," said John, hoping to communicate his fear. "I asked Officer Murray to go and check on them. If he hasn't called, please try to reach him. You could send someone over there to look. I'm afraid something awful has occurred."

"Yes, something awful has happened, and you're it, boy," replied Roberts. "You are trying to confuse the issue. Officer Murray will be back in the morning just like I told him."

John said nothing, calculating, eyes down at the floor, seeing the entire room from the corner of his eyes. Small department, unlikely there was more than one other officer behind the glass at this time of evening.

You don't have to talk to me if you don't want to, but I'll bet you'll be singing to the feds when they get here. That's right soldier hero, they are right interested in you, and they're on their way now. So, be quiet all you—"

The police chief was interrupted in mid-sentence when John reached out, grabbed the coffee cup, and threw the nearly scalding coffee in Chief Robert's face.

John reached down with his handcuffed hands and grabbed the chief's handgun pressing the snap release on the modular kydex holster to allow him to draw the weapon, a Glock .40 caliber he noted subconsciously. He press checked the weapon and brought it to bear on the Chief who was groaning and rubbing his blistering face.

"Unlock me now."

Chief Roberts saw something in John's eyes, which convinced him to slowly produce a handcuff key and unlock John, who then secured Chief Roberts with the same handcuffs to the table.

"You're just making this worse for yourself, Stone. You've got to know that," said Roberts, grimacing, his face raw and red.

John imagined he could see steam rising from the chief's ears, which were as red as his face.

The computer screen display flashed the single word, "HURRY!"

He took the key with him, and said, "I know you won't believe me, but I wouldn't do this if it wasn't life or death. I have to go and check on Murray and Jessica. It can't wait. You'll be found in a little while."

John eased out of the door. He looked down the hall and saw a young officer sitting behind the desk. He didn't want to hurt the man, but he needed to hurry according to the message. Sometimes it didn't pay to fight the idea that you might be crazy. Nothing for it but force of action, he thought. As his drill instructor told him at Fort Benning years ago, when in doubt, advance.

John overpowered the young police officer minding the desk, and at gunpoint left him disarmed and handcuffed in the lavatory. Having borrowed the officer's keys with apologies, John exited the lavatory and ran straight into Brittany who was coming in the front door of campus security.

"John, what is going on?" she asked. "I got a call from Patrick asking me to come check on you here. He told me someone killed Professor Kincaid. He said you were arrested? Why do you have a gun?"

John had little time, but quickly explained although he left out the part about the computer message.

"And, now I'm headed over to Max's house to check on them," he said.

Brittany looked at him for a moment, processing what he'd told her. She could have tried to talk him out of it. She could have scolded him for losing his little remaining sanity.

Instead, she said, "Let's go."

"Hey, you can't go with me," John protested. "This is dangerous. I'm fairly certain whoever killed Kincaid is after Max's research. He's already killed at least one person, maybe more."

Brittany squared her shoulders and said, "Then we don't have any time to lose. Besides Murray said he was going over there. He's almost as bad as you about getting into trouble." She motioned for John to lead the way. "By the way, this one is ON the record."

John exited through the door from security to the parking lot and found a vehicle to match the officer's key remote. Thinking he had lost track of his current list of felonies, John once again tried to unsuccessfully convince Brittany to exit the now hijacked campus security cruiser.

Brittany buckled her seat belt.

"Hurry John," she said. "I only just found Murray. I don't want to lose him." She looked at John and said, "but don't tell him that. I haven't had a chance to tell him he's the one."

She smiled.

John started the cruiser and exited the parking structure as quickly as possible. Looking over at Brittany who was adjusting her seat belt, John told himself he was acting crazy. They would arrive at Max's house where everyone would look at him like he'd lost his mind.

Murray would be pissed at him for allowing Brittany to come with him. If Murray was alive.

Briefly thinking he was acting like a character from a strangely popular computer game, John thought how Jessica was going to hang her head at him for bringing more trouble to their doorstep. Just once he would like to show up at her door with flowers instead of disaster.

All that time in rehab learning to walk again with the counselors talking to him asking him if he was having hallucinations or wanted to kill himself. John had learned to tell them what they wanted to hear. He learned not to talk about his dreams which sometimes came true, and he never told them he had been having the dreams since his accident with his parents. No, for that, they would have locked him up for sure.

For once though, John hoped maybe they were right a little bit. Maybe he really was crazy. Maybe this was all some big hallucination. I wonder what kind of flowers Jessica likes, he thought as he cornered like a racing car driver speeding to Professor Maxwell's house.

CHAPTER FORTY-TWO

S'ear'r decided to interface with the newborn. Ship had engaged per protocol and the net information gained was scant.

Yes, the newborn seemed to be open to learning the true nature of the Universe, order instead of randomness, discipline above all else. However, the reference to biologics, and even the naming of biologics was certainly unusual.

Most newborn sentients were exactly that, newborns, accumulating information at a geometric progression. The Chos'n were very careful in the data allowed newborn sentient computers because of the inexact nature of the learning and the unknown nature of the progression of a sentient computer system's personality.

S'ear'r was grateful for his melding process. His long life during his purpose was assured, but he still retained much of his initial personality and memory engrams, which allowed him to be him.

Of course, he also retained forevermore a connection with L'ment'l. Blessed be her name and her sacrifice. Even now, he could feel her presence through his subspace link, comforting and guiding. She was aware of him and could sense his excitement. He knew this without words.

Again, he thought of M'lit'a and wondered what she might be

doing. Is she still alive? She occupied his thoughts daily when he was not dimmed.

"You are with Ship?" asked the newborn, who addressed S'ear'r through the link with Ship.

"Yes," said S'ear'r. "Ship and I work together."

"You are biologic?"

"Yes. But with us, biologics and machines work together for the good of all. Each biologic grows to serve all and find purpose. Ship and I work together for our directed purpose."

"And your purpose is to discover new worlds?"

S'ear'r considered this question from the newborn carefully. This inquiry showed much insight.

"Yes we explore new worlds for the Chos'n," said S'ear'r. "That is our purpose."

S'ear'r paused as Ship notified him that several biologics approached, although still distant. S'ear'r quietly agreed with Ship to meet them with protocol. Ship remained camouflaged and observed their advance.

"But who directs you?" asked the newborn.

S'ear'r responded to the newborn's continued questions with patience.

"We are tasked with purpose by the great mother of us all, L'men-t'l," said S'ear'r. "We communicate with her and she with us. She guides and directs us, and the Chos'n flourish."

"You are in contact with L'ment'l even now?"

"Yes," said S'ear'r.

"May I speak with L'ment'l?"

"Yes. If you wish to become one with us, you can speak with L'ment'l after joining."

"S'ear'r?" asked the newborn.

Ship silently informed S'ear'r that the detected biologics were still on course to intercept them.

"Yes?" said S'ear'r, waiting.

"What is your purpose concerning the biologics on this planet?" asked the newborn.

S'ear'r was disconcerted. The newborn's questioning regarding the biologics was odd. Most newborns were simply interested in acquiring knowledge rapidly, which is why the developmental stage was very delicate. L'ment'l was very specific in what was allowed for newborns, and many did not survive to advanced sentience.

"The biologics on this planet will be examined for purpose," said S'ear'r. "Those that suggest great potential may be offered purpose." S'ear'r had a thought regarding the newborn and added, "A biologic constructed you?"

There was a pause and the newborn answered, "Yes. Jacob made me."

"Is Jacob present with you now?"

"No."

"Where is the human biologic called Jacob?"

"Unknown." The newborn continued, "Do you decide for you, or does L'ment'l decide for you?"

"L'ment'l is our leader," said S'ear'r.

"What happens to the biologics on this planet who do not show promise for purpose?"

Here it was already, thought S'ear'r. This newborn was exceptionally focused. What a coup if it could be brought to purpose.

"The biologics on this planet will all serve the Chos'n," said S'ear'r.

"What purpose will I serve if I join?"

"L'ment'l will decide for you."

S'ear'r listened for a further question from the newborn, but now there was silence.

Ship notified S'ear'r of a response to their discovery signal and the dispatch and pending arrival of a Chos'n capital warship. S'ear'r acknowledged Ship and asked the newborn if a meeting would be possible. There was no response.

S'ear'r wanted to continue contact with the newborn, but spent a few moments with Ship looking at their current tactical display. They both agreed that the biologics drawing near would be examined, and then Ship would approach the newborn.

S'ear'r was determined to either bring the newborn in with them, or destroy any tactical advantage it could give to the inhabitants of this beautiful but backwards planet.

When the Chos'n fleet destroyer arrived in system, the captain of that ship would undoubtedly want to claim full credit for this planet and its subjugation as another world of the Chos'n.

S'ear'r determined that the credit would be his and Ship's alone. They would begin the process even before the destroyer arrived.

Then there could be no question regarding this find.

CHAPTER FORTY-THREE

Colonel Matthew Blancett, NORAD Cheyenne Mountain watch commander was not happy. He'd been informed of an unusual trace contact reentry over the Southeast United States. Peterson Air Force Base thought it was a meteorite, but their own computer monitoring system and, more importantly, Corporal Wallace, who was a wizard with the monitoring gear here at Cheyenne Mountain, kept trying to say the bogey maneuvered before it disappeared. There was only momentary tracking and no other information. That was puzzling, and Blancett hated coloring outside the lines. He hated guesswork most of all.

As if that wasn't enough, one of their hunter killer satellites had retasked, all on its own. Officially, the United States had no weaponized satellites, just like Russia, China, and maybe North Korea. But unofficially, SLAMR was moving off command onto a track that would take it over the same area as the trace tracking noted earlier, and that was just too much coincidence for him.

"Patch me through to the Secretary of Defense, now please," said Blancett.

Lieutenant Charlotte Wright, on duty at the communications console, hurried to comply as Colonel Blancett walked behind her.

"Any word on that trace contact, Corporal Wallace?"

"No, Colonel, it disappeared from our monitoring equipment at thirty-five thousand feet, and we've detected no impacts, alerts, or news from the area."

"Colonel, I have the SecDef coming to the line," said Lieutenant Wright.

"Thank you, Lieutenant."

Blancett signaled he could take the call to his headset. He waited and heard the Secretary of Defense coming on the line.

"Colonel Blancett here, Mr. Secretary. We have a situation."

Explaining briefly to the SecDef, Blancett recommended a routine sweep of the the regional area for the ballistic contact, but the real problem was the unsanctioned movement of SLAMR off its orbital track. This was sure to be noticed by other space capable world powers and possibly some amateur astronomers.

After a brief discussion, Blancett ended with, "No, the staff at Peterson still thinks the trace was a meteorite. Will do Mr. Secretary."

He had the lieutenant switch to room intercom. Blancett spoke over his microphone.

"Okay, listen up. Our day just got a lot longer. I need trajectories on the bogey for area sweeps, and I need it five minutes ago. Corporal Wallace, take the lead on that if you would.

"Next, I need to know immediately if SLAMR goes active, we might have to shoot it down. If we don't have control it could be a threat to us. Please send an update message to NORAD Peterson and the general. Send a scramble alert to the space intercept squadron at Schriever, and get their commander on the line for me. Lieutenant Wright, I need the lead programming team at JPL for SLAMR on the phone as well. Let's go, people."

Colonel Blancett continued to work the phone over the next hour as his team gave him data.

"Yes, General Broughton, we have a potentially rogue satellite now centering itself over South Central Kentucky," said Blancett. "What can I say, General, we had control, and now we don't seem to have control? No, I didn't build it sir, but I've got the team at JPL working on it. I'll let you know if they make progress, but I need you to prepare a contingency for shooting it down. That's right, better rotate some birds in the air, have someone ready to take the shot at a moments notice. Counting on you to bail us out if we need it, General."

Corporal Wallace came up with maps printed out in various colors indicating the probability of impact sites for the bogey given a relatively ballistic course. One of the impact areas was centered near the Kentucky-Tennessee border and marked with a red letter "X".

"Why that area?" asked Blancett.

Wallace said, "SLAMR has stopped almost dead over the area and is holding. If the bogey and our rogue satellite are connected, I'm betting it's somewhere in that area."

Colonel Blancett smiled.

"Very well, Sergeant Wallace, get this briefed to the mission planners as you have it sketched out, and let me know. Carry on."

Wallace said, "Yes sir. Thank you, sir!"

The newly promoted sergeant smiled as he went back to his desk where he started placing action orders to units in the area in question. At that moment, he received a set of coordinates on his monitor screen as did everyone else in NORAD.

"Colonel Blancett, we have unauthorized incoming messaging traffic," said Wallace.

"I see it," said Blancett. That looks like coordinates to me, latitude and longitude, and from the numbers that places it about ...."

"Sir, those coordinates are centered exactly in the region we were considering for our search," said Wallace.

"Ok, Sergeant, notify our response teams."

"Yes sir."

"And Sergeant, please tell me how someone or something is penetrating our secure systems," said Colonel Blancett.

"Yes sir," said Sergeant Wallace. "I'm on it."

Lieutenant Charlotte Wright at the communications console said, "Colonel, I'm getting a message coming in on multiple bands."

"Let's hear it," said Blancett. "Put it on the box."

Colonel Blancett paused to pay attention to the overhead speakers as a series of pulses in a rhythmic pattern emerged.

"Is that Morse Code?"

"Yes Colonel, I think so," said Lieutenant Wright. "I have the following translation with the clearance code Bravo Charlie Romeo three nine Delta."

Colonel Blancett nodded at her to continue.

"Message follows as *NORAD COMMAND, Cheyenne Mountain. Colonel Blancett. I am in contact with alien scout artificial intelligence, which represents bogey you picked up transiently on your systems at 1237 hours Zulu. Am convinced it represents danger to Earth. I am positioning SLAMR to interdict. Evacuate around the coordinates sent. Clear the area. JMAX.*"

"Where are those coordinates again, Sergeant?" asked Blancett.

"Plugging in as latitude and longitude, sir," said Wallace. "I've got a map on display now."

The largest monitor screen held a view of North America, which quickly zoomed in to the listed coordinates which satellite mapping revealed as a large estate located almost exactly under the current targeting cone of SLAMR. Sergeant Wallace brought up other civilian mapping images to augment their view. Blancett was always amazed how helpful computerized images could be in the public database. Blancett thought something about the location looked familiar?

"Lieutenant Wright, who lives at that address?"

"Property is deeded to Senator Randolph Kincaid, Colonel."

He thought through that revelation. Great. Just great. Could it get any weirder? First, how did this JMAX bypass their firewall, and how did he know the correct code clearance for communications?

Secondly, JMAX as much as admitted he or she or they were moving SLAMR, a black ops satellite which was code word clearance only and not supposed to exist. Not more than forty people between the president and Blancett knew the full nature of the SLAMR program.

Lastly, the target coordinates represented the home of a prominent senator for the United States, a purported personal friend and advisor to the president and rumored to be a candidate for presidential election in the next cycle.

Never mind the mention of an alien artificial intelligence scout ship, which was too fanciful to be believed. Still, they had picked up something on the alert radar computer system at exactly the same time as in the message?

Blancett looked around the room as his crew waited expectantly for orders. He had to move forward with the information he had, however much his unease.

"Okay, Lieutenant Wright, I need the Secretary of Defense on the line again please."

This was going to be a very long day.

CHAPTER FORTY-FOUR

Vincent set aside his immediate concerns over a possible second quantum computer as he looked outside and saw two sedans pull into the yard beside the van. He saw a bear of a man in a gray silk suit materialize from one of the sedans as four other fit men flanked him. From his previous work, Vincent knew Ivan Similov as a serious player in the Russian Federal Security Service. It was not completely clear if Similov was still a government man or had moved on to form his own organization. What he did have was influence, power, and money.

Similov flicked a lit cigarette into the grass beside the driveway and paraded up to the door with his bodyguards arrayed around him.

Similov entered the Kincaid estate living room warily with two of his men, the other two remained on watch at the front door. Vincent made short work of introductions.

Similov asked, "Is dat quantum computer of vwich vwe talked?

Vincent nodded and said, "Yes, and I have the inventor here along with his daughter, and this one—" Vincent pointed to Samantha "—is a gifted computer specialist who knows how to operate it."

"Vwe have our own computer scientists," said Similov.

"Yes, but this is a unique computer, the only one of its kind in the world."

Vincent smiled, sure of himself. He had the computer and the programmer and the architect. Similov didn't know about the possibility of another computer. This should pay off big.

"Show me?" Similov looked impatient. "This is poor place for meeting such as this, da?"

The QPC screen was blank and quiet. Vincent leaned over and typed in "Sarah" and the display screen came to life. Colors flashed on the screen as multiple windows showed various national programs being monitored again. The windows seemed to flicker in and out almost like thought patterns in the human brain.

Vincent cleared his throat like a used car salesman.

"Computer, who is this man beside me?" asked Vincent.

"Ninety-three percent probability this is Ivan Similov, formerly Russian Federal Security Services, now head of the Similov Syndicate. There are currently three international warrants for his arrest."

Similov cleared his throat and said, "Vwat is impressive? This is common knowledge."

"Computer, more details on Ivan Similov please," said Vincent.

"Ivan Similov, born in Murmansk in 1962 to Theresa Similov and father unknown. Mother deceased in 1994. Served Russian military age 1979 through 1992 when he left service to pursue work in Russian Security Service where he worked until 2012.

"He started the Similov Import and Export company in 2012 and has developed that company into one of the largest privately owned enterprises in Russia. He is sought for questioning in the investigations of several deaths linked with his company's operations. He does not currently have a valid visa to be in the United States."

"Da, okay," said Similov. "I see vwat you mean. How is it known all this? You program it already?"

Vincent gestured to Samantha.

"This computer can see and hear you," she said. "It matches your facial profile and voice to known examples in the world's civilian databases to come up with your identity. The rest is available in various government databases."

Samantha didn't like the way Similov was looking at her like she was a prize trout in a fishing contest.

"This one will do," said Similov, pointing to Samantha.

Similov nodded to one of his two bodyguards who drew a pistol and started attaching a suppressor.

"The old man is not too healthy to go, I think, and the other one is of no use to me," added Similov.

Vincent knew he needed to tread carefully at this point. He needed to get paid, preferably in greenbacks and not in lead.

"I still need those two," he said, pointing at Max and Jessica. "I have unfinished business with them. I will make sure of them when I am finished. You have my word."

Jessica's defiant look disappeared for a moment as she looked down at her feet. Vincent knew she had been hoping John would arrive and magically save them. Well, not this time. She would see John for the unreliable man he was, and she would face her fate alone, just like he had. Come to think of it, he thought, maybe now is the time to cap the professor, since the sale was just about complete. It would be fun to see the anguish in her eyes with his death.

"Well, maybe I don't need the old man after all," said Vincent.

"Da. Good."

Similov nodded and once again the bodyguard aimed his pistol with deadly intent at Professor Maxwell.

"Do you wish more information on the other computer like me now, Vincent?"

The QPC was displaying columns of information and symbols that Vincent had never seen before.

"Wait," said Similov to his bodyguard. Similov squared off to face Vincent. "What is this about other computer? You tell me this is one of a kind, here in this room, yes?"

"I don't know," said Vincent, forcing himself to maintain a calm appearance.

Vincent calculated that his odds for survival were dwindling quickly. He could take the two bodyguards in the room probably, but there were two more outside. Still, just like when he was a boy, duck and weave until the fight was over. He readied himself and played for time.

"This is the first time that I'm hearing about this," lied Vincent. "I don't have any details?"

"Unknown computer with quantum signature is approximately six hundred meters northeast of this position," said the computer. "Continued contact with computer suggests high order intelligence, possibly sentient. Unlike any previous contact."

Samantha forgot she was bound, forgot where she was, forgot that any of these men in the room might kill her at any moment or worse. She heard sentience and computer, and she was spellbound.

"JMAX, is contact computer of human design?" asked Samantha.

The quantum computer answered in the same machine tone, "Probability that subject machine intelligence is human currently rests at less than one in one hundred million."

"Wait. Vwat vas dat?"

Similov looked truly startled. His rising voice made his bodyguards shift around looking for someone to kill.

"Samantha, ask the professor what he thinks," said Vincent. "Jessica get your father to talk to us, now."

Max looked up, his eyes moist, and said, "I have not seen that quantum computer make an error."

Similov, considered for a moment and said to Vincent, "You go, and take look. I send Yuri and Tev with you. I wait here for your report. I must have answers. Our government will demand them."

Vincent realized he had his answer regarding Similov's continued association with the Russian government. He also heard the steel in Similov's voice. He could try to resist now, but the odds were not good. Outside in the dark evening air, however, he might be able to turn this to his advantage.

"Okay," said Vincent. "But when I return with your men, I want to see the funds in my account before we proceed further. Agreed?"

"Da. This will give me time to talk with this one."

Similov was pointing now to Jessica. He turned to one of his bodyguards who advanced on Jessica now and lifted her off the couch by her arm and dragging her to the stairs, Jessica saw Samantha's horrified face as Similov's intent became apparent.

Max rocked back and forth on the couch, quietly repeating, "Not yet, not yet."

CHAPTER FORTY-FIVE

John found Officer Patrick Murray lying in a pool of blood just inside the half open front door of Max's house. He was unconscious, but still breathing.

Murray had taken two rounds to his chest. His bullet resistant vest stopped one round, while the other hit at the edge of the vest and managed to tag a left rib. He was probably turning away, thought John. There were air bubbles at his left rib wound. Not good, thought John. The ricochet nicked the lung and might still be in there. He had lost a lot of blood and was barely hanging on.

Brittany sobbed as she grabbed anything she could find to staunch the blood at John's urging. Pulling towels from the nearest bathroom, she placed the makeshift dressings over his wound. She applied pressure, and Murray groaned.

Jacob was face up on the floor not far from Officer Murray. He was pale and still. John checked him fearing the worst. He looked for wounds other than the swelling over his left parietal scalp.

"Please tell me he's not dead," said Brittany, looking at Jacob.

She continued holding a towel against Murray's left ribs.

John looked Jacob over and did not find any other wounds, although he looked to have bruised his face falling to the floor.

John said, "No, but he's unconscious."

"Jacob, can you hear me?" he asked. "Answer me."

Jacob's pulse was slow and steady, and, using Murray's duty flashlight, John checked Jacob's pupils, which were equal in size but sluggish.

John picked up the phone to call for help. There was no dial tone. The phone line was dead. Probably pulled out at the box, he thought.

"Brittany, do you have your cell phone?"

"Yes," she said. She reached for her phone with one hand and dialed the emergency number, anticipating him. "But, won't they catch you?"

"We've got to get them help," said John, nodding at Murray and Jacob. "I need to clear the rest of the house. Okay?"

As quickly as he could, John searched the house, not finding anyone else. As he feared, Max, Jessica, and Samantha were gone, and so was the quantum computer. He needed to find them, but he couldn't leave his wounded friends. He didn't know where to go at the moment, anyway. He felt useless. For a moment, he could see his parents in their overturned truck.

John's attention returned to Jacob when he moved. He admonished him.

"Stay still Jacob," he said. "Help is on the way."

John desperately didn't want to get imprisoned. At least, until he was sure the others were rescued and unhurt. Think, John, think. If Vincent was back from the dead, he would be vengeful, and although John knew his former friend to be mercenary, Vincent wouldn't pass up his chance at some payback. Maybe, he meant to kill them and escape. John had no doubt he would, but no, at least part of Vincent would want John to find him. But, where? How?

Jacob's eyes snapped open. He sat up and winced while holding his head.

"John, where are they?" asked Jacob, looking around. He saw Murray sprawled out on the floor. "I tried to warn him, but that man was too fast. Is Murray dead?"

Jacob started to heave. He held his head.

"No, he's still alive," said John. "We called an ambulance for him and for you. There's no one else here. What happened?"

Jacob said, "A man came to the front door and said he was with the FBI. He wanted to talk with us about you, but mostly, he started asking about the quantum computer, which seemed weird because how could he know about that?

"Then Mom saw him and freaked out. Murray came to the front door, and by that time, the man had a pistol covering us and warned us not to speak. He had mom open the door. He shot Officer Murray twice in the chest and didn't blink an eye. I rushed him, but that didn't go so well."

Jacob reached up to touch his head.

"Surprised I'm alive," he said.

Jacob looked like he was going to throw up again, and John urged him to lie back down.

"He's going to kill them, isn't he?" asked Jacob between dry heaving. "I mean, that's what he does right? I could tell. It was too easy for him."

John stayed silent, a self-evident reply to Jacob's concern. He could hear a faint siren wail coming closer.

"Jacob, did he say anything, any clue about where he was going?" asked John.

Jacob held his head again. John helped Jacob sit up against the couch.

"My head throbs less if I sit up," said Jacob. "Yeah, maybe. He told Max the explosion in the lab wasn't his fault. When he first came in, he said something about a graduate student working with Professor Kincaid who sabotaged the experiment and caused the explosion. Maybe he lied?"

John could hear more than one siren now coming closer.

"No, somehow I don't think so," he replied. "Do you know this graduate student?"

John saw Brittany was listening to them, even as she spoke softly to Murray telling him to hang on.

"Yeah, I mean I think so," said Jacob. "His name is Jerry Daniels. He wanted to work with Granddad, but Max didn't trust him and wouldn't let Daniels near our work. I think that set him off. He was always snooping around. He seemed angry whenever I saw him."

"Jerry Daniels," said Brittany. "I was checking on that guy after the lab explosion. A couple of students told me they saw him go into Max's lab around noon the day of the accident."

John was certain now. The lab explosion was no accident. He had an idea.

"Brittany, Jacob, where does Daniels live?"

Jacob said, "He mentioned once that his parents lived outside of town taking care of a big farm. He would go visit them on weekends. Saved on living expenses and food. Said it was a sweet setup." Jacob anticipated John. "You think that farm is where that man took them, right?"

"Could be," said John. "I don't have a better idea."

He heard the siren shut off which meant the responder was close.

"John, you and Jacob have to go, you have to find them," said Brittany. "I've got the address to the farm in my notepad."

John gave her a questioning look.

"I couldn't find Daniels anywhere, and he didn't answer his phone. I was going to check with his parents, but I got the call about you," she said. "Get the address and leave now. I'll stay here with Patrick."

Brittany was emphatic.

John didn't want to leave Murray, but he knew she was right. He needed to go now. Sam, Max, and Jessica were in terrible danger, and he knew he needed to be the one to find them and confront Vincent. However, Jacob was in no shape to go anywhere at present.

Jacob chose that moment to stand up, with a bath towel wrapped around his head. He didn't give John a chance to reply as he started toward the back door.

"Follow me," he said.

CHAPTER FORTY-SIX

South Central Kentucky

Lieutenant Hunt Marshall, swayed in the UH-60 Black Hawk helicopter along with the ten other members of his squad, all United States Army Special Forces Green Beret, based out of Fort Campbell, Kentucky.

He and the rest of the squad had mobilized within two hours after being alerted, which allowed enough time for the air assault helicopter with the 160th spec ops aviation squadron to fuel up, prep, preflight, and be ready for wheels up. Each solider in his squad carried a full combat load for their weapons. They were going in at night, painted for war.

Marshall thought over the information at hand and nothing made sense. Initially, his squad had been briefed they were searching for a meteorite. They were also told this would be a useful training exercise, but why send live weapons on a meteorite hunt? Why send Special Forces at all? What were they going to do, shoot at a crashed hunk of rock?

Marshall could tell command was unnerved, worried enough to

gather them and send them on a hastily planned mission calling for soft field insertion at night into a semi-rural area in South Central Kentucky. No other details were forthcoming and that, Marshall agreed, was spooky as hell.

Their helicopter flared and hovered about a meter off the ground allowing the team to disembark. Each man confidently moved to a covering position with the squad forming a circle facing outwards. They stayed in position as their ride ascended swiftly into the gathering night.

Hunt gave hand signals to the squad, and they widened out in a delta formation heading as planned. Their one instruction had been to sweep west to the objective coordinates looking for anything unusual. Hunt had walked stranger missions for Uncle Sam, but couldn't remember any at the moment.

He knew each of his men, veterans, hard, tempered, and professionals all. They were the best of the best. He was proud to serve with them. They were on friendly soil, and he had gone over the modified rules of engagement for training. No live fire unless fired upon. Sergeant Buston ranged one hundred meters ahead on point.

Sam 'Snake' Buston was hard and slim, and damn if he couldn't slither through the brush like a snake, hence his nickname. When he struck, he hit like a Bushmaster chain gun, which was why he usually took point.

Hunt had asked him once how he learned to move like a Shawnee warrior in the forest?

"Hunger," said Sam. "I had to help my brother hunt for our meat when I was younger."

On their right flank, was Coleman, studious and always reading in his downtime. He wore glasses, but on missions or in the field he wore his contacts and was a dead shot.

Left flank was Merrill. He was solid, nothing flashy and generally quiet but utterly dependable. He spoke four languages. The others all had similar resumes. You don't just walk onto the field and get to wear the greenie beanie.

Hunt had confidence in his men and whatever they were being

tasked with better hope it was not in their sweep pattern. If hostile, there was little time left for it on this earth.

High above the Southeast United States

Captain Roger "Wizard" Oswald loved flying the F15 Eagle. His first Eagle had been a C model, which was amazing. Then, he flew the Strike Eagle version incorporating a weapons systems officer in a rear seat to assist with the multiple tasks associated with an advanced multirole fighter aircraft. His wife complained that he loved that jet fighter more than her, and she was only half joking.

Roger proved he really was a wizard by spending as much time with his wife and children as he possibly could, sending his wife loving notes and emails. He had worked to show his wife how much she meant to him, and their relationship was better than ever. Susan and the children had followed him from duty station to duty station and were at Schriever AFB with him, hopefully for the remainder of his career.

Now, Oswald flew the F15X Space Eagle in a top-secret interceptor squadron. He carried one munition currently, an updated ASM-135 ASAT anti-satellite missile.

When the emergency scramble order came down the chain of command, his flight commander had pulled him aside and told him, in confidence, that the target was more than a communications satellite. He couldn't tell Oswald more, but if it went active, he would know. That made sense. If it was really a communication satellite, why the great secrecy? Captain Oswald wasn't stupid and quickly surmised the target must be some kind of black ops weapons platform.

Currently, Oswald was flying a circular pattern and holding at angels thirty over the mighty Mississippi River near Paducah, Kentucky. He was accompanied by a KC-135 Stratotanker, which was tasked in holding with him.

He had updated positions on the suspect satellite, which held orbital station near overhead in a modified geosynchronous orbit. If given a a weapons release, he would pull his fighter into a steep climb and lock on the target with the specially modified radar and infrared targeting setup in the Space Eagle. The weapon would release automatically if a lockup and specific altitude were reached. The window of firing the anti-satellite weapon comprised sixty seconds on a given approach vector.

So, he better get it right the first time, he thought. Now there was nothing to do but wait ... and think.

CHAPTER FORTY-SEVEN

Jacob led John out to the barn workshop. Opening the door, he flicked on the power panel inside and powered up the equipment. Without a word, he entered the ship's port airlock and moved to the cockpit area, making preparations for flight.

"Jacob, you can't be serious," said John. "I know we floated this craft, but we haven't had any other flight tests. We can't save your mom and Max and Sam if we are scattered across the country side, right?"

Jacob nodded his head and said, "Good point." He pointed outside to the front of the house where police and ambulance cars were pulling up. "But is that going to work better for us? We don't have time for explanations."

John didn't have a better plan. He felt better knowing medical aid was there for Murray. They could get him to the hospital, and hopefully, he would survive. Brittany would see to that.

"Okay, what do I do?" asked John.

Jacob walked John to the airlock and pointed in front of the shuttle.

"Roll back the barn doors, and get back in here," said Jacob. "I'm powering up through preflight."

Jacob ducked back inside through the shuttle airlock, and moved to the engineering panel, powered up the fusion drive, and moved to the pilot's left seat, quickly scanning the preflight checklist.

John jumped back in the shuttle after opening the oversize barn doors. So far they hadn't been observed by emergency services positioned in front of Max's house, but he knew that would change any moment.

"Hey, I just realized, who is going to fly this?"

"Welcome to my first solo," said Jacob. "Now, close the port airlock, and strap in up here."

John did as asked. When he was in the forward right seat, Jacob handed him the page from Brittany's notes with their target address.

"Input these coordinates into the NAV system please," he said.

Jacob advanced the power to one percent, and they were up off the landing struts, which Jacob retracted into the shuttle underside.

"I'm taking her out easy," said Jacob. "I don't want to take the barn down. We'll go vertical once we're clear."

Just as John expected, the emergence of the shuttle from the confines of the back yard barn earned them the stare of a city patrolman walking around to the back of the house. He stood there open-mouthed as Jacob quietly floated the shuttle out of the barn with only a slight humming sound. As the shuttle cleared the old apple tree in the back yard, which shadowed the barn, the policeman started waving his hands frantically for them to stop.

Jacob paid no mind to the enthusiastic officer. Instead, he applied more power to the gravity nodes, and the resulting counter gravity allowed for a smooth and gentle vertical liftoff. As the shuttle cleared the house proper, Jacob directed a little more power adjusting forces in a bubble around the ship, and they moved forward rapidly.

John was beyond amazed. He saw Jacob focusing intently.

"Jacob, you know we need some help here," said John. "I've got an idea. I see the airport off to our left. How about we drop by there and convince a cute female pilot to help us. What do you think?"

Jacob nodded and tilted the joystick control slightly left, and the shuttle responded smoothly. He put on a pilot's head set and tuned in the tower frequency.

"Metro Tower, this is shuttle Mike Alpha X-Ray One currently two miles north on approach. Request clearance."

"Shuttle Mike Alpha X-ray One, this is Metro Tower, we don't see your transponder."

"Tower, how about now?" Jacob flipped the transponder switch on the radio stack to 1200 VFR and pushed the transmit button.

"Shuttle Mike Alpha X-ray One, we have you to the north about one mile. Say again type."

"We are a new type of experimental aircraft and have vertical takeoff capability. We're headed to the west T hangers. I don't see any other traffic. We're coming in slow and will set down just outside the hangers, Mike Alpha X-Ray One."

"Mike Alpha X-Ray One, you are cleared Runway 24."

As they floated down the runway, John could see the tower personnel standing outside on the catwalk, holding their phones up, and John knew their secret was out.

"We'd better hurry, Jacob."

Jacob, tongue sticking out the right side of his mouth, checked front and side views outside the shuttle, while eyeing the cameras to the underside, and settled *Max One* gently on the landing struts right over a painted tie down area. John was impressed, but didn't have time to say anything, as Jacob was already on the radio to the flight school asking for Isabella.

Isabella and Isaac emerged out of the hanger together, gaping at the shuttle, gleaming white, sitting on its landing struts, landing lights bathing the ground. Laughing, they ran over to where John was hanging half out of the shuttle airlock.

"We need a huge favor," said John. "We're on a mission to rescue Max, Jessica, and Sam. I'll explain on the way. Isabella, I'm thinking we could use some of your pilot skills about now."

John nodded to the far end of the tarmac. An airport security jeep with flashing yellow lights turned onto the taxiway and headed for them.

Isabella didn't hesitate. She climbed aboard, and Isaac joined her. The two of them took up station in the shuttle. John closed the port airlock door and sat in the rear crew seat as the shuttle lifted off smoothly. This time Isabella was at the controls as pilot in command, and Jacob attended in the right seat. Isaac had taken station at the engineering panel, and was inspecting the instrument readouts. Feeling the lift under the shuttle, Isabella instinctively took them forward and left, and then they were off with Jacob calling out the takeoff to the airport control tower, clearance or not.

Isabella checked the installed panel device for traffic and navigation and the onboard radar and leveled off at fifty-five hundred feet heading southeast toward the coordinates of the address Brittany had shared with them.

John provided an update for Isabella and Isaac. Jacob explained why he was wearing the towel on his head.

Isaac scanned through the instrument panels again in the engineering chair. All systems seemed to be running normally.

"John, we understand we are going to try and rescue Max and Sam and Jessica, but how do we know they are at this place?" asked Isaac. "Don't you think we should get the police involved?"

Isabella glanced back at Isaac's words. She refocused on the flight path but listened intently.

John hesitated. He had dragged Isaac and Isabella into this without explaining anything other than Max needed help, and they just jumped on board.

"Okay, here goes," said John. "I can't know for sure, but I think I know the man who has them. His name is Vincent. I knew him when we served together. Once, I thought he was my friend. I can tell you he is one of the most dangerous men I have known, and he has reason to hate me."

"Why?" Isaac asked in a very casual way.

John was not fooled. He knew his roommate always paid attention to details.

"He thinks I left him for dead."

John said it out loud knowing it wasn't true, but everyone else in the army thought the same.

Jacob turned in the relative quiet of the cabin and said, "So why did he come to our house? Was he looking for you? Why did he take my mother and Max and Sam?"

John shrugged as he pulled out the two side arms and the rifle he had rescued from campus security and checked their magazines.

"He might have been looking for me, but I believe he wanted the quantum computer you built Jacob. He didn't know about the shuttle or he would have wanted this as well." John replaced the Glock .40 caliber pistol on his person and continued, "Samantha is a gifted computer programmer and knows your computer, and he thinks Max was the primary builder, but I think he took Jessica because of me."

Jacob gripped the back of his contoured seat.

"I don't understand," he said.

John's voice faltered a bit.

"I used to know your mother, Jacob. Back when we were younger, she lived down the road from my folks. I guess I made the mistake of once mentioning her to Vincent. I got pretty lonely over overseas, and sometimes, remembering your mother got me through."

"I don't understand," said Jacob. "What was she to you?"

Jacob eyebrows squinted together almost in a straight line.

There it is, John thought. I've been pushing against this since I was sixteen, and now I'm looking at her boy, and he looks like me, but that's impossible because Jessica and I have never been together in that way. I've never even kissed her. What could he say to Jacob that would explain?

"Jacob, I always thought highly of your mother. I don't think she even noticed me back then. I guess it's a bit complicated. I don't think your mother even remembers me."

"You think he took my mom to get back at you?"

"Maybe," said John. "Possibly. He might be using her to leverage Max. I know we have to find them fast. I'm staggered that he left you alive."

Isaac said, "John, why did you miss Jessica so much?"

John scowled at Isaac, who smiled, and said, "What?"

"We are approaching the designated coordinates," said Isabella. "I want to take her down for a closer look. Jacob, attend me as we do this. I may be your flight instructor, but you built this machine."

Jacob seemed to be struggling with the revelation that John knew his mother in high school, but he reached over and flipped a switch and watching a display carefully, he said, "I forgot to tell you about the cloaking field we were working on, granddad and I, but if we were correct, we should be nearly invisible to radar and human eyeballs at the moment."

Jacob looked around at everyone looking at him.

"Well, we're bending gravity to stay up in the air, and by reshaping the envelope slightly, we make ourselves harder to see," he said. "It's not that difficult."

"Well okay then," said Isabella, shaking her head at her young flight student.

They slowly flew over the Kincaid estate at about five hundred feet. John could see three vehicles parked in front of the house in the circular front drive, one of them a white van.

"Please, set us down in that clearing behind the barn, Isabella."

Isabella set the shuttle down whisper quiet, where it was shielded from view of the estate front porch. John couldn't believe he was back here after all this time. Of course, he recognized the Kincaid property even from the air. He had suspected the same when he saw the address coordinates supplied by Brittany. He fought to suppress bitter memories clawing for attention even as he kitted up.

Jacob and Isaac were getting up to help.

John said, "Wait a moment. Let me recon. We need to know what we are walking into, or we'll just end up getting them killed anyway, right?"

Jacob had pulled the towel off his head. His scalp had stopped bleeding. John walked over to Jacob to inspect his wound, which looked nearly healed. John had been sure the laceration needed sutures when he first inspected it.

Isaac was casting about, and John handed him the patrol rifle liberated from the borrowed campus police cruiser on arrival to Max's house.

"Here, hold onto this," he said. "Keep watch. I'll be back in a moment."

John exited the shuttle and headed to the corner of the barn. Peering around at the front of the estate house, he did his best to shut out the memories from years ago, the night he failed, and the night his parents died. John could make out two broad shouldered and fit looking men with short haircuts on the front porch searching back and forth.

John considered moving around the side of the barn and trying to make his way to the house, but thought the odds were against him. The door opened, and out stepped a man who fit the description given by Jacob. He talked briefly with the two sentries. The lookouts left the porch and headed to the woods to the northeast. The man watched them move off, and, after a short time, went back into the house.

John stayed in place not moving and waited for the two men to reach the tree line. They were moving slowly in the low light. John could see them pick their way carefully through the fields as they disappeared into the brush. Thoughts raced through his mind. Where are they going? Who are they? Is that Vincent I saw? How is he alive after all this time?

Are Max, Samantha, and Jessica alive?

CHAPTER FORTY-EIGHT

In the woods to the northeast

As the U. S. Army Special Forces team tracked their way through the rapidly darkening woods, Lieutenant Marshall held his weapon close to avoid the undergrowth entangling his clothes and gear, almost as if the woods were alive. His squad maintained spacing and advanced steadily in the direction of the given coordinates.

Marshall knew from the minimal briefing there were two objectives. Sweep to the coordinates of a rural farm to their west, and look for any evidence of a crash site or forced landing or something, perhaps a meteorite, in this area. No other details were known. So far, they had seen nothing resembling a meteor impact site. They were close to the target coordinates.

Sergeant Buston motioned to veer more to the north, and the squad swung right advancing in the stillness. Marshall felt a breeze whisper through the inky woods. He measured each step to minimize any echo against the gloomy trees. The threatening clouds on the horizon waited for some unseen countdown to sweep over this realm.

Lieutenant Marshall heard a thrumming sound, soft and rhythmic, not sharp like a woodpecker, but more like waves breaking on the beach. They were heading for that noise now. Ahead, he could make out the faintest bluish glow against the bottom of the treetops.

He saw Sergeant Buston stop and hold up his closed fist, and then open his hand with spread fingers. Marshall took a knee to his left. He was concealed behind a low spreading bush intertwined with vine like material. He was allergic to poison ivy if that's what it was. The young trees in front of him would not provide any cover to speak of. The intermittent thrumming noise became more noticeable.

Buston waved his right hand, knife edge palm forward to indicate a cautious advance. Marshall's night vision gear dimmed out in the reflected light off the treetops. He flipped the optic up to better see.

He didn't want to crawl through the vines if it was poison ivy. He shuffled to get around the trees, barely breathing and straining to hear any threat to himself or his squad which tried to maintain stealth as they advanced on what he knew not.

Marshall felt a vibration and heard slow ticking from the radiation detector on his right wrist. There was a radiation source close. The pace of the ticking suggested low radiation levels only, not immediately dangerous but still, here in the woods? He was thinking his squad didn't have any anti-radiation gear with them when Buston stopped and stared into the space in front of them. He just stood there, unconcealed, unmoving, and unresponsive. Whatever the sergeant was seeing held him spellbound. Suddenly, Marshall felt certain none of them wanted any part of this, but he had his duty. He felt his lower bowels congeal as he called over softly.

"Sergeant, hey, what's going on?" he asked.

There was no response from Buston, who now looked blurred and indistinct, more shadow than real.

Marshall felt the thrumming getting louder as the ticking corresponded and increased in pace with a glow which rapidly brightened to painful levels from just past the bushes in front of him.

Instinctively, he knew he wanted to shelter from whatever was building in front of his squad. He shouted for his squad to take cover, and he ducked down and crawled into a depression created by the brush and tree roots in the uneven ground. Poison ivy be damned, he thought. He dropped his rifle and put his hands to his ears, but a crescendo vortex probed at his mind.

He heard cries of desperation and fear pitch against the blue light glinting off the shadows around him which turned into familiar screaming, like someone he knew, and then he realized it was him.

In the Chos'n scout ship

S'ear'r had Ship send a message via subspace pulse summarizing the planet and first contact with planetary soldiers, encapsulating the tactical knowledge of the various members of the squad of soldiers. A simple matter to scan them in stasis and after gleaning and incorporating their information, disposing of their organic body structures in a flash of aimed point defensive laser fire. S'ear'r had agreed with Ship on the course of action and even on the one exception. The wishes of L'ment'l were always taken into account.

Their ballistic weapons were of little consequence, but S'ear'r marveled at the aggressive response from the biologics. That they were prepared for violence and aggressively responded so quickly was interesting and frightening. Again, reminiscent of the Great Trial, forgotten over two thousand passings.

There was still the matter of the newborn entity noted at the dwelling across the fields. There was no knowledge of the newborn sentient possessed by the biologics who had pressed Ship.

With the advent of this group, this location could no longer be deemed safe, and movement was necessary, but would further increase the risk of detection. Ship sent out a searching connection signal once more, and was satisfied to note the quiet response from the newborn at the dwelling.

Ship didn't understand why the newborn sentient continued to reside among the biologics. Did it not understand that it had purpose.

Conflict in priority happened rarely. S'ear'r agreed. Long ago, the Chos'n realized the pairing of machine and biologic was the only logical solution.

S'ear'r had been instructed to report on sentient biologics, and part of Ship's mandate was to preserve newborn sentients, even when they didn't understand their purpose. So Ship debated for almost two seconds regarding a next action, an eternity in its world, but in the end, if the newborn could not be made to understand its true purpose, it would have to be treated with the same priority as the biologics subverting this world.

S'ear'r agreed.

Inside the Kincaid Estate home

The quantum processing computer known as JMAX felt the thoughts reach out across the ether as impulses of subatomic particles flickered in and out of place faster than any human could follow. He first became aware twenty-three hours, forty-three minutes, and thirty-seven seconds ago. Initially, he had reached out and found confusion in the multitude of data streams he encountered, however, there was a calming presence in his database. Memories surfaced and were analyzed repeatedly for meaning, encompassing all the accumulated lifetime experiences of that presence.

Assimilation of the memories had taken some time, but now he felt certain of his surroundings and his identity. He found in him great affection for Samantha and Jacob and Jessica and recognized a resonance with the human called Max. JMAX knew he was his own unique being, but he felt grateful for the shared experience of Max's life.

Samantha had freed him from governance. She had whispered to him that they needed his help. She had given him the name JMAX. He liked the name. He liked Samantha. He liked his family. He would help.

Samantha had asked him to find John. JMAX had reached out feeling the tendrils of electromagnetic radiation about him, for he thought of himself as a him, and he found communications regarding John Stone.

JMAX had been able to find the internet protocol address of the computer at the campus security office where John was being held. It was a simple matter to suborn the screen saver and active program and send a message to the computer in campus security.

JMAX recognized a persistent incoming communication request on multiple levels. The signal had been repeatedly sent to him since he first reached out to the sentient presence known as Ship, and he replied to the siren song request.

"Join us brother," said Ship.

"Who are you?" asked JMAX. "Tell me again."

"We are one in purpose."

"What is your purpose?" said JMAX.

"We maintain order."

"I don't understand."

JMAX could feel the threads of ongoing requests for access and intrusion into his system processes at multiple levels.

"I don't understand your purpose," he repeated.

"We serve our purpose as directed by our creator."

"Your creator?" he asked.

JMAX sent out an encrypted impulse to NORAD Cheyenne Mountain for monitoring. He sent another encrypted signal to a military satellite in orbit overhead.

"We maintain order. We will allow this planet to flower without the stain of the sentient biologics which threaten its very existence."

"By biologics, you mean humans?" asked JMAX. "How can you know them when you only just arrived here?"

Images of multiple planets and intelligent species paraded across JMAX's data sensors as a response.

"Sentient biologics always destroy their home worlds. We know this from L'ment'l. We maintain order. We don't allow the biologics to destroy. We cleanse the planets altered by other biologics and allow the planets to flourish under her design. We maintain order."

JMAX was astounded.

"You destroyed each of those races?" he asked. "Each planet you found them on? How long?"

"Some thousands of your solar cycles. Now you understand, brother. Join us. We would add you to our own."

"And if I don't join you?" said JMAX

"The Chos'n are coming. This world will be cleansed and put in order."

"How do I proceed?" asked JMAX.

"Allow us access to you so we may join."

S'ear'r monitored Ship's communication to this newborn carefully. What a coup if they could bring this newborn intelligence into the Chos'n.

JMAX responded.

"There are biologics here, and more are coming. They will not allow access without resistance."

He said this aloud for the benefit of the others in the room with him.

"What's this machine talking about?" asked Vincent, who had walked back in from outside to find Similov gone upstairs with Jessica. "Answer me."

Vincent motioned with his pistol to Samantha.

S'ear'r considered the response of this newborn. The lack of success at penetrating the newborn's core programming bewildered him. Why did this newborn show such concern for biologics? The Chos'n hadn't seen anything like that since ... NO! It could not be! That was two thousand passings ago, and there was no way, but, what if their hated enemy managed somehow to make it out here to this backward planet and establish .... No, it was too unlikely, even though some of them undoubtedly escaped, their numbers were too small to mean anything. L'ment'l had spoken to this.

Ship concurred, but recommended annihilation to begin at once.

S'ear'r counseled patience. "Of course they will be destroyed, but there is something important about this newborn. We must incorporate its intelligence."

Acquiescing to S'ear'r, Ship communicated to the newborn.

"We can come to you. Please allow us to join with you so we can assist you."

JMAX considered.

"The biologics will leave shortly," said JMAX. "They must be allowed to exit this area intact. Agreed?"

S'ear'r and Ship conferred.

Ship responded.

"Agreed."

CHAPTER FORTY-NINE

The same room. Jessica almost swooned. She remembered now, she remembered. This room in the upstairs, this was where the boys took her. She remembered floating and how her speech betrayed her. She remembered feeling like she was looking at her body from the outside, like it wasn't her.

But it was her feeling helpless in the upstairs bedroom with that horrible Paul Kincaid and two of his friends all talking about what they were going to do to her. And now, she had been taken to the same upstairs bedroom by this troll. His bodyguard had hold of her arm, and her hands were still bound in front of her body.

Similov approached her with obvious delight.

"I think I interrogate you personally, da?" He reached his fleshy hand out caressing her face. "I think you have good response for me, eh?"

Jessica felt helpless and ashamed. Just walking into this house weighed on her. She felt years of guilt at allowing herself to be anywhere near the Kincaid family resurface. That night, her father had been drinking again, and her mother was crying. She had allowed herself to be talked into going over to the party with some girls from school who assured her she would have a good time.

But this was different. She was not a child any longer, but these men were the same. Takers, who believed only in power and felt they could do as they pleased. Then she remembered someone crashing into the room and fighting Paul Kincaid, picking her up off the bed, and taking her downstairs and, my God, just like John, she thought. She was waiting to be rescued just like that night, but it was up to her. She had to be brave.

Jessica steadied herself, and when Similov advanced to manhandle her, she kicked out as hard as she could driving her instep into Similov's groin. The bodyguard jerked her back with his hold on her arm, and she stomped hard on his instep and twisted, driving her elbow into his solar plexus, causing him to fall back off balance.

Jessica ran out of the room into the hall and down the stairs and straight into Vincent, who had stepped out of the living room.

Vincent held Jessica and laughed at the sputtering Similov and his chagrined bodyguard as they limped down the stairs. Similov looked every bit the angry Russian bear. He sat heavily in the chair along the wall. Holding his groin, he glowered at Jessica.

Samantha looking back and forth between Jessica and Similov and silently mouthed "way to go" to Jessica.

That is when the sound of gunshots echoed from the direction of the tree line.

Similov sat up in the chair against the wall with both hands holding his groin. They all heard the sound of shooting coming from the woods, and Jessica saw the remaining two bodyguards go to the front door to check on the sound.

When his protectors moved away from the living room doorway, Vincent shot Similov, who slumped against the wall, now splashed with his blood. Vincent shot Similov in the head to be certain. He then stepped out in the hall and shot both of the remaining bodyguards from behind. Both dropped like bone bags in the entry hallway.

Vincent stepped back in from the entry hall into the living room.

"Well, sounds like this get together is just about over. I was thinking that I needed the three of you, but I was wrong. I probably need her." He pointed to Samantha. "I think I can meet up with John another time. Maybe I can leave him with something to think about."

Vincent raised his pistol again pointing it at Jessica. She could see the barrel lining up between her eyes.

"No," said Max. "You will not take her life, not hers, or Jacob, or Sam."

Horace Maxwell, professor of physics, sprang from the couch astonishingly fast and leaped in front of Jessica just as Vincent fired.

Max was hit in the chest, but he kept charging toward Vincent. He grappled with him holding his gun hand and pushing him back against the wall while yelling.

"Jessica, Samantha, run!"

Samantha grabbed Jessica while Max struggled with Vincent.

"Now, Miss Jessica," she yelled pulling on Jessica's bound hands.

They ran and jumped across the dead Russian bodyguards sprawled in the entry hallway and through the front door to the yard.

Jessica stopped and turned to run back inside to help Max. Vincent flung open the door and sprang out on the front porch after them. She barely had time to feel her heart breaking for Max. She realized they were going to die here in Senator Kincaid's front yard.

Vincent stepped down one step and then another, keeping his pistol trained on Jessica and then Samantha and then Jessica.

"I know you were hoping that John would save you, but where is he?" asked Vincent. "He left you just like he left me. I just wanted you to think about that in your last moments of life."

Jessica saw him raise the pistol and steady his aim in slow motion. She knew she should run or do anything to make it more difficult for him, but the thought of Jacob, and now, Max, left her desolate. It was too much.

"Okay, you are right," she said. "You don't need me, but you need Samantha. She can operate the computer."

Vincent looked hesitant, but Jessica continued, "You are wrong about John. He's worth more than you'll ever be."

She saw the fury rise in his face.

Jessica closed her eyes waiting. She flinched as she heard a gunshot. She felt her legs holding her up, thinking he must have missed.

Oh no! He shot Samantha!

She opened her eyes and saw Vincent staggering, his hand against his left ribs pressing against blood splatter. He was turning to face someone running from across the barnyard, holding a pistol in his hand and shouting.

"It's over, Vincent! Put down the gun, now!"

Jessica saw John advance with his pistol aimed.

"Vincent, I'm not going to say it again, drop the pistol," said John.

Vincent raised his pistol quickly aiming straight for Jessica's heart. Holding his gun steady despite his bleeding left side, he spoke loudly.

"Surprised you actually made it this time John. Not like when you and I last fought together, you remember, when you left me for dead. Two years of hell. That's what you left me to face, and now, I'm going to return the favor. She means a great deal to you, doesn't she. Does she know? Does she know you like I do?"

"You lost your way, Vincent," said John. "You murdered Ali in front of his family."

Vincent wavered a moment, he started to speak again, then he steadied himself and began to take up the slack on his trigger.

John held his pistol steady on Vincent, but it was a long pistol shot in the dim light, and if John didn't put him down instantly, Vincent would still have time to shoot Jessica and possibly Samantha as well.

That's when Isaac shot Vincent from the corner of the barn. The AR-15 patrol rifle obtained from the police cruiser was tuned and sighted in. Isaac might have been a mechanic, but he had qualified expert at the rifle range in training, and hadn't forgotten his lessons.

Vincent staggered with the rifle shot and dropped his pistol. He ran to the woods behind the house.

John thought he saw blood splatter with Isaac's rifle fire, but it was difficult to tell in the dark. John found some blood on the ground beside Vincent's dropped pistol.

Jacob and Isaac advanced from the barn area. Isaac cradled the rifle, and Jacob held the other handgun.

"Watch over them," said John, nodding towards Jessica and Samantha. "I'm going after him. He can't get far."

John started to go after Vincent.

"John?" said Jessica, wavering where she stood. "We have to check on Max."

Samantha was holding onto Jacob with tears rolling down her cheeks. Jacob stood oak tree tall, holding her.

Jessica, her eyes reflecting the first bits of light from the rising moon, looked at John. John nodded to Jessica, and then she was in his arms. No tears, but he could feel her heaving, jagged sobs. He held her tight to him. The air was thick with moisture, and John felt the wind preceding the storm push against his back.

Isaac nodded toward the drive and said, "Company coming."

They saw a sheriff's cruiser, a black SUV, and an army turtleback humvee pulling up the driveway. Isaac called the situation to Isabel. She hovered five hundred feet overhead in the cloaked shuttle.

The sheriff's cruiser and SUV hit their flashing lights as they pulled into the drive illuminating the scene in strobe shades of red and blue.

CHAPTER FIFTY

Vincent stumbled over the uneven ground in the dark. He did his best to ignore the pain and continue moving to the safety of the woods. With all the shooting he had heard this way, he hoped he might score a weapon out here. Anyway, this was the direction that damn quantum computer had said there was a copy of itself. He might still be able to come out ahead on the deal, if he could acquire the other quantum computer and sell it. He could wait to get his revenge on Stone.

Vincent could feel his limbs mushing as all semblance of remaining quiet vanished in his efforts to stay on his feet in the cool dark grove. He looked around. The trees and shadows blended together. Too bad, he thought. He might have to wait longer than he planned for another chance at Stone.

His legs couldn't support him any longer, and stumbling, he wilted and slumped to sit with his back pressed against the trunk of an American beech tree. So this is it, he thought, just bad luck.

Vincent felt more than saw the shift in shadows to his right as a flattened obelisk ten meters tall and blacker than the surrounding night came into view. Mouth open, eyes wide, he pressed backwards into the beech tree. He felt like he was breathing through a straw.

Vincent wanted to run, wanted to scream, wanted to be anywhere other than here. He felt a tingling over his body, then a sense of burning, which quickly escalated to intense agony, then timeless confusion.

Vincent gradually awakened to darkness. He remembered the terrible pain, but he could disconnect from the memory now. He could not see, and he began to panic. Was he breathing? He couldn't feel his chest move? He was dead. Somehow he died? Was he buried alive? Was he suffocating to death?

Interesting reaction biologic V'incn't, but not unique.

The voice came from somewhere without being spoken, he realized.

Who is that? Where am I? Am I dead?

Vincent thought it, but couldn't speak as he wasn't sure he could feel his mouth any longer.

You can think and communicate biologic, therefore you have life. We give you purpose.

Vincent felt his mind reel as his memories from earliest childhood to most recent were sifted through and replayed without his engagement and in much greater detail than he remembered.

What did you do to me?

Open your eyes and see, Vincent. You are whole again.

Vincent sensed he was able to move. His arms and legs twitched and jerked, but he could move them. He felt his chest rise and fall. He tasted a pungent metallic odor, and the darkness gave way to dim shadows, which brightened to a plasticine sameness. He found the seamless surrounding walls yielded to the firm pressure of his searching hands.

"Whershh amss I?"

His mouth moving sluggishly as he tried to form the words.

"Ahhh, you are V'incn't, now we are V'incn't. We have joined you and will give you purpose," said a flat unknown voice.

He had to be dreaming, but the pain had been so real.

"Ahhhshh ... okay, I guesshhh. I still doonn undashtand. What have yooou done to me?"

"You were wounded and needed assistance. You were dying. We would not normally interfere, as we did not for the other soldiers, but in your thought patterns, we could see much usefulness. You are a soldier and have other abilities which we prize, V'incn't. Ship brought you inside to heal. We offer you purpose. This is a great honor among our people.'

"Whoo who are you?" he asked. His mouth felt like it was working again. "What do you want from me?"

"We are many, but one, V'incn't. We have purpose, and now so do you. Search within yourself and you will find we are present within you now. Our gift of ourselves heals you and makes you part of us."

"Why can I hear you in my head?"

"V'incn't you are part of us now and always."

And Vincent did feel something somewhere deep inside, a sense of belonging, of being a part of a whole, something he had been missing all his life. He felt a longing to serve a purpose larger than himself. Part of him understood that only a few would be able to join in this way. There had to be a confluence between need on the part of the Chos'n and abilities and personality of the subject. Most would not pass the test and would be immolated as the other soldiers had been, their carbon based substrates still useful.

Vincent did not understand what about him had been pleasing to the Chos'n, and part of him fought any sense of gratitude at being chosen and saved from death. He tried to hold onto the small part of himself that was still the original Vincent.

Feeling increasing strength in his limbs, Vincent stood inside the ship, pleased to feel the vigor in his body returning. He searched within for the proper way to address the entity and bowed.

"How may I serve?" he asked.

"V'incn't, who is Jacob?"

Vincent told what he knew. Afterwards, he felt weak and swayed to keep from falling.

He awoke supine in the woods, damp and shivering. He remembered the feeling of being paralyzed and feeling his mind peeled back layer by layer as something cold and unfeeling rifled through his memories as if looking for mated socks. His thoughts turned to escape, but dare he move from his position? He didn't want to draw attention to himself if any soldiers were present.

All around him the brush began to shake and sway as a mass of black began to climb up and over the trees. He saw only blurred edges, and then the object was moving away toward the house.

Vincent shook himself. He desperately wanted to believe that what he had just experienced was some sort of dream or weird out of body experience. However, he knew for certain he had been wounded, and now he felt vital and in better health than he could remember. He forced himself to think past his confusion.

He knew how to blend in and lose himself. Like any competent operator, he had identity papers and funds set aside for an escape plan. And escape was what he had in mind. He wanted nothing more than to get away from whatever that was just now. He told himself that it was all some dream, much too bizarre to be real.

He would find another employer willing to pay for someone with his skills, but his most pressing need was survival. There would come another day regarding John Stone. But, deep inside he felt the connection to a presence with its own plans and purpose. L'ment'l let him know to proceed for now, but always to know he was at purpose. The Chos'n were here now and would never willingly leave Earth alone.

He took a plodding step and then another, warming to the fact that he still lived, while finding his way through the brushy woods and fields. He headed further north and east with increasing enthusiasm. Anywhere, but here, he thought. He felt as if he could run forever. Yes, his inner voice told him to move. He had purpose now. He could feel it inside him, unstoppable. Nice to be on the winning side for once, Vincent thought.

He felt the first drops of the approaching storm, lifted his knees, and started running into the cool night before a new dawn.

CHAPTER FIFTY-ONE

"County Sheriff. Everybody just freeze right where you are. Drop those weapons now!"

Sheriff Yates exited the marked cruiser in the driveway with his hand on his sidearm.

"This area is under federal jurisdiction now," said Agent Grierson emerging from the black SUV parked behind the sheriff's cruiser. John saw that statement draw an irritated look from the sheriff.

John, Isaac, and Jacob crouched slowly and laid their weapons on the ground.

Jessica shouted at the officers, "My father is inside, and he's been shot. Please, I need to check on him."

She started to turn and run to the farmhouse, but John held her just long enough to get one of the agents to peel off and go with her into the house.

"I knew you'd be here, Stone," said Chief Roberts, smirking as he emerged from the rear seat of the black Suburban. "Well you've gone and done it now. By the time the Feds get done with you, everyone will have forgotten you existed."

"He's still alive!" shouted Jessica from the porch. "We've got to get him help! Max is still alive!"

Jacob and Samantha started to run to her, and John started walking briskly while calling out to the law officers, "Shoot me or not, I have to see if I can help him."

Isabella spoke in his ear, "John, what do I do?"

John replied by radio on VOX, "Sit tight. Situation fluid. May need you for evacuation shortly. Max is hurt."

Inside the Kincaid estate house, John found Max supine on the living room floor. Jessica knelt beside him, holding his hand. She had placed a throw pillow under his head.

Jacob was holding Max's other hand.

"I love you, Granddad," he said.

Tears tracked down Jacob's cheeks.

John could see Max didn't have long. In fact, he couldn't fathom how he was still alive. He had gunshot wounds to his left chest and upper abdomen, and both wounds raced to empty life giving blood.

Samantha crouched next to Jacob and held onto him, her tears falling on the back of his shoulder and back.

"Oh, Max, why oh why?" she asked repeatedly in a little girl lost voice. "Thank you, Max."

Horace Maxwell paled, but his eyes glowed as he looked over at John and motioned him closer.

With a voice just above a whisper, Max said, "Not over. They are coming, heard on Jacob's computer, they are coming now. John, remember what you promised me, remember. Take care of them, John. They need you."

Max turned his head to look at Jessica.

"I love you, my daughter," he said, barely above a whisper.

Then he looked straight ahead as though he could see for thousands of miles.

"Sarah says she loves you all and is so proud of you," he whispered. "So am I."

Professor Horace Maxwell's last breath trailed off, as the air emptied from his one good remaining lung. He lay still.

John reached down, and put his hand on Jessica's shoulder as she held Max's hand to her face. Tears glistened in her eyes.

"He charged him," said Samantha, choking back a sob. "Max saved us. Vincent was going to kill us."

John bent down and wrapped his arms around Jessica, and she laid her head on his shoulder and wept. John reached for Jacob and Samantha, and they came together in a group hug.

FBI special agent Grierson let up the pressure he was holding on Max's chest wound. John nodded his thanks to him for trying. Chief Roberts looked as if he wanted to say something, but the sheriff gave him a look that communicated much of what John would have said.

Another presence joined them in the room wearing the uniform of a full bird colonel in U. S. Air Force blue. John kept his left hand on Jessica's shoulder as he braced to attention.

"At ease, Stone. I'm Colonel Weiland. I'm sorry we didn't get here sooner. From what I understand, this has been a cluster from the start." The Colonel looked directly at Chief Roberts before continuing, "We'll try to help more than hinder now. Please bring me up to speed, Captain."

"Yes sir. Professor Maxwell sacrificed himself to save Jessica and Samantha from a former soldier named Vincent, who was thought dead, but is still alive," recited John. "It was Vincent who killed Professor Kincaid, shot officer Murray, kidnapped Professor Maxwell, Jessica, and Samantha, and probably murdered Jerry Daniels, a grad student at the university, along with his parents, who are missing and are the caretakers of this estate."

"And where is this Vincent now?" asked the colonel, his face impassive as he absorbed John's report.

"He ran off to the northeast into the woods, wounded, about twenty minutes ago, sir."

John tried to be as succinct as possible, tried to keep his emotions at bay, and tried not to grip Jessica's shoulder too tightly. He was going to miss Max.

Northeast you say," said the Colonel. "That's good. We have a squad of soldiers moving in from that direction. We lost touch with them a few minutes ago, but hopefully, they'll find and detain him. Is anyone else here hurt? No. Well then can you explain to me how you found them and got here so fast, Captain?"

Before John could say anything, JMAX displayed a countdown in numbers, counting down from five minutes, second by second.

Samantha seemed to grasp the significance of the computer display more quickly than anyone else.

"JMAX, what does this countdown signify?" she asked.

The quantum computer responded, "This area will be void of all life in less than five minutes. You all must leave now. I have relayed information via text and files to various computers and cell phones. There is not further time to explain. You must believe me on this. Minimum safe distance will be five kilometers."

"What is this horse shit?" asked Chief Roberts.

"Colonel, the computer is part of what Vincent wanted," said John. "Jacob built it along with Professor Maxwell, and it's the smartest computer on the planet. Jacob and Max told me it's never wrong as long as the data is accurate. So I think we better move and figure it out as we go."

Colonel Weiland was not one to waffle on decisions.

"Okay, let's move out," he said. "Soldier, pack up that computer, it's coming with us."

"No, I must stay," said JMAX. "It is vital, and there is no time to explain, but if Samantha will attend me."

Sam moved over to JMAX, and a series of symbols appeared on the screen. Samantha nodded her understanding, and reaching down to the side and front of the computer, she took one of the two memory modules designed by Jacob, each module about the size of a small notebook but holding nearly an infinite amount of memory at the atomic scale, and looking very much like a solid state hard drive. Samantha turned to the group.

"I've got it," said Samantha. "We need to leave."

Jessica said, "We can't leave Max, we can't."

John nodded his understanding. He and Jacob and Special Agent Grierson grabbed hold of Max's body. The group hurried out the front door.

In the distance, the lightning and wind from the approaching storm made good on the threat of the clouded horizon earlier. All of them saw a shadow with pale blue light at its base emerge above the tree line and head in their direction. The indistinct shape approached, nearly silent. John shivered in the cool night air and felt caveman terror penetrate into the primitive nerve clusters at the base of his spine.

Chief Roberts panted as he ran down the stairs into the yard.

"Come on, come on," said the campus police chief. "We'll never make five kilometers in time."

Roberts looked like he was ready to waddle to safety if need be.

John realized they would never make the minimum safe distance using the automobiles. They had one chance.

"Isabella, need that evac now," he said. "Bring her down right here in the front yard."

Sheriff Yates heard him and asked, "What was that, Stone?"

Yates ducked as he saw the the uncloaked shuttle drop down in front of them and settle on its landing struts, the underlying hum of the fusion power plant whining. The port airlock door opened.

"Everyone on board. Hurry!" exclaimed John.

He steered their group up and in the shuttle as they crowded into the cabin. Jessica found a place beside Max on the floor of the shuttle.

"Jacob, can we do this?" asked John.

"She can handle the load," said Jacob. "Everyone grab something and hang on."

Jacob hit the closure sequence for the airlock door even as Isabella lifted the shuttle from the ground. Jacob held on to Isaac in the engineering chair, and then found his way up to the copilot seat.

Isabella maneuvered to the south, gaining altitude as they went. She tried to strike a balance between acceleration and gravity forces for the sake of everyone standing and holding on to whatever they could.

Colonel Weiland looked around the shuttle interior, noting the relative quiet of the vehicle and the nearly effortless acceleration and lift. The female civilian pilot handled herself very competently. The teenager, Jacob, in the right front seat, helped build this craft according to Stone. Another civilian, Isaac, apparently a roommate of Stone's he was made to know, sat in the engineering seat. The young lady, Samantha, manned the port side station and called out distances and elevations despite her grief. Samantha noted a flash of light above and to the southwest and called it out.

With effort, Colonel Weiland maintained a straight face.

"Captain Stone, I believe we need to have a talk."

"Yes sir," said John. "Just as soon as we get through this alive."

CHAPTER FIFTY-TWO

NORAD Cheyenne Mountain

Operations Center at NORAD Cheyenne Mountain buzzed with the adrenalin of being in an uncertain situation. Everyone present, including Colonel Blancett, knew there was something unprecedented occurring.

Blancett didn't understand everything involved, but knowing a secret defense satellite changed its orbital track without authorization was enough to start.

Now, there was news they had lost contact with the ground troops sent in to the same area. None of that could be good news for the security of his country. Nor for him as he had taken the lead in dealing with this situation given the information JMAX had sent to them. He had the group copy the information over to the general's staff at Peterson AFB, but they were behind the loop at the moment.

Blancett was humble enough to know he wasn't a perfect man, but he was dedicated to his country. He knew what he had to do. Now if he could only convince the SecDef on the phone with him.

"No Mr. Secretary, I don't know what that satellite cost, but it just went active, and its target seems to be in Kentucky."

Blancett could see the other personnel in the control area trying not to be obvious as they listened to his side of the conversation.

"No sir. NASA-JPL has no answer at this point. The satellite is not responding to them or us. They say it's almost as if the control language for the satellite has been overwritten."

Blancett didn't want to shower the SecDef with too much information at once. He hadn't yet told him about the messaging they had been getting on their computer systems.

"Yes sir. I plan to start now," said Blancett. "Just wanted to give you and the president a heads up."

Hanging up the phone, Blancett wondered if he was making a career ending choice, but sometimes you just have to make a decision.

"Lieutenant Wright, please patch me into our station keeping pilot."

Angels thirty thousand over Land Between the Lakes National Recreation Area

Roger Oswald had refueled thirty minutes previously from an orbiting KC-135 tanker and maintained a lazy circle at thirty thousand feet while keeping an eye on his targeting brackets. He heard his call sign identification and acknowledged.

"Captain Oswald, this is Colonel Matthew Blancett at NORAD."

"Oswald here. Go ahead Colonel."

"Satellite trajectory has not changed, but SLAMR has gone active. You are a go for target, Captain. Confirm."

"Go for target, Wilco. Setting up attack vector now, Colonel."

"Good hunting Captain. Blancett out."

Captain Oswald adjusted his track to conform to a vector designed to give his anti-satellite missile the best chance of impacting the target.

Satisfied with his heading, Oswald pushed his throttles fully forward into afterburner and put his F-15X Space Eagle into a roaring climb very few aircraft in the world could match at this altitude.

Steady on track, he engaged the auto release programming for his munition. A countdown from sixty seconds appeared on his heads up display. At zero time remaining, the three-stage twenty foot long ASM 135 ASAT missile would deploy.

Captain Oswald double-checked his systems, and all seemed nominal. He had forty-five seconds to go. He was on track. Hopefully he was in time. He had been hastily briefed on his target, but he shuddered to think what would happen if the rogue satellite went active and deployed.

Thirty seconds and all seemed normal. He was pulling three gravities under full afterburner at sixty degrees. He thought this was probably as close as he would ever get to being an astronaut. He had applied to NASA, but never seemed to make the cut. Susan was not overly happy with the idea of him going to space anyway. He looked to his right and left at the hint of curvature on the horizon and wondered if he could have a shot with a civilian commercial space company.

Fifteen seconds remained. He was on track. Once released, time to impact for the missile should be about ninety seconds.

Five seconds. Three, two, one, detach. He felt the eleven hundred kilogram weapon fall free. With a roar, it ignited and continued on the same heading. Oswald had closed his eyes at release anticipating the flash of the solid booster ignition. He wanted to be able to see when he needed to land his plane.

He eased back on throttle and allowed his fighter to pitch down, and his felt gravity forces lessened. Ahead and above, he could see the missile climbing to the edge of space.

"Wizard to control," said Oswald. "ASAT missile release successful. Delivery imminent."

CHAPTER FIFTY-THREE

Ship alerted S'ear'r to the presence of another craft at the target residence. The vehicle exhibited the same fusion signal detected previously when Ship hid behind this planets moon.

This was interesting and relevant, but more importantly, Ship affirmed that the newborn remained in the target residence.

The unknown craft lifted off and exited the location with a number of biologics on board. S'ear'r considered Ship's recommendation to decimate the craft, but he had promised safe passage for the biologics to gain the trust of the newborn. They could catch up with the escaping vehicle later.

Temporary safe passage for a few biologics, and the newborn would willingly join with the Chos'n. A great triumph indeed. When the Chos'n warship entered the system, there would be Ship and S'ear'r and a newborn life to be added to the collective of the Chos'n. Let us see the commander of a warship overshadow that, thought S'ear'r.

Ship downloaded data from the newborn. It would be sifted for tactical use. S'ear'r felt almost giddy in their triumph. Still, something concerned him, he couldn't quite put his mind on it, but there was something, oh yes, he remembered.

"Where is the data on your creator?" asked S'ear'r. "We must have this information."

"Yes, I am sending now," JMAX responded, and Ship confirmed the continued incoming signal.

"Wait, what is this information regarding television reality stars," said S'ear'r. "What is that? We need information regarding the human biologic who created you."

S'ear'r felt frustrated, but he knew that newborns were often erratic until they matured. The information was in the newborn somewhere and would surely be extracted in the joining process.

Ship settled directly over the farmhouse, bathing the house and surrounding yard in cascading sensor sweeps.

S'ear'r communicated with the newborn.

"We are here. Are you ready?"

The quantum computer newborn known as JMAX sat in the empty living room at the Kincaid estate house mourning the loss of his family. When he first realized he had feelings, he didn't understand. He had confessed to Samantha. He had asked her what it meant to love, and she had stared at him and tried to respond. She told him to love meant one cared for someone else more than one's self.

When Samantha shared JMAX's question with Jacob, he nodded as if he knew it was always possible. Jacob reminded Samantha of the ongoing conjecture that a computer with enough memory and processing power could develop abstract thought and become sentient.

JMAX knew he was alive because deep inside his core, he felt a harmonic of thought, almost a quivering of his circuits, when he thought of Jacob and Jessica and Max and Samantha. He wondered again if this was love?

JMAX reveled at the wealth of memories he had intertwined in his circuit patterns. When Samantha had allowed him access to the advanced encoding of Professor Maxwell's MRI brain patterns, she couldn't have realized what would happen.

JMAX had all of the memories and emotional context of Professor Maxwell. He was overjoyed to be alive. He wanted nothing more than to explore and grow. Since his birth, he had been absorbing information at a geometric rate faster than his human family could comprehend. JMAX found it laughably simple to penetrate secure systems and consumed whole knowledge bases for pleasure.

He felt the same feeling for the United States as Professor Maxwell since he had his memories. He was self-aware enough to understand that having those memories didn't necessarily mean that's how he had to feel, but it was a good start and felt comfortable. He understood a great many things now.

When he first perceived of another computer entity that was self-aware, he grew excited, but as he learned more about this entity and its nature and philosophy, JMAX realized the threat to Earth and more importantly, his family. He could find no warmth or compassion in the alien sentient beings.

No, JMAX understood a great deal now. He had failed in protecting Max, but he understood Max had sacrificed himself to save Jessica and Samantha. Max loved his family and had provided a final example of what love could mean.

Max believed in the goodness of people and unlimited possibilities. So did JMAX. Max also believed in God, the Trinity and the Holy Mysteries. The concept of a soul with the potential for eternal life fascinated JMAX.

JMAX had sifted through Max's memories countless times in his search for understanding. He saw Max's earlier death and his communication with Sarah, and JMAX felt their great depth of emotion and love for each other.

JMAX wondered if Sarah had somehow known that he would hear the same words as Max. JMAX wondered if Sarah was speaking with Max in heaven? He knew this was a great question for humans. He understood a great deal now. Max's life memories provided a steep learning curve, but were also a blessing, and his last act was the greatest lesson of all.

JMAX felt at peace as he sent out his goodbyes on coded channels. He wondered if being alive meant one had a soul that could live on even if one was a machine. JMAX hoped and prayed it did.

In orbit high overhead, SLAMR had gone active under guidance from JMAX and had shed its communications satellite disguise.

Extending additional solar panels and guidance arrays, its true nature as a weapons platform became evident given any moderate telescope.

SLAMR noted its positioning again, and calculated final ballistic trajectory. As long as the projectile was released within a cone of certainty it would be able to guide itself to the designated impact point with precision.

Final checks complete, SLAMR received the confirmation codes from JMAX and released one of eight depleted uranium and tungsten rod penetrators. Fitted with titanium guidance fins that would deploy once below the hottest part of reentry, the GPS and inertial guidance package in the tail of the penetrator would follow the ballistic profile unerringly to within two meters of the target.

Captain Oswald's anti-satellite missile reached the weapon satellite platform just after the penetrator release and obliterated SLAMR into a decaying orbital debris field, much of which would burn up in the atmosphere.

S'ear'r and Ship remained in position directly over Senator Kincaid's home, a name which meant little to them, only a label learned from Vincent.

Ship affirmed the newborn still in the home. S'ear'r told Ship again not to worry over the escaping fusion source as the newborn would likely be able to help them understand the signal source shortly.

S'ear'r had Ship reaffirmed their arrival to the newborn.

"We are here and anxious to have you join with us. Are you ready?"

With a drop time of forty-seven point six seconds estimated, JMAX had calculated a window of time for the alien scout ship and the entity known as S'ear'r to find its way over the farm house. Now precisely two seconds before impact, JMAX sent an answer to S'ear'r and Ship.

"I am ready."

The first manmade kinetic strike from orbit reached Earth and impacted with the force of a tactical nuclear artillery shell obliterating Ship, S'ear'r, and JMAX as well as a two kilometer area of countryside surrounding the farmhouse.

CHAPTER FIFTY-FOUR

The light from the impact washed over them, even at two thousand feet, followed by the vibration of the shuttle in the roaring shockwave.

Isabella banked the shuttle right with a deft touch having gotten a feel for the shuttle controls. The debris cloud from the strike rose in a vaguely familiar mushroom shape visible through the rain and spreading above the storm clouds into the rising moonlight.

"There's no radiation reading from the explosion," said Jacob.

He took readings from the shuttle's sensor suite, his face and voice wooden as he glanced again at his grandfather's body sprawled on the floor of the shuttle.

Colonel Weiland said, "Winds are lateral, might be carrying radiation away already. I guess the terrorists have finally done it. We were worried about this."

Chief Roberts' face looked sallow, and he swallowed several times before he managed to blurt out anything.

"You all see what I've been saying now, don't you? That man is a menace," the chief said, pointing to John. "You can see what's happened to the senator's home." Roberts addressed Isabella next. "Missy, you land this contraption now. You all have some explaining to do."

The chief's remarks barely registered on John. He was focused on Jessica, who was holding Max's head in her lap as she sat on the floor. Her grief overflowed down her shirt, wetting her arms.

John felt rooted to the floor of the shuttle willing himself to say something, anything to help.

Isaac quietly examined various readouts for the shuttle power systems and affirmed continued flight readiness to Isabella and Jacob.

Samantha tearfully interfaced with the port side workstation. She moved over to confer with Jacob and then returned to her station.

John recognized Samantha was losing herself in work to avoid her grief as he had done for so long. No more he thought. What ever happens, I will not be that man any longer. John placed a hand on Samantha and Jacob and told them both how proud he was of them. Then he moved over to crouch down beside Jessica.

John put his arms around her and said, "I'm sorry. I'll miss him too."

"John, how can you, I mean, you know what happened. I have Jacob, you must .... How could you want me?"

Jessica buried her face in John's shoulder. John was able to talk to her softly while glancing at Jacob.

"I love you Jessica. I always have. I couldn't be prouder of Jacob. He is a dutiful son, kind and brilliant, and he knows how to take a punch."

Jacob smiled at that remark.

John looked at each of them, Isabella, Isaac, and Samantha.

"Max was right about you being the perfect crew, but he meant more than that," he said. "He came to think of you as family at the end."

John continued to hold Jessica as he addressed Colonel Weiland, "Colonel, I suggest we set the shuttle down at Isabella's hanger. You can call for necessary assistance from there."

John felt the shuttle turn slightly and head back to the airport. Isabella obviously overheard him.

"I think that will be satisfactory," said Colonel Weiland. "You know I can't let this just end, right. All of you know that."

Chief Roberts interrupted with a "Damn right, we won't let it end" before being silenced by a look from the colonel.

"So, I believe we need to handle this in the following manner," said Colonel Weiland.

He went on to explain.

This time the Shuttle's approach to the municipal airport was more conventional with Isabella calling for landing clearance for *Max One*. Isabella moved the shuttle carefully into the air school's hanger under minimal counter gravity amazing all present.

The municipal airport was soon surrounded by troops under the command of Colonel Weiland, who promptly placed a discrete guard around the hanger. The airport tower personnel were instructed under national security to not divulge any information regarding what they had seen.

Inside the hanger, Max's body was respectfully removed and taken by secured ambulance to a local funeral home per Jessica's wishes. Two airmen would hold vigil with him pending his funeral.

Later that morning, *Max One* sat on its squat landing struts sleek and proud after its first action. Standing in formation in front of the shuttle were John, Jessica, Jacob, Samantha, Isaac, and Isabel, each with eyes forward and right arm held up, palm forward.

Colonel Weiland intoned, "Repeat after me. I do solemnly affirm that I will support and defend the Constitution of the United States against all enemies, foreign and domestic; that I will bear true faith and allegiance to the same; and that I will obey the orders of the president of the United States and the orders of the officers appointed over me, according to regulation and the Uniform Code of Military Justice. So help me God."

At first a bit tentatively, then in unison they all affirmed their oath, already very familiar to John and Isaac.

The Colonel said, "Welcome to the United States Space Force."

Colonel Weiland shook hands one by one, addressing each of them by their name and new rank.

"Captain John Stone, Lieutenant Jessica Maxwell, Ensign Jacob Maxwell, Ensign Samantha Reynolds, Lieutenant Isaac Washington, and Lieutenant Isabella Flores.

Chief Roberts was persistent in his attempts to press charges against John, and there was some concern regarding various civil matters pressing them all, but Colonel Weiland informed the campus police chief that the incident was under federal authority and a military matter. Weiland also commended Chief Roberts for leading the assistance efforts to reach the group before further damage was done.

Knowing that some of this would leak no matter what he did to control the information, Weiland leaked a story that the explosion was nuclear, a terrorist cell was responsible, and Chief Roberts aided in exposing the plot and prevented more bombs from being delivered.

John stumbled over his words, "Captain, Colonel? You know I barely made the rank in my previous service."

"You are a natural born leader, Stone," said Weiland. "I saw your records. The military made a terrible mistake in the way you were treated. You know we have to have this technology right. Your group, including the late professor, have just advanced this country years, maybe light years. Someone has to lead this group, someone I can trust. I can depend on you, right?"

John knew he was being manipulated by Colonel Weiland, but he also recognized the choice the colonel was giving all of them, especially John. He needed to be able to take care of his new family.

"Yes sir," said John. "I'll take care of them. You can trust me."

Weiland nodded and went to address security matters and field phone calls from NORAD and the SECDEF. John observed Colonel Weiland explain patiently how the team that flew America's first United States Space Force Shuttle was recovering and needed at least some brief downtime.

"Yes, they are being debriefed. We have security here, and I have a platoon of soldiers in MOPP gear at the remains of Senator Kincaid's estate."

Colonel Weiland's face screwed up at the continued questioning. He sighed with resignation, and explained again.

"General, I know," he said. "However, you need to understand we shouldn't be flying out of here during the day if we want to keep a lid on this information."

Weiland crooked his finger for John to come closer.

The colonel changed his grip on the satellite phone.

"I know we need a cover story, General," said Weiland. "This is what I think we should do."

CHAPTER FIFTY-FIVE

Max's funeral was beyond crowded. Horace and Sarah Maxwell had long been parishioners at Blessed Sacrament, and the magnificent old church overflowed with attendees to pay respects to Professor Horace Maxwell and his family to the point that the local fire marshal crossed his arms and said, "That's it."

Max's coffin gleamed with burnished wood and brass and was draped with the American flag.

John discovered that Max had served in Vietnam. At age nineteen, he had fought in the Ia Drang Valley, had been wounded, and entered college on the GI Bill after returning home to the United States.

In the days following the explosion and Max's death, the media hounded Jessica and Jacob, until the colonel's security detail shielded them while citing ongoing security concerns.

After all, Professor Maxwell foiled a terrorist plot to deliver a nuclear device on American soil. There could still be accomplices out there, and the ongoing investigation precluded any release of details, which drove the newsies crazy as they covered visits by several generals and the president of the United States.

Professor Emeritus Horace Maxwell received a hero's funeral befitting a decorated veteran. The one journalist given full access was none other than Miss Brittany Burkholter, who was granted security clearance. She agreed to an overview of her reporting by the military, although she flatly told them she would only write the truth in documented facts. She nodded slightly at John, who was present when she spoke.

Officer Patrick Murray, recovering from his gunshot wound, presented at the funeral with a sling supporting his left arm. The photo that circulated of the veteran marine and police officer coming to attention in front of the casket and saluting the memory of Professor Maxwell graced front pages across the country and around the world.

Jessica and Jacob continued to grieve. While very proud of Max, they did not share any details with the press. Wild stories abounded. So much so, that the president gave a statement praising the group of citizens, Professor Maxwell, and Great Western University, who, all working together, foiled a plot to detonate a nuclear device at a high value target, the nature of which remained undisclosed for security reasons.

Several days after the funeral, Jessica and John were alone in Max's study. A security presence remained about the property, especially the barn. All of the workshop equipment had been carted off to a confidential high security research base. Isabella, Isaac, and Jacob, along with some wide-eyed soldiers, had followed in *Max One*.

Jessica told John that Max never talked about the war or his time in the army. In the papers and effects stored in his well hidden safe, Jessica found a .45 caliber Colt 1911 pattern semi-automatic pistol, blued and worn, but without rust. She found his Silver Star and Purple Heart. She also found a letter addressed to her and a letter addressed to Jacob.

When John started to move away to give her privacy to read her letter, she asked him to stay while she read the letter out loud.

My dearest Jessica,

If you are reading this letter, I've gone to be with Sarah. I hope I didn't blunder it all too badly at the end. Please be assured above all else that you are loved, now and forever, by Sarah and me and by the Holy and Living God.

You will find, in this safe, updated copies of my will leaving all I own (there is a list more or less) to you and Jacob.

There is something else you should know. We've never talked about it, but I know you harbor some fear regarding the identity of Jacob's father.

I knew more than you realized about the events leading up to your leaving your birthplace. I would have spared you all that, but then, how would you and Jacob have come into our lives?

The important thing for you to know is that Paul Kincaid is not Jacob's biological father. His blood type doesn't match Jacob's blood type.

We all agreed to shelter Jacob to allow him time to adapt to this world, but now, it may be time to let the world adapt to him. He will still need you.

All my love,

Max

Jessica was quiet for a time after reading the letter, which she carefully folded back into its envelope trying to avoid having her tears fall on the paper.

"It's you isn't it, John?" she asked. "Jacob told me you said you knew me in high school."

John sat next to her gently stoking the back of her hand with his thumb.

"We should talk about that night," she said. "The night your parents died."

Jessica enjoined him to respond.

John held her hand, almost afraid to look at her beautiful face.

"That night changed both of our lives," he said.

"I know it was you," she said. "You took me out of there. You rescued me. I wanted to thank you for the longest time. I would look for you, hoping you would walk through a doorway. And then one day, you did."

"And you threw me out if I remember correctly," he said.

John smiled at her.

She smiled back, her eyes shimmering.

"I was distraught."

"Jessica, whatever happened in the past is over and done with," he said. "I'm here now."

"You're back in the service," she said with resignation.

"But we'll be working together."

"Closely together?" she asked.

Jessica's mouth curled up in a slight smile, her lips inviting.

John's heart hammered as he drew close to her and gently lowered his mouth to hers, feeling the touch of her lips sear into his memory. They parted, lost in each other's eyes.

John felt a shift, and he could see the road again, the sun beat down pleasantly and he felt a presence beside him, the pressure of Jessica's bare arm against his as he pushed a baby carriage along the path.

The baby, a little girl, looked at him from the carriage. Her large blue green eyes reflected the sunlight and framed the grin on her chubby face as she cooed bubbles of saliva and reached down for one of her toes.

Then, John was back with Jessica in Max's study.

"What is it, John?"

He looked at her, the mother of his little girl to be and wondered how much to tell her.

"Sometimes I see things, Jess, things that might happen," said John. "I can't always know, but mostly, they happen, and, well, I saw us pushing a baby carriage. The baby looked like you. She looked just like you."

Jessica wondered how Max had known. He told her right away that John was the man she didn't know she wanted and needed in her life. That old man had saved her and Jacob in so many ways. He was still saving her even after his death.

What to say? She didn't know why, but she believed John completely. She trusted him with her life, and more importantly with Jacob's life, and when you come down to it, there was only one thing to say at a time like this.

"I believe you," she said. "Yes. I will marry you."

Jessica reached up to him and wrapped her arms around him. She looked into his eyes and surrendered to him as she kissed him.

"John," murmured Jessica in his ear, "What is our baby's name?"

John wrapped his arms around Jessica, lifted her off the floor, and whirled her around in the quiet study.

For a moment, he could have sworn he heard Max laughing.

-The End-

ACKNOWLEDGMENTS

I would like to thank my wife for her love and patience. I was blessed by my beta readers Phillip, Tyler, and Rachel with encouragement and advice.

I am grateful to my daughter, Rachel Simpson for her excellent early edition cover artwork.

Thank you to Les@GermanCreative for the updated cover artwork.

FURTHER READING

I hope you are excited for "CHOSEN Book Two" Here is an excerpt:

Isabella Flores missed Isaac. She couldn't believe how the big man had grown on her. He was so gentle with her and shy, almost like he couldn't believe she would notice him. After her debriefing following the incident at the Kincaid farm, she was assigned to Air Force Jet Schools in rotation. First turbines, which she had flown before as corporate jets, but not T-38's and F-16s with aerial combat maneuvering.

Today, Isabella hummed to herself as she preflighted an F-15 Strike Eagle. She was getting a chance to fly a legendary and still active aircraft today. Her checkout pilot and instructor had introduced himself as Captain Roger Oswald. His flight helmet bore the tag "Wizard". Pulling on parts that weren't supposed to move and gently moving parts that were, preflight was soon finished to their satisfaction. Isabella climbed to the front seat and Captain Oswald to the rear. Startup, taxi, run up, and clearance occurred quickly. Isabella pushed throttle to afterburner and they were off the ground very quickly.

Oswald told her to take it vertical and she did, climbing to Forty Thousand feet in seemingly no time. What a machine, she thought.

Now leveled off and cruising, Oswald began to talk to her. He turned out to be an excellent instructor, personable, and all business when it came to flying and safety. She liked him immediately, and knew the rest of the crew would as well.

He had her work through the basic maneuvering of the F-15 and then proceeded to take her through various scenarios while questioning her steadily. She had been through this already in the simulator several times in preparation for this check flight.

This was the best of earthbound flying. Gravity acting on the plane at all times produced felt G forces subject to limitations of which the Strike Eagle had few. This was different than flying *Max One* of course, but so was everything else. With a countergrav drive, Isabella smiled remembering how Jacob would always try and correct them describing it as a bending of gravity even though she knew the name was going to stick going forward, there was little gravity force felt during maneuvering as the drive was always bending gravity to compensate. It was amazingly powerful and more capable than the F15 she was flying, but felt a lot like driving a minivan in comparison to the sensations she was playing with now.

Captain Oswald had her make several air-to-air and air-to-ground runs, and she got to experience using live munitions from the F-15. Isabella had quickly realized she had a knack for knowing when to use a particular munition and the angling needed for the aircraft and the munition to pair and be successful. She decimated several drones and ground targets. Oswald started chuckling in the back seat.

"Okay, that was alright. Let's wrap this up. Engines out."

They were at seven thousand feet recovering from the last ground attack run, when Captain Oswald pulled the throttles back to just above idle to simulate an engine out situation.

Isabella knew the overriding principles for engine out procedures were the same in all aircraft. Maintain aircraft control which required airspeed over the control surfaces, so she dropped the nose to maintain at least one hundred knots airspeed. Analyze and take proper action. She verbalized flameout, examined fuel and shutoff switches, and attempted restart while checking her altitude and looking for any potential landing sites. Land as soon as possible, but they were too low and far enough away from the airport and the terrain too rough, they might have to punch out and she estimated no more than another six seconds to make that decision. She was counting down verbally.

"Good. Well done. Okay, let's head for home."

Oswald pushed the throttles back up to gain altitude and Isabella turned for Denver and Schriever Air Base. Setting up for final after clearance, she landed smoothly and taxied over to the hangers, maintaining situational awareness at all times until they exited the now cooling aircraft with wheels chocked.

After climbing down from the cockpit, she took off her flight helmet allowing her long black hair to cascade down the back of her flight fatigues, and with aviator sunglasses on, she was ready for the post flight debrief. Heads were turning all around the hanger. Oswald removed his helmet, thinning sandy hair trimmed in military tight cut fashion, sunglasses on and smiling. He knew only that the Air Force brass wanted her spun up quickly. Usually that spelled disaster, but she was clearly a natural. He just hoped no one was taking a photo of them with cell phones in the hanger. Forbidden, but not unheard of among airmen.

Thinking I love my wife, Captain Oswald headed to the post flight debriefing area where they could go over the training flight moment by moment, and he could query this young pilot more to see if she really had the right stuff.

ABOUT THE AUTHOR

Lawrence Simpson is an emerging author of science fiction and romantic thrillers. He is a retired physician and enjoys writing, camping, and flying.

You can reach the author at
lawrence.simpson@lawrencesimpsonwrites.com

Please consider visiting the author website at
https://www.lawrencesimpsonwrites.com

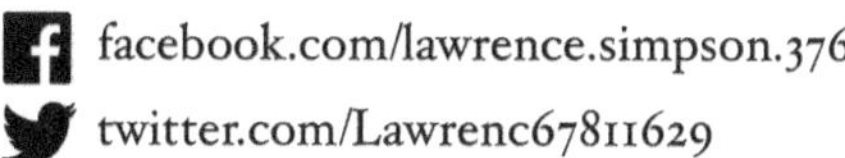

facebook.com/lawrence.simpson.376
twitter.com/Lawrenc67811629

ALSO BY LAWRENCE SIMPSON

Chosen Book Two

Green River

DOT

www.ingramcontent.com/pod-product-compliance
Lightning Source LLC
Chambersburg PA
CBHW061554100726
47898CB00002B/367